THE GOLDEN ROAD

We are the Pilgrims, master; we shall go
Always a little further: it may be
Beyond that last blue mountain barred with snow
Across that angry or that glimmering sea.
White on a throne or guarded in a cave
There lives a prophet who can understand
Why men were born: but surely we are brave
Who take the Golden Road to Samarkand.

James Elroy Flecker

ONCE A PILGRIM

The True Story of One Man's
Courage Under Rebel Fire

Will Scully

HEADLINE

First published in 1998
by HEADLINE BOOK PUBLISHING

10 9 8 7 6 5 4 3 2 1

British Library Cataloguing in Publication Data

Scully, Will
    Once a pilgrim : William Scully, Mark Bles
    1.Scully, Will
    2.Sierra Leone – History – 20th century
    I.Title II.Bles, Mark
    966.4'04'092

    ISBN 0 7472 2257 6 (hardback)
    ISBN 0 7472 7515 7 (softback)

Typeset by
Letterpart Limited, Reigate, Surrey

Printed and bound in Great Britain by
Mackays of Chatham PLC, Chatham, Kent

HEADLINE BOOK PUBLISHING
A division of Hodder Headline PLC
338 Euston Road
London NW1 3BH

This book is dedicated to the memory of my father, William James Scully, who fought but sadly lost the fight against multiple sclerosis and whose fire still burns with us.

Acknowledgements

Describing what I did has been easier than exposing the feelings that accompanied my actions, but I guess that sense of vulnerability comes with publishing a book about yourself. Extreme situations generate extreme reactions, and I have done my best to explain how I felt about what happened to me. This is a very personal account, partly because for one long and critical period I was alone, but I would not want readers to think that I am unaware of all the others who were involved and who contributed so much to what went on in Sierra Leone. A number of people gave me crucial support at the time, and others helped more recently during the writing process. It is impossible to mention everyone, and some would not want their names in print, but I am particularly indebted to the following:

Roger Crooks for trusting me, especially with a lot of money at a very difficult time for him; Steve Lawson for helping us both on the day and beating my drum later; Martin Greenwood for his Yorkshire grit, booming voice and firefighting (among many other things with Roger and Steve) with a group of equally brave Lebanese whose names I don't have. They spent a long day on all floors of the hotel putting out fires caused by 200-plus RPG strikes; Lincoln Jopp for his courageous support at the hotel and subsequent friendship; Murdo McCloud for being there in Conakry, who talked the East German pilot down in thick mist, or nothing might have been written, and who has turned out to be a good friend; Corinne Dufka and Liz Blunt for their satphones; Peter Penfold, the British High Commissioner, for his support and putting my case; the US Marines, who turned up just in time;

my wife Veronica ('Ronnie') for her love and understanding, for tolerating my lifestyle and for being there when I thought about her; and my sons Daniel and Maxwell who I am immensely proud of; my brother James for being a brother and all those early morning and late night trips to Heathrow for this and most other escapades; my mother Jean for her love, unwavering faith and support; and George for loving and cherishing her; Peter Dickson for his brilliant sense of humour; Chris Ryan and Geordie who prompted me to start the project; and Dominic Anciano and Ray Burdis for critical encouragement, friendship and enthusiasm; and Peter 'Monster' Malmstrøm and Christian Okenclaus too; a load of great friends from my time in the Army for the times when I learned my 'trade' but most of whom I don't see from one year to the next; Barbara Levy, my agent, too; Heather Holden-Brown and Lorraine Jerram for their remarkable patience and sense of humour; Louise Cort for assistance during our research; Hirondelle Candle for the fax; Mike Shaw for an opportunity offered (and accepted); and finally Mark Whitcombe and Mark Bles without whom this book could not have been written.

map1

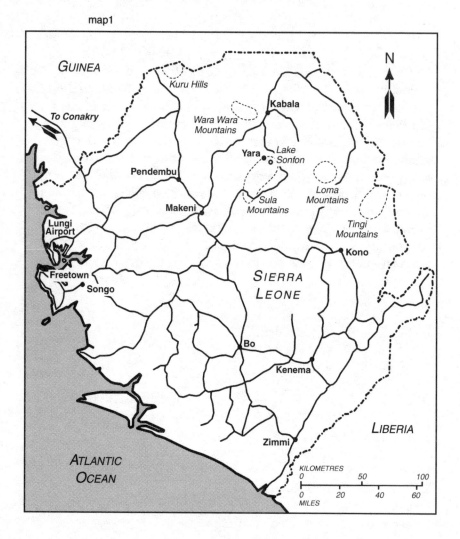

Sierra Leone

Gold and diamond smuggling, and an endless guerrilla war between soldiers, rebels and foreign mercenaries, make Sierra Leone one of the poorest, most corrupt, dangerous . . . and exciting countries in the world.

This small West African country is on the Gold Coast between Liberia and Guinea and at first sight seems an idyllic tropical paradise of surf, beaches and lush green jungle. Inland, savannah woodlands rise over rolling hills to blue mountains cut by a mosaic of farmland where villagers have for generations provided most of the country's food.

The reality is very different.

The capital, Freetown, is a hotchpotch of decayed colonial buildings and corrugated tin shanty ghettos. It was founded in 1787 by British anti-slave trade abolitionists who bought land from local Paramount Chiefs to settle 400 freed British slaves. The stark contrast between these high ideals and the realities of life in this small tropical country was established right at the start when all but thirty died of disease or infighting with the local Temne people. In 1792 more freed slaves from America and Jamaica arrived, and by 1808 the country came under the British government's influence. By 1833, Freetown was being used as a base to sail out and capture foreign slaver ships working along the Gold Coast. The freed slaves were brought back to settle in Sierra Leone which quickly developed a violent, mixed society speaking English, Creole, Mende, Limba and Temne. In 1896, the British declared Sierra Leone a Protectorate and in the years after the First World War a variety of Europeans, Indians and a sizeable Lebanese community established themselves in the country.

Gold has always been mined in the mountain ranges of Sierra Leone but it was, and still is, under the control of local Paramount Chiefs – a potent combination of tribal chief and witch doctor – who ruled day-to-day life in the hinterland. The lure of gold is strong and the overall quantities in the country are interesting but most of the trade has been conducted by petty diggers in villages in the interior under tribal control and smuggled out of the country by individuals, so investment was never attractive to major foreign businesses.

However, in the 1930s, serious alluvial diamond deposits and other rich mining areas were discovered in the Kono region east of Freetown which quickly became Sierra Leone's principal source of foreign exchange: and a magnet for tough foreign adventurers. They flocked into the diamond areas and competed with local prospectors to find the rich streaks of mud which contained the diamonds, while the government tried to control the lion's share through the National Diamond Mining Co. As the years passed, important discoveries proved that Sierra Leone has staggering world-class diamond reserves. In 1970, two million carats were exported legally, let alone the smuggled gems, and in 1994 an enormous 172-carat diamond was sold at auction for US$2.8 million.

Unsurprisingly, moves for full independence began at the same time as the discoveries of big mining reserves. These bubbled on through the Second World War but in 1951 a democratic constitution was approved giving everyone the vote and elections were won by the Sierra Leone People's Party (SLPP). After ten years of relative calm, on 27 April 1961 Sierra Leone became an independent state within the British Commonwealth. However, this fragile democracy was hopelessly stretched to cover the extreme poverty of the majority of the people who were, and still are, self-reliant on the ages-old slash-and-burn method of agriculture, and the dazzling fortunes to be made from the diamond, bauxite, rutile and iron ore mines. Almost inevitably, after only seven years the civilian government fell to Sierra Leone's first military coup, followed by a counter coup in 1968 which temporarily restored the elected government. The country lived on the edge for a few more years, survived another failed coup in 1971, but finally succumbed to a one-party presidential system with military backing and no opposition in 1973. This fatal combination and the world oil crisis in the 1970s – Sierra Leone is heavily dependent on fuel imports – set the country on course for steady decline and economic ruin.

In 1985, the Army took over and Major General Joseph Momoh obtained 99 per cent of votes cast in the presidential elections. For seven years Momoh jockeyed to stay in power, playing off the Army and civilian politicians with various appointments to positions of importance. The period was characterised by allegations of coups, arrests, executions, accusations of corruption, and all the time the country's wealth was robbed inside and out. Illegal fishing of important reserves by vessels from neighbouring Guinea, Liberia and Nigeria went on unhindered, the rutile mines producing titanium oxide, an essential ingredient of paint, the bauxite concessions, for aluminium, and iron ore mines all suffered from administrative corruption and the annual diamond exports dropped to only 132,000 carats in 1989. Meanwhile, social conditions took Sierra Leone to the bottom of the international league, with one of the slowest economic growth rates of any country since 1975, the lowest life expectancy in the world (only thirty-six years for men), as well as the highest death rate (25.7 per 1,000) and the highest infant mortality (169 per 1,000) by a long chalk.

In 1991, terrorism stepped into this increasingly grim social, economic and politically sterile picture. Catalysed by the violence which wrecked neighbouring Liberia, a guerrilla movement styling itself the Revolutionary United Front emerged under the loose command of Foday Sankoh. Using the excuse that they disapproved of Freetown supporting foreign Liberian troops inside Sierra Leone, the RUF grabbed villages in the border areas, and de-stabilised the delicate agricultural balance of rural life by roaming across the east of the country, pillaging, raping and killing local people with whom they had absolutely no tribal or political connections. Foreign investors abandoned the rutile and bauxite mines, unable to compete with management inefficiencies and the rampaging depredations of the RUF. Desperately, the government hung onto the diamond areas.

Another coup in April 1992 put a military junta in power led by Captain Valentine E.M. Strasser, but the fighting seesawed back and forth in the interior as the RUF extended their control while political chaos reigned in the capital. The Sierra Leone Army fought back, lost and regained some areas of jungle in the Eastern and Northern Provinces while a million refugees fled their farms to escape the rape and pillage perpetrated by both sides, most flooding into Freetown. This influx created new ghettos and greater poverty in the capital, and these villagers' contribution of agricultural produce to the country's export trade fell rapidly, from 28 per cent in 1984 to only 5 per cent in 1994.

Desperate for help, the government asked British and Israeli Army officers for military advice on how to fight the rebel RUF, but in January 1995 when the RUF seized the valuable mining areas on which nearly all the country's foreign exchange depended – and doubtless more than a few bank balances of those in power – and with the RUF in Songo only 35km from Freetown, Strasser sought the more focused assistance of foreign mercenaries. He also invited in the armed forces of Guinea and Nigeria, both of which had a less than altruistic view of the rich diamond reserves. Fifty-eight Gurkhas who had served in the British Army and a much larger number of South African mercenaries working for Executive Outcomes, a South African company, joined the conflict on stiff commercial terms revealed in this book. Gradually, the balance began to turn again in favour of the government.

In May 1995 Songo was recaptured, by the end of June government forces had retaken the mining areas of Kono and Bo, and by September the RUF was seeking a negotiated settlement. However, new political upheaval in Freetown upset these advances. Another coup attempt was suppressed in October and, amazingly considering the chaos inland, new elections were announced in December. Strasser was accused of planning to restrict voting so he was suddenly replaced in January 1996 by another military junta headed this time by Captain Julius Maada Bio, a previous Chief of the Defence Staff. While endless reports of massacres and human rights violations inland poured down to the coast, general elections were held in February and in March when a new civilian government was inaugurated under President

Ahmed Tejan Kabbah. Astonishingly, a cloud of international observers declared the process, 'As fair as you would expect in this part of Africa considering all the circumstances.'

In April after the elections, Kabbah further surprised everyone by announcing that the government and the RUF would agree to a permanent cease-fire on various conditions. Plainly, there had been some hard negotiations about who controlled the country's mining wealth. However, the RUF continued to rob and kill as before and Sankoh refused to recognise the new government until May when he accepted peace on condition that the mercenaries left the country. They had tipped the balance against his disparate, undisciplined forces and he wanted them out. Local tribal fighters, called Kamajors, joined this mess, like candidates in a real-life *Magnificent Seven* protecting their villages to fight off the attacks of dissident soldiers and rebel RUF alike. Their highly successful efforts at repelling rebel attacks apparently provoked resentment from the Sierra Leone Army, but this probably arose because the Kamajors understandably saw no difference between rampaging rebel RUF or soldiers.

Ahmed Kabbah was the new, duly elected president who had reinstated the 1951 democratic constitution and he enjoyed the support of both Great Britain, traditionally always highly influential in Sierra Leone, and the United States, which held the international monetary and social assistance purse strings. In November 1996, at meetings at Abidjan in the Côte d'Ivoire he forced Sankoh to lay down arms or he would resume military operations. Sankoh signed a peace agreement. In a spirit of new democracy, Kabbah had secured peace for Sierra Leone, the only state in which the true wealth of the country could be exploited for the good of the people.

By February 1997, a national commission was established to monitor the peace settlement, all foreign troops were to be withdrawn, the RUF would cease hostilities and lay down their arms, and all the mercenaries would leave Sierra Leone.

None of this happened.

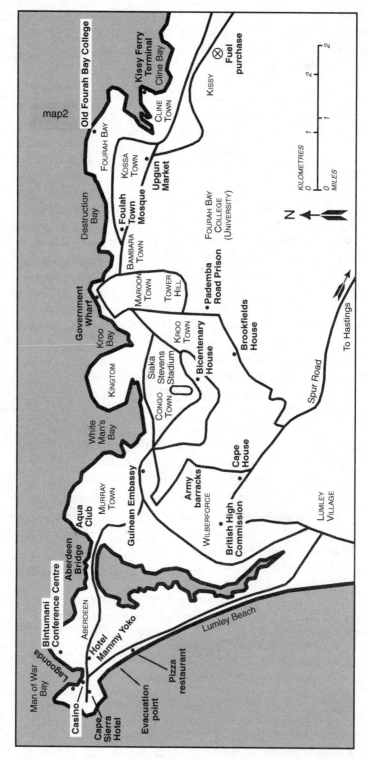

Friday 16 May, 1997

At Freetown's Lungi airport, ten dollars got me past the immigration police, twenty dollars in fives smoothed my way through beaming customs officers without a bag opened, and I was feeling quite pleased with myself till the local fixer arrived just as I was leaving the terminal. She was late but made it clear at once that I should have waited for her. She started shouting and made such a scene that the officials I had just bribed began to take an interest again, like vultures, seeing the chance of further handouts. The last thing I wanted was for them to search my baggage. Quickly, I paid her another ten dollars to shut her up. Mollified, she calmed down and ushered me from the terminal, as if her magic alone was responsible. This was normal; this was Africa.

Another fifty dollars bought me a ticket on a Russian helicopter, a big white and blue Mi-17* piloted by Russians, for the short ride from the airport across the Sierra Leone River to a hotel a couple of miles away the other side of Freetown. We climbed away from the airport over the dirty, grey river and I looked out the window, to get my bearings. A crowd of black people stood about at the jetty at Tagrin, as if they had been there for days, waiting for the wood boats with outboards to ferry them across

---

* Mi-17, export version of Mi-18 Russian military transport helicopter (in use in the FSU and fifty-seven other countries) which was based on the earlier extremely successful Mi-8 Hip (NATO designation). The Mi-17 is powered by twin 1,417 kW TV3-117MT turboshafts, with telltale bulbous twin intakes above the pilots' cabin, for a ceiling of 4,500m, maximum speed 250kph, range 425–520km, and carries 28–36 people, entering through 'clamshell' rear doors.

1

the river to the town. Even from the air, Freetown looked a mess. Decayed old colonial buildings marked the centre, while on the outskirts squalid huts and tumbledown buildings clustered haphazardly along the roads, looking as if they had been shoved into Freetown by some vast bulldozer working from the green jungle inland. In a sense they had. Sierra Leone's guerrilla war had driven more than half a million people to live in the capital to get away from the fighting up country where guerrillas, government, smugglers and mercenaries fought to control the diamond and gold trade, Sierra Leone's chief and most attractive source of foreign currency. This was the sort of place I liked.

The Mi-17 beat round south of the town making towards a peninsula which jutted out into the sea. Here was the upmarket quarter of Freetown, where the rich, including a good many expats and a large wealthy Lebanese community, had their villas and where several better-class hotels had been built by the sea. We circled and landed on a helipad at the side of the Hotel Mammy Yoko, reputedly Freetown's best. I jumped out and found Murdo McCloud waiting for me.

Murdo was a Scot, tallish, of medium build with dark curly hair cut short, British service style, and a cheerful, expressive face. Plainly, he enjoyed the sense of frontier chaos in Sierra Leone – he was known as 'mad dog McCloud' from his reputation as a gung-ho Harrier jump-jet pilot in the Royal Air Force during the Falklands campaign, but his manner could never quite shake off the years he had spent as a squadron leader, an executive officer rank in the RAF. We had spoken on the phone but never met, so we shook hands and he helped me unload my bags from the helicopter.

I had several large suitcases of my own and a bag full of radio kit, including six Motorolas, for Murdo, which is why he had sent the fixer to the airport to get this equipment through the customs. Experience of this sort of work told me to come prepared and my own luggage contained enough clothes and gear to cover all eventualities, from plain fatigues and bush shirts, all carefully non-military in case the customs got curious, tough non-military boots, and other useful pieces of gear which I had collected and refined over the years training soldiers in the jungle, to the other, *haute couture* end of the activity scale with natty summer suits, short-sleeved shirts, lightweight shoes and smart ties to work in a bodyguard role in the town. I felt pretty organised, but I would not have felt so at ease had I known that quite shortly I was to lose the lot.

We left the hotel in Murdo's old Mercedes, crossed the Aberdeen Bridge into Freetown and I saw that my first impressions from the air were right. Freetown is the pits. The air was tropical-warm and smelled thick and sweet of decay. The roads were narrow and in a terrible state of repair, congested with people wandering along the beaten red earth at the side or milling about by stalls set up between mounds of rotting vegetables and rubbish, selling bananas, yams, casava, beer, whisky, brandy, varieties of cigarettes, shirts, pots, pans, shovels – in fact anything. Some people had even set up stalls on piles of fresh earth while it was still being thrown out of the holes in the road where a gang of sweating workmen were digging, flinging soil with their long-handled shovels and shouting at the vendors to go away. The colour of the beaten-hard earth reminded me of the rich red soil of Hereford where I lived. This analogy with one of England's finest cathedral cities goes absolutely no further, although everything seemed coloured this reddish brown in the fading afternoon light: the people, men in filthy slacks and T-shirts and the women in patterned skirts ambling along the side of the road barefoot, the ropey, battered old cars, the buildings which were falling apart with clumps of weeds growing out of cracks in the walls, the roofs and the animals scuffing in the dirt, goats and chickens – all were the same dusty reddish brown.

Murdo drove through the larger, but no less decayed buildings in the centre of the town and into a smarter area on a hill on the opposite side of the peninsula where I had landed at the Mammy Yoko. Large villas lay hidden behind dusty walls topped with rusting barbed wire and concealed by palm trees and thick tropical bushes. In Spur Road, he turned into a gate marked 'Cape House', drove up a sweeping drive and pulled up under the impressive portico of an enormous white-painted mansion complete with decorative neo-classical pillars. This was the base of

Cape International, the company Murdo and his partner Fred Marafono had started together.

'My headquarters,' Murdo announced rather grandly, gesturing at the house and large derelict garden.

At once, I noticed the double front doors were heavily reinforced and the big downstairs windows were fitted with bulletproof glass. This was expensive glazing, very. Whoever installed this was expecting trouble.

Inside, the grand impression faded. Our steps echoed on wide, dusty floors, all tiled, in vast rooms empty of furniture and, in spite of the warmth outside, the atmosphere inside was cold, damp and unlived in. At the back was a terrace onto the garden. Murdo camped on the second floor, presumably because he felt safer one floor up, with his girlfriend, Beth Dunne. They had chosen the only room with any sort of air conditioning, a lazy fan burring round and round in the middle of the high ceiling over a truly huge double bed. Next to this was another big room with just an HF* radio on the floor, a desk covered with papers and a small Psion personal computer and a telephone. This was Murdo's 'office'.

He showed me to another enormous bedroom bare of furniture except for one immense double bed covered with garish African prints and a desperate-looking sixties-style settee covered with worn cream and chocolate brown fake leatherette shoved against the far wall. I threw my bags on the floor and Murdo gave me a can of *Castle* beer, the local brew.

'EO had this house,' he explained casually. 'I took it over from them after they had to leave at the beginning of the year.'

I had heard something of this. The Sierra Leone government had recruited Executive Outcomes, a South African company, to supply mercenaries to fight rebels of the Revolutionary United Front (RUF) who were trying to control the Kono diamond mining area, about 250km from Freetown east of the Liberian border. The mercenaries, over 200 experienced combat soldiers

---

* HF, high frequency radio set, for long distances, the waves either direct 'line of sight' or 'bounced' off the ionosphere (therefore not effective at night).

from South Africa and Britain, were more than a match for untrained rebels, no matter how much posing as soldiers they did, and by November '96 they had forced the RUF leader, ex-Corporal Foday Sankoh, to sign a peace accord with President Ahmed Tejan Kabbah. Part of the agreement was that the mercenaries leave Sierra Leone, and most had gone by February '97. However, the lure of diamonds and gold was too strong, especially in such a heady atmosphere of chaos and anarchy, maybe the most seductive drug of all. Some stayed. Murdo had worked for Executive Outcomes as an air logistics administrator during the fighting against the guerrillas in '95 and '96, and although he had had a serious disagreement with the company it was none the less glad to let him buy Cape House in Spur Road. Executive Outcomes left and he remained in Sierra Leone to pursue his own project.

He wasn't the only one. After our beer, we jumped in Murdo's old Mercedes to go downtown to find Murdo's partner, Fred Marafono, another of the ex-Executive Outcomes mercenaries whom I knew well from our mutual background in the SAS in the British Army. We crossed the town again which was lit with ghastly neon and the occasional street lamps which still worked, crossed Aberdeen Bridge and came to an apartment block in the Cape Sierra Hotel down by the beach where we found Fred doing business with some local people in an apartment. Fred Marafono was a big-boned, powerful Fijian with a broad honest face and years of SAS experience training and fighting all kinds of friends and enemies in rough places all over the world. A fearsome fighter with fists or weapons, he none the less had a great sense of humour and always developed immense enthusiasm for the people he worked with. Seeing him with his thick black hair grown out all over the place and down to his shoulders, and dressed in a pale cream Katanga-style safari suit which looked quite bizarre on his large frame, it was clear he was very far from the constraints of the British Army, and it seemed to me that Fred had at last 'gone bush'.

I guessed later that Fred's businessmen were diamond dealers, but I never had time to work out what the meeting was all about as it ended quickly and became confused in a lot of angry shouting with some guards outside so Fred pulled us all away. Outside, he was typically delighted to see me again, smiling and shaking hands, and we drove back into town. On the way, we made a simple plan to drive together up country the following day to the gold mine at Yara in the Sula Mountains, about 225km from Freetown, which was the project base for the time being. I was used to events moving quickly when you first get to a new place, but I was beginning to feel that I wanted to know more of what I was going to do in Sierra Leone.

In London, my mate Jim Murphy, another Hereford* man, had told me he was going to train indigenous troops to fight rebels in the jungle, which appealed to me a lot, so that when he himself was knocked over by a car as he left a pub, and had to drop out, he called me. I was delighted to take his place. I faxed my CV to Murdo in Cape House in Freetown, and he replied inside two hours from his 'office' with the offer of a job at $4,000 a month to work in a jungle training camp. These are pretty bad wages in this market but there was the chance of some interesting opportunities and I reckoned the job worth looking at. Unfortunately, Fred had other plans for the evening and we dropped him at his own apartment which he shared with a Liberian contact.

Murdo and I went to find Beth and we all went to an open-air pizza restaurant on Lumley Beach, an expat haunt where I noticed a couple of US marines at a table near us. I guessed they had come in the US Army Hum-V† vehicle parked outside. Beth had been one of the few women operators in British Army intelligence but she had given all that up and was now working for one of the numerous aid agencies in Sierra Leone, called Merlin. With her was a friend who was wasting away with chronic dysentery after stupidly accepting the fantastic advice of another aid worker that the local water was clean to drink. Beth was

---

* Hereford is the town where the SAS is based and the name is often used as a synonym for the SAS Regiment itself, e.g. so-and-so was *at Hereford*.
† Hum-V, or HMMWV (high mobility multi-purpose wheeled vehicle), big, broad vehicle which replaced the Jeep, with powerful four-wheel drive for any terrain.

trying to persuade Murdo to help buy drugs to cure her and I was forcefully reminded how deep the disorganisation in such countries can run. The chaos is not merely political but drags down every aspect of social life. Eating pizzas and chatting by the beach, as ordinary an evening as any in that part of the world, little did any of us realise how close Sierra Leone was to the brink.

Saturday 17 May

The following day, in the clear early morning African light which somehow magically made the place seem vibrant and new, we breakfasted in colonial style on the terrace: eggs and bacon, Marmite on bread and coffee, all served by the local cook-cum-garden boy. After a brief explanation from Murdo, I was ready to go, my small daysack with a few essentials and a change of pants and socks handy and all the rest packed in bags in the hall.

Fred turned up during breakfast grinning broadly as ever, his long black hair held back over his shoulders with a bandana, and super-exotically dressed to match his soldier-of-fortune image in an olive-grey combat suit with horribly tailored trouser leggings which he had stuffed into the tops of his combat boots. He and I flung my bags in the back of a pickup-style Landrover, ex-military, which was in a shocking state of repair. Many of the scrapes and dents must have been due to the appalling roads outside Freetown but I am sure Fred was responsible too. He was never a good driver and the owner of the mine had banned him from driving any of his company vehicles.

Makeni, where we had a rendezvous, was the first and only significant town on the route, about three hours' drive from Freetown. The road led at first through thick tropical swamp jungle in the Sierra Leone River valley, overhung with lush green trees and palm fronds. Fred drove in his usual happy-go-lucky style, swerving left and right round potholes and stones, waving cheerfully at the local people walking along the red earth at the roadside. He talked non-stop about the fighting against the rebels the previous year, and with irrepressible enthusiasm about his plans in Sierra Leone. As one of the mercenaries working for

Executive Outcomes, he had taken part in most of the fighting alongside the current Sierra Leone Minister of Defence, Captain (retired) Sam Hinga Norman. He and Sam Norman had played a very significant role together in the principal action near Makeni in which the RUF rebels had been soundly defeated and which had led directly to their agreeing to cease-fire terms and a cessation of the violence which had caused over 10,000 deaths since 1991. Fred, therefore, was very close to Norman, and popular for his energetic and idealistic commitment to the country. He was convinced his own future lay in Sierra Leone alongside the present government. The fact that he had felt this way about every country he had worked in, from Borneo to Dhofar in southern Arabia, and to Belize in Central America, was forgotten. Now, Fred planned to settle in Sierra Leone, and, in a way which probably took him back to his roots in Fiji, he talked enthusiastically of buying land, sharing it with the people, farming oranges and date palms and rearing cattle.

Rounding a corner in the forest, we were stopped at an army road block outside Makeni. Scruffily dressed soldiers wearing baseball boots, carrying AKs* and one an RPG† rocket launcher stood about in the road waving us down. I knew from past experience in Africa that the soldiers were only interested in what they could entice, or even rob from us but I was more concerned that if they got us out and searched the Landrover, they would find the old Chinese AK which Fred had hidden under his legs on the floor. Carrying illegal weapons was a guarantee of arrest, even in a country as chaotic as Sierra Leone, and a long,

---

* AK (Automat Kalashnikova), the Russian assault rifle, with thirty-round curved magazine of 7.62×49mm rounds, found all over the Third World. A useful, reliable platoon weapon which is easy to fire and use, simple to clean and maintain. The only problem is the safety catch, which is on the right hand side.

† RPG-7 (Reaktivniy Protivotankovyi Granatomet) Russian anti-tank rocket launcher. The RPG is an olive green 40mm tube, length 95cm, weight 6.3kg, with a simple pistol-grip firing mechanism halfway along the tube. The rocket, weight 2.2kg HEAT (High Explosive Anti-Tank), is a bulbous conical charge, fitted on one end, and the firer must be aware of the backblast, which can injure people behind. Maximum range, 900m, effective range, 300m.

disagreeable sentence in a Freetown jail did not appeal. As the newcomer, I took my cue from Fred. He had a unique approach.

'Hallo there, my brother!' he shouted at the corporal in charge as he slowed to a halt. The corporal looked uneasy. Unfazed, Fred continued, beaming hugely in a way which was hard to resist, 'Don't you worry, this is my country! I fought for this country, I am buying land and you're all my brothers.'

The corporal looked unhappily from us to the other soldiers. They could see we were expats, and therefore almost certainly involved with diamond or gold mining, and by comparison with their own miserable poverty we were rich, but this wasn't what they wanted to hear. Fred kept up this disarming initiative, scooping up several packets of Lucky Strike cigarettes in one enormous hand from the shelf under the dash where we kept them for this sort of occasion and the corporal took them with a half-embarrassed grin, like a child. The other soldiers peered in the back of the pickup, and through the window at us, more with frank curiosity than any malicious intent. Still calling them 'Brother!' Fred waved goodbye and eased off slowly up the road. Scorching off fast from a group like that would only invite them to start shooting, though I felt sure Fred was oblivious to the danger and was convinced they were indeed his fellow brothers.

We drove through Makeni, a mess of mud-brick huts with rusting corrugated iron roofs, chickens and goats roaming the streets, broken-down trucks grinding up the potholed roads and masses of people just standing about or sitting in the hot sun. A few miles the other side, we came across Ken waiting in the heat of the midday at the side of the road in another Landrover.

One look at Ken convinced me I had taken a job with a bunch of fruitcakes. He was a Maori of medium height but probably weighed at least 17 stone and was built like a brick shithouse. He was solid muscle, with biceps as thick as my thighs. He wore jungle slacks and an olive green skinny weightlifter's gym vest to show off his immense chest and shoulders. He had a massive head, shaved to above his ears, with the long black hair above swept back into a ponytail and he sported a ridiculously tiny Spanish-style goatee beard on the peak of his enormous square chin. The 'Hercules' image was complete with a pair of

Terminator 'I'm gonna kill you!' wrap-around dark glasses. Beside Fred, the two looked like Trackers from Hell and I was suddenly in the movies.

We swapped Landrovers and Ken carried on to Freetown, for a day or two of 'I & I',* while Fred and I drove on to Yara, another three hours away in the Sula Mountains. The road was now just a narrow dusty track and we crept along slowly, bouncing and winding back and forth between the ruts and holes. This was rural Africa as I had seen it in Cameroon, Chad, Zaire and Rwanda. The dense green tropical jungle was now behind us, and we climbed into low hills. In drier, more semi-deciduous forest, the road passed through endless small villages of mud huts. Sierra Leone is among the poorest countries in the world and the clothes the people wore were often nothing more than rags. The little children went naked – as did most of the women, at least from the waist up. In each village we saw female development from birth to death, from flat-chested kids running alongside our Landrover with peaky plaited hair, to firm-breasted young girls in their early teens considered in their prime for childbearing, often with tiny babies at their breasts as they watched us pass, and finally to the older women generally busy round the fires, whose wrinkled faces made them look a hundred but who were probably not much more than forty years old, which is the average life expectancy in Sierra Leone. They went naked, proudly showing off their shrunken, sagging paps as proof of the many children they had produced. Those who were clothed with dresses or trousers had rips, holes, patches, straps and buttons missing.

And it was all dusty brown, baked in the African sun like a sepia print. The people were brown; the mud huts with their thatched roofs were brown; the goats were brown; the chickens were brown; and the ground was brown. Even clothes hanging on washing lines were brown, and exactly the same colour as the clothes the people were wearing. The adults mostly sat about, especially the men, watching us pass. As it was by now late in the

* 'I & I', Intercourse and Intoxication. More pertinent, and agreeable, version of the American 'R & R' – Rest and Recuperation – made famous during the Vietnam War years.

afternoon, we saw people preparing their main meal of the day, sitting round fires they had built on the ground in front of their huts. The favourite dish was *lasa* rat, a local delicacy, spitted on sticks, like meat brochettes.

We reached Yara in the late afternoon, and I suppose the clear evening light in the hills made the place as attractive as it could ever look. The village, a tiny group of scruffy mud huts like all the others we had driven through, lay on the left of the road among trees and our camp had been built on the right, on a small hillock in a large area of cleared ground. It was trying to look like a fort from *The Last of the Mohicans*, with a wood picket fence erected all round the hill and wattle huts with thatched roofs inside.

We drove through the entrance, past the small guard hut, and parked by a bigger wattle building. I got out stiff after hours in the Landrover on such bad roads, stretched and saw at once a familiar figure emerging from the cookhouse and crossing the baked earth of the compound to meet me. This was Duke MacKenzie, a Kiwi who had been in the New Zealand SAS. Murdo had used the HF radio from Freetown to warn him of our arrival while Fred told me on the way that he was on the project. I was looking forward to seeing him. We had not met since '84 when he had come over to Hereford and we had worked together on training and courses and got on well. It was a real pleasure to see him again and we laughed at the changes we both saw in each other. I swear he had put on some weight but he was still very much the same fair-haired, stocky, cheerful and practical Kiwi I remembered from before, with a typical New Zealander's obsession with rugby football.

We walked over to the cookhouse for a brew and to chat over old times and it turned out he wasn't very well at all with a severe dose of malaria. I looked around the hut. It was nothing more than a thatched roof perched on wood poles joined by waist-high thatch walls to protect the two battered chest refrigerators which were wrapped with heavy chains and padlocked to stop locals liberating food for themselves. The table we were sitting at was covered with a mess of brewing essentials, tea bags, sugar, powdered milk, and mugs kept scrupulously clean against disease in noticeable contrast to everything else. Duke flicked on the electric kettle supplied by the generator which burred away constantly on the other side of the compound.

'How's it going here?' I asked.

He pulled a face and just looked at me with an expression which told volumes. 'Come on,' he said heaving himself upright. 'I'll show you round.'

The mine workforce slept in the large thatch-roofed hut by the gate. The walls were made of wattle woven with wood slats, quite strong and effective though you could see through chinks between the slats, and inside the men slept on rush mats strewn on the ground. Beyond this, three old lorry containers had been dumped on the ground, two of which had been converted into stores. 'Windows' had been cut in the sides with oxy-acetylene torches round three sides of a square, peeled and beaten open on the fourth side and metal grilles welded on for security. These stores could be properly padlocked to prevent theft so Fred had occupied the third for his own personal room and office. Nearby, some rusty old vehicles were parked in a way which gave the distinct impression they had not been used for years. Next to this high-tech 'facility' was a concrete block-built shower house.

Our own 'accommodation' seemed to be in a state of constructional flux. Originally, Duke said, there had been no camp on the site at all and they had lived in a couple of tents. Then they had put up bamboo roofs over the tents to keep off the worst of the tropical thunderstorms, and added big lazy turning fans. Then, thatch walls had been started around the sides, though they were not finished. Inside, the arrangements were basic too: US Army cot beds under mosquito nets, and clothes kept in bags on the ground. Catching a look on my face, Duke pointed to a site across the compound where some derelict-looking concrete posts stuck out of the ground and a couple of locals were mixing concrete with a tangible lack of enthusiasm. He explained that this was part of a plan to build more permanent accommodation, 'But it ain't happened yet.'

'And doesn't look like happening either,' I retorted. Within a very short time of being in Yara, I was getting bad vibes about this job.

Certainly, the place had magic. Yara was on high ground

between the Sula and Wara Wara Mountains and in the pale, crystal clear evening light I could see rolling hills covered with green jungle stretching away for miles into the purple haze in the direction Fred and I had driven up from Freetown. This was a view people pay hard-earned money to enjoy, to relax in a cane chair in the warmth, under the vast blue dome of the African skies, listening to chirruping crickets and birds in the trees, sipping a cool beer or a cocktail and chatting about old times and places you've been. Actually, Duke and I made another brew of tea in the cookhouse and sat down to enjoy this view in two smelly old car seats with their springs bulging out. I looked at him and said, 'So, tell me what's this all about?'

Duke explained. Although there had been a cease-fire, the rebel RUF inevitably continued to plague country districts and, if there was any doubt before, it was now plain that they were an anarchic, disparate group of criminals with little central control from Sankoh who by this time was under house arrest in Lagos, Nigeria. The rebels were only interested in seizing control of the diamond mining areas and terrorising the population. There had been several incidents not far away in the uplands of the Sula, Loma and Tingi mountain ranges where RUF rebels had attacked and robbed villagers, raping the women and in one case lopping off the arms of their victims. After years of attacks and killing, the people were tired, but suffering was never a sufficient catalyst to stir a civil population on its own to find change and it needed the success of the mercenaries in '96 to give the government the idea to extend their control of the interior and the diamond mines. Responsibility for this naturally lay principally with the Minister of Defence, who was Sam Norman.

'This ties in with some stuff Fred was talking about on the way up,' I said, though it had all seemed rather far-fetched at the time. Fred, leaning heavily on his friendship with Sam Norman, had claimed he had cooked up the idea of training local hunters called the Kamajors to fight the rebels in place of the South African mercenaries. The principle behind this was simple enough. RUF rebels claimed to be revolutionary freedom fighters who were to set free the people of Sierra Leone, but in fact they were strangers to the areas they terrorised, with no interests, family or tribal connections, whereas the Kamajors were local people, well-respected hunters and many were Mende, from the same region as Sam Norman. Sam was convinced by Fred's enthusiasm that he could use his experience of training the Dhofaris of southern Arabia into *Firqat*, the militia groups who fought so effectively for the Sultan in the insurgency war in Dhofar in 1970–75. There, the SAS had managed *Firqats* in various tribal areas all over the *jebel* above Salalah town on the coast, training men who only days before had been fighting for the guerrillas against them but who, with impressive financial inducements from the Sultan for every rocket, grenade or bullet they brought with them from the enemy, had changed sides. With the commitment of men like Fred Marafono who were prepared to work with people who days before had been trying to kill them, these Dhofaris made excellent soldiers and they became a crucial element in the final defeat of the communist insurgents from the People's Democratic Republic of the Yemen. Fred's vision for training the Kamajors in Sierra Leone included the same game plan he had seen work so successfully in Dhofar, with heavy weapons training, helicopter raids and the demolitionists' favourite, triangular ambushes. Sam Norman, fired up by Fred's idealism, was delighted at the prospect of having his own personal Special Forces unit.

There was another piece in the jigsaw which supported this plan. President Kabbah's government was one of the few African governments which could justifiably claim it had been elected by a proper democratic franchise, and the British High Commission, principal among other international observers who had watched the elections on 26 February '96, had believed the voting was as fair and reasonable as could be expected in any Third World country, and better than most. However, not surprisingly this fragile new democracy found no favours among the hard-liners in the Army which had ruled Sierra Leone under military dictatorship for so many sterile years in the past. Sam Norman was the Minister of Defence but he had supported the foreign mercenaries against the RUF rebels over and above the Sierra Leone Army; he was an appointee of the civilian President Kabbah and he knew he was not popular with the military hard-liners, many of whom, like Captain Valentine E.M. Strasser (dictator from

April '92 to January '96) and Captain Solomon Musa, were living in England but remained a serious threat to the state. So, the plan to train the Kamajors was made not just to block the threat of the rebel RUF, but also to balance the power of the Army itself. Kabbah could see the advantages of a civilian militia which was supported by the people and he backed it.

'But nothing's happened,' I observed. 'And why are we anything to do with a gold mine?'

'Well, the grand plan ain't started yet, so the mine's a cover,' said Duke shrugging. After a pause, he grinned and added, 'Actually, I reckon it's to keep Fred in beer money, and it gives him and Murdo an excuse to bring Regiment guys across.'

The mine, named with stunning simplicity the 'Gold Prospect Mining Company', belonged to a Cornish entrepreneur called Nick Worrel who had a mine in Cornwall and who had picked on Sierra Leone to explore for gold prospects. Worrel came to Yara and courageously spent weeks on his own moving round the whole region searching for traces of gold in the prominent quartzite structures which stuck out of the ground like meteorites landed from space. He realised Sierra Leone was still a very tribal society, with many of the population in the rural areas still animists, their beliefs hardly changed at all by Christian or Muslim missionaries or any other modern influences, and he could do nothing without the support of the local people. In a style reminiscent of the first explorers in Africa, he brought gifts and money and ingratiated himself with the local headman, called a 'Paramount Chief', and he did this so successfully he was himself made a Paramount Chief. This gave him the right to own land. With the support of the local Paramount Chiefs, whom he involved and supplied with new cars, Worrel bought 110 square kilometres of Africa where he had identified significant gold prospects.

The area had always been somewhat 'on the edge' – it included Lake Sonfon, a sacred lake a few kilometres away reputed to contain great spirits to whom virgins were sacrificed, at least until quite recently when the government obliged them to switch to goats instead – but the rebels' terrorism had driven the geologists away and now they refused to come up at all.

'So, what do you do up here?' I asked, genuinely puzzled as to how Duke could have spent so long in a place like Yara with so little to do. He had been there for three months.

Duke shrugged again. 'Nothing, really. Nothing to do anyway. Ken goes down to the village, drinks beer and shags the local girl.' He smiled, 'And I mean *the* local girl. She has a face like a bag of ferrets, she ain't young, and with AIDS like it is in Africa I've got to say he's got more balls than me. Or, maybe he's desperate. He's been up here for five months.' He looked tired, malarial. 'But really, only the mine manager, Mike North, comes up occasionally now, but he's bloody difficult. He sees us as the "enemy". He's a typical long-term expat. He was a copper years ago and tried to do the security here for the mine, but Nick Worrel is under Fred's spell and gave the contract to him instead.' In fact, Nick also got on very well with Duke, as they both shared the same obsession for rugby football.

'So the "plan" is you just sit about waiting for Fred and Murdo to persuade Norman and the President to come up with a contract for these Kamajors?'

Duke nodded like a man who has been caught doing something stupid and embarrassing. 'Yep. Like you, I thought I was up here to train guys to fight the rebels, but so far what you see is all you got. Meantime, we keep an eye on the gold mining.'

Being a guard on a gold mine was not what I had expected and did not appeal. Being a static guard on anything is extremely dull and I wanted something more interesting. However, I had told Murdo I would see how the job went and decided to give it some more days before coming to any conclusions.

In the next couple of days, Duke showed me round the area. As we walked towards the lake across flat dry earth between tall trees, a black head suddenly popped out of the ground ahead of us. Away on our left, another head popped into view. These were miners working 'bell shaft' mines. Once a gold vein was suspected, they dug a small hole and then enlarged it sideways underground, making a bell-shaped cave beneath the surface. As the ground was hard, the diggers could hear our footsteps approaching and would stick their heads out to see who it was, like gopher rats from their burrows. Rebels had been known to

18

catch the miners and it paid to be on the alert for trouble.

They washed the mined material back at camp with techniques probably unchanged since before men first killed each other for gold. Although the concept of specific gravity was not recognised by Archimedes in his bath till around 200 BC, the fact that gold is heavier than most other substances has of course been known for ever along Africa's Gold Coast, and this is the principle behind washing the mined material. In a corner of our camp, one man put the muddy, stony material in a wide shallow metal bowl held by another man doing the sifting, and then he added water from a hose while the sifter swung the bowl in a continuous circular motion, rattling the muddy stones round the battered shiny bowl. As he rotated the bowl, he brushed the stones to one side with his fingers and washed out the lighter earth and mud over the side of the bowl. The other man added fresh water and they repeated the process, working in rhythm, humming and singing, rotating the bowl, washing out the mud until finally they had reduced the mined material to a few heavy stones which they picked out of the bowl between finger and thumb and put in a bag on the ground.

All this activity was carefully watched by a supervisor who was supposed to stop theft and corruption. I reckoned this was a vain hope. There has never been any significant corporate investment in Sierra Leone's gold deposits, except in the late eighties till it was driven out by the violence which started in '91, and the reason was simple. It was impossible to stop corruption, theft and illegal gold trafficking. Corruption, it seemed, touched everything in Sierra Leone. I resolved to make a detailed written assessment of the situation and go to Freetown to discuss matters with Murdo. Fred had disappeared somewhere, and although I had told Murdo from England before coming that I would come out for a month to see how it went, the story I had heard from Duke and what I had seen gave me no confidence at all that anything would ever happen. This job had all the hallmarks of being just another desperate lost cause which attracts so many excellent ex-soldiers to rot their time away in desolate, malaria-infested places all over the world.

Fortunately a couple of days later, on Tuesday 20 May, Murdo called from Freetown on one of the daily HF radio schedules to say that Mike North and a geologist wanted to be escorted up from Freetown on Thursday. That gave me the opportunity to drive down on Wednesday and have things out with Murdo in Cape House. I spent Tuesday working on my military appreciation of the situation, to get my thoughts clear. As I worked, the sense of something missing grew.

I collared Duke again: 'Tell me if I'm wrong, but this whole thing, it doesn't add up.'

'What d'you mean?'

'Listen, I've been going through what the grand plan is all about and there just isn't enough money about. It's just not realistic. I know the Sierra Leone government isn't flush with cash, but where's the resources, cash and backup?' We were being paid $4,000 per month and I knew guys were getting much more on other work abroad. For example, security work in Algeria was typically paying a monthly rate of $10–12,000. I agree we had all accepted our wages before starting work, but having seen what was involved, this was not the sort of money you could expect to pay for good quality guys to set up an elite counter-guerrilla force and then ask them to fight rebels. If that was the level of the pay, then it didn't say much for the financial backing, or the job.

Duke nodded, 'Yeah, you're right. I had a long chat with Nick Worrel when he was out here last. He's a good guy and we got on well. He asked me how much I was being paid and when I told him he said he thought we were being paid $10,000.'

I nodded. This would be more like it. Our pay was low which was not uncommon in these really 'frontier' type of deals, and it was normal for the people who ran such contracts to take a percentage for administration, project development and profit. Quite likely, Fred and Murdo needed a good deal of ready cash to secure the bigger government contract with Sam Norman to train the Kamajors, but it seemed they had cut the pay to the blokes to the bone. I asked, 'What did he do about it?'

'Well, he thrashed it out with Murdo,' Duke said. 'He was really pissed off Nick had been talking to me.'

'But nothing happened?'

'No.'

I knew why without Duke telling me. Nick was a likeable

Cornishman with plenty of guts himself. Coming out to Yara all alone to look for gold was proof enough of that. He got on well with Duke and it suited him to have guys like Duke around his gold mine as the threat of rebels was never far away. But Fred was Murdo's partner and he liked Fred too. Nick was another one who had been carried away with Fred's idealism, with his talk of buying land, helping the villagers farm the land, protecting them, training the Kamajors and saving Sierra Leone. Fred himself believed in his vision, he was a huge, big-hearted enthusiastic Fijian, a fighter, a larger-than-life character, and Nick had bought into the legend.

On Wednesday morning, I took the Landrover down the long potholed road to Freetown. I noticed more army road blocks than before but thought nothing of it. On the way, I went through in my head all the points which made the job a disaster and all the ways in which it could be saved. On reflection in the camp at Yara, I believed the job could work, but there were so many chaotic elements typical of these contracts and certainly typical of Africa which were racked up against it that I had decided that unless there were significant changes I had no option but to call this one a failure, pack up and go home. I had better things to do in life than sit about and mind an empty camp.

In Freetown, I drove straight to Cape House in Spur Road and pinned down Murdo in the big empty room he called his 'office'. He looked defensive and I launched straight into him.

'Listen, Murdo, I was expecting a training camp in the hills, training local hunters to fight the rebels, with on-the-job live ambushes. That's what I was led to expect. I knew about the gold mining company but I never realised that's all there was!'

'It's a cover for the real job,' Murdo retorted in his Scots burr.

'It's not working,' I told him. 'Even the geologists won't go there.'

'One's going up tomorrow, with Mike North.'

'That's the first time in months! Ken and Duke have been up there stagging on in the jungle all this time going mad and doing nothing.' Furthermore, there was no time off. When Ken and the others came down to Freetown for a break, Murdo expected them to sit in Cape House on radio duty, just in case.

'It's only a question of time, believe me. I'm absolutely sure,' Murdo insisted, sticking to his dreams of a government contract.

'Ray Harris didn't think so,' I continued relentlessly. Ray, another guy from Hereford, had been there months before, seen the desperate stagnation and left, furious at being taken for a fool and disappointed at the same time, especially with Fred whom he had always respected.

I sympathised with Ray, but the real reason he had left was because he too believed he was not being paid enough of the contract value and blamed Fred and Murdo.

However, I did not tell Murdo I knew all this. I suppose I did not want to rock the boat too much. After all, it was work for some of the guys, like Ken, and even if I left the job myself, I did not want to queer the pitch for Duke. But there was more to it than Ray had imagined. Out at Yara, Duke had gone on to explain that Nick Worrel had given Murdo and Fred a choice: a contract worth either $15,000 per month per man or $10,000 per man plus a share in profits from his gold mine. The fact was that Nick Worrel liked having ex-SAS guys looking after his mine in Sierra Leone and wanted them to stay on, so had tried to make his offer as attractive as possible. He had been there longer than the rest of us and maybe he could see how quickly the country could get dangerous. Murdo and Fred had taken the second option of $10,000 and Nick's offer of shares in his mine.

Murdo and Fred were partners but they spent their cash rather differently. Murdo used the money to flit back and forth to London, often for the weekend, while Fred stayed in Sierra Leone, often up country, and mostly distributing the project's funds in largesse to the chiefs and villagers. He was a big, generous man who loved to be loved, and there was no better way of making the Africans love him than by giving them money, cigarettes and gifts of cattle or goats.

'The fact is there isn't a contract,' I told Murdo bluntly. 'There's no plan, no structure and no backup to suggest it'll work anyway.'

In town, Murdo lived in a vast empty house, and the only 'backup' was his Psion computer and the old HF radio on the floor in the corner of the room which looked so out-of-date it almost had valves in it. They had no satcom for an emergency link with the outside world, and no weapons except the three old Chinese AKs and a mere five magazines each full of ammunition so worn and polished I wondered it would fire at all without serious danger of stoppages or blowing itself apart. This was hardly a basis for mounting a project to match the dreams he and Fred were trying to sell, and I hated to think what would happen to us if we were arrested for carrying the AKs illegally.

In desperation, Murdo rummaged about in the papers on the table and pulled out a letter. 'We have got backup,' he insisted, waving the piece of paper at me. 'This letter gives us full authority to take whatever weapons and ammunition we need from the Army's main armoury in Freetown, and it's signed by the Minister of Defence personally.'

I admit I was surprised and read it carefully. Quite clearly, it gave Cape International authority to carry arms legally and permitted us to go into the government armoury in Freetown to take whatever weapons we required. This was at least something, in fact quite impressive. Plainly, it was the result of Fred's close relationship with Sam Norman, and, even if there was nothing else, this letter seemed to assure the resources we would need to train the Kamajors.

'We don't want to use this authority till we get the contract,' Murdo explained. It might have given the game away. He was well aware there were elements in the Sierra Leone Army who would have opposed the plan to train the Kamajors.

He gave me a copy of the letter, as a protection in case of trouble at one of the frequent road blocks if someone discovered our AKs. Encouraged a bit by this, I switched to my summary of the things which could make the contract work. I told him frankly that I did not want to fire off all these criticisms without offering some constructive ideas as well. I ran through a list of actions I believed would transform the project, such as getting decent HF and hand-held radios, a satcom telephone, a list of training stores, like weapons, magazines, ammunition, plastic explosive, batteries, wires, initiation switches, screws, nails, hinges, targets, and all the personal equipment we would need to do the training. I told him we needed helicopters, both in training and in support for operations against the rebels, and I gave him my notes on A4 sheets about how to structure the work, allocating time on duty up country to train and fight, and time off for the guys, either in Freetown or an option to go home for a short break. This would be a long-duration project and efficiency was lost if guys stayed on the job all the time. As an ex-RAF pilot Murdo understood about logistics, especially heli support, but even though he had seen how the mercenaries with Executive Outcomes had worked, his RAF background was no good to him in planning this sort of army special forces project. Fred, who acted very much as Murdo's sergeant major, was no help. Even if Murdo could have dragged him back from the jungle, Fred had no interest in office work whatsoever.

I also told him he would need a couple of extra guys and should pay them more. I explained the scales of pay which I thought would be fair, both in terms of the contract in Sierra Leone, and in relation to the international 'market' of ex-regular special forces soldiers, to attract the right people to do the job. There are a large number of ex-special forces soldiers out and about in the world now, some with the sort of excellent operational experience which he wanted to use on this project, but there are a lot of others, and civilian hangers-on, who are space cadets and Walter Mittys, men who would take a job at any price just so they could tell colourful stories about themselves in the bar back home. They would be useless in training and likely enough thin out very rapidly once the real shooting against the rebels began.

'Frankly, Murdo, the $4,000 per month you're paying us isn't enough to get and keep the right men. For this sort of work, it should be double that.'

'That's all good stuff, Will,' Murdo said, impressed. He had listened carefully and positively to my comments, and was probably using the funds to develop the overall contract, but finished by saying, 'But we could never afford it.'

I just looked at him. I guessed he received about $50,000 per month and was paying out $16,000 to Ken, Duke, me and Fred. I thought the management share was too high, but that was typical on a lot of these jobs so I said, 'Okay, that's up to you, but this job isn't what you said it was going to be. It's not just the money, but everything else as well. It just ain't working. That's why Ray left; that's why Duke is going at the end of this month; and that's why I'm leaving. So, book me a ticket back to the UK, Murdo. I'd like to be on a flight at the weekend.'

There had been no shouting, just a calm, blunt discussion. I gave him my passport and the open Sabena ticket and he reluctantly agreed to book me on the next flight home. With Ray Harris gone, Duke going and now me, he was understandably not happy, but I had better things to do with my life.

I spent the night at Cape House again, and next day I met Mike North, the GPMC site manager. He was a typical hoary 'I've seen it all' expat: lean, tanned, thin grey hair slicked back, in his fifties and wearing a tropical safari suit. He carried a 9mm pistol discreetly under his jacket in a brown tooled leather holster and had spent nearly twenty years in and around Sierra Leone. He was another one who was not happy with Murdo or Fred. Nick Worrel had hired him and, when the violence got too bad and he was looking for someone to secure his investments, Mike had put in a bid to run the security at the mine using local people. He was convinced his qualifications as an ex-policeman and long experience in Sierra Leone would guarantee him the job which would have been a good earner. However, a policeman's image is nothing against the exotic lure of the ex-SAS and mercenary excitements which Nick so enjoyed being associated with, nor could Mike compete with Fred Marafono's persuasive ebullience, but he was furious when he lost the job to Murdo and Fred's Cape International company.

Mike became bitter. Routinely, so Duke told me, he would find any fault with Cape International work, and he refused to take advice about when it was not safe to drive up to Yara on the roads. Since the Executive Outcomes mercenaries had left the country under the terms of the cease-fire agreement, the rebels had, inevitably, broken their word and re-infiltrated into the mining areas in the Northern Province, round the town of Kabala. Supposedly freedom fighters, the RUF were nothing more than groups of bandits who lived in the hills beyond the control of the Army or the government and they had started ambushing and robbing again, slowly moving further and further south. Recently, they had been seen near Kondembaia, which was only 15km north of Yara.

On Thursday 22 May, in the morning, I had to escort a 4-ton truck of food stores up to Yara in my Landrover, bringing Mike North along with the convoy in his Range Rover. He drove up at Cape House in the morning, in a bad temper, and the geologist with him stayed in the car. I was never introduced but, looking through the window, I could see he was really very overweight and he did not look at all happy.

I tried to discuss the convoy arrangements, the speed and order of travel, and what we would have to do if we ran into trouble on the road, but Mike North would not listen. He turned abruptly away, got into his Range Rover and by the time we had cleared the edge of Freetown, after passing through several army road blocks and travelling fairly slowly at the speed of the truck, he put his foot down and disappeared in a cloud of dust into the distance.

In sweltering heat, my Landrover and the truck trundled and bounced for hours over the appalling roads, through Makeni, past numerous army road blocks which always cost a few dollars or handfuls of cigarettes, and reached Yara as the sun was going down.

'Where's Mike?' I asked Duke.

'I thought he was with you,' he replied.

We had lost him. At least, that was the way it would look, as he was our responsibility in principle even if he made it impossible for us to help him in practice. We got on the HF set and radioed back to Freetown where Ken was on radio stag in Cape House as usual, on a few days' leave in town with his local girlfriend Sonya.

'The geologist is dead,' the big Maori's voice crackled through the headphones.

My heart sank. This was absolutely not what I wanted to hear. With Duke leaning over my shoulder, I asked, 'Where's Mike North?'

There was a pause, then Ken answered, 'They aborted the trip.'

'What happened?'

Ken laughed, a strange noise over the poor HF link, 'The geologist was so terrified about being attacked by rebels, and so fat and so hot, he sweated himself to death.'

'He what?' I shouted into the mike.

'He had a massive cardiac arrest in the car and died, before they reached Makeni!'

'So where are they now?' I asked, relieved in spite of this unfortunate news. At least he had not been shot by rebels. 'Are they stuck in Makeni?'

'Better than that! Mike didn't want to answer a lot of stupid questions by the police, and I guess no one deserves being left in a Makeni morgue, so he drove the dead geologist back to Freetown in his Range Rover.' There was another pause and some snorting which did not sound like static. 'He dragged the body onto the back seat of the Range Rover but the geologist was so fat he kept rolling off the seat onto the floor every time Mike went over a pothole. Mike said the body kept wedging tight behind the front seats. In the end, he just left him stuck on the floor and drove back to town!'

I felt sorry for the geologist, but the vision of Mike North stopped on the side of the road, back door open and sweating to heave the dead man off the floor onto the back seat, worrying all the time that an army patrol might turn up any moment and arrest him for murder, was just excellent! Duke and I were still smirking when Mike turned up the following day for a short visit. Perhaps understandably, as he must have known what we were thinking, he was even more surly than usual and hardly said a word to us all the time he was there till he left on Saturday. His attitude towards me was quite different when we met up a week later.

After he had finished telling us about the geologist, Ken added that while we had been driving back to Yara, Murdo had disappeared off to the airport and flown back to London. For a long weekend. I marvelled that the big Maori felt no jealousy or irritation that Murdo could do this leaving him to sit on the HF radio all the time, but maybe Ken was happy enough with his 'night fighter' girlfriend and the whole of Cape House to play in.

'Did he book my flight back before he went?'

'No,' said Ken. 'I've got your passport and old ticket here. He left them on the table.'

I was not surprised. Nothing seemed to be going quite right in

27

Sierra Leone. The place was jinxed. I resigned myself to getting my return flight fixed the following week when Murdo got back.

Then Fred turned up again that evening, out of the blue. I think he had been doing more deals with diamond dealers over by Kono, and now he wanted to act the 'laird' of Yara. He had taken it into his head to drive round the villages to find a young calf and because Duke was so ill with malaria he persuaded me to go with him. 'You see, Will, we need to know where to buy good food for the team, two-year-old calves are what we want, and we can help them with up-to-date rearing methods.' He was irrepressible.

That is how I came to spend all Friday and Saturday with Fred, driving for miles out of Yara through the mountains on appalling tracks in that Landrover looking for two-year-old calves to slaughter and eat. Both days, we spent bone-shaking hours in the Landrover. Every time we saw a beast that looked remotely like a calf in some scruffy patch of grazing near the road, we had to go off into the bush to find the owner in some desperate little group of mud huts and talk cattle rearing and prices. The local people were desperately poor. They saw Fred as a source of cash, and were as cheerful and polite as you would expect. He saw them as fellows, the good people of Sierra Leone, as committed to the land as he saw himself. He called them 'Brother!' and he examined the calves they offered him with obsessive care, grabbing them, inspecting their mouths, their ears, picked up their hooves and stroked their flanks or backs to check for disease. He was in his element.

Late on Friday afternoon, we found a calf, Fred haggled a price and we agreed to come back the following day to pick it up. He and I drove all the way back on Saturday morning only to find the man had sold it to someone else. We started all over again. We followed someone else's suggestion where to find a sale of other calves, and drove for more hours through the hilly forests over more bumpy roads in the boiling sun, dehydrated and battered in the old Landrover, only to come across a big crowd of people shouting and milling round a tractor which had broken down and totally blocked the narrow road through the forest. We turned round and drove all the way back. Fred did not mind: he loved it.

I hated it! If I had wanted to be a farmer I would not have joined the SAS and I certainly would not have come to Sierra Leone.

Eventually, we found a calf and brought it back late on Saturday afternoon. Fred supervised its slaughter, we cooked and ate some of it. It needed hanging more but I must admit we had a good dinner that night.

Sunday 25 May

Next day, Sunday morning, Fred disappeared again. He drove off early, just after dawn, in a cloud of red dust, waving at us through the Landrover window, away to see his diamond dealers in Kono. Duke and I stood in the compound and watched him go. Fred had used nearly all our dollars and our stock of Leones, the local currency, paying for the calf, and in generous handouts to the endless villagers we met during our endless bone-shaking drive around every bloody track in the area looking for it. So Duke and I were left with a few bits of calf meat and a store of tinned food off the truck. We were stuck in Yara with nothing to do except stare at great lumps of quartzite sticking out of the ground. They may have been worth millions, but we could not help feeling they had been there millions of years; they were still there; they would probably be there for another million years; it did not matter whether we guarded them or not, and we were broke.

We wandered back to the cookhouse, had a brew of tea, and went to hear the routine morning HF call from Ken in Freetown. It was not routine.

'I can hear shooting in town and explosions,' he said, the urgency clarion in his voice even with the static. 'I think there are mortars too. It started before dawn and it's been going on all morning.'

'What's happening?' Duke asked him.

'I dunno,' he replied. 'And I can't very well go and have a look as I'm here on my own.' He sounded worried. After a slight pause, he added, 'There isn't much food in the house and I've got no money.' Ken was obviously wondering what he would do if he was obliged to leave Cape House and fend for himself. Typically,

31

Murdo had left him with neither instructions nor dollars, the only true means to get things done in places like Sierra Leone.

We told him to sit tight in Cape House. It seemed the best thing to do, and we agreed that rather than let the whole day go by till the usual evening call, Ken would call us at 10 a.m. to let us know what was happening. It seemed to me things were sliding rapidly out of control.

When we stopped talking to Ken, we immediately re-tuned the HF set to pick up the BBC World Service. Within twenty minutes, the news bulletin on the hour informed us, 'There has been a military coup in Sierra Leone.' We listened to the classic, clipped, British tones, reaching out from Bush House in London, 'Early this morning, Sunday 25 May, in Freetown, the capital of Sierra Leone, soldiers overthrew the civilian government of President Ahmed Tejan Kabbah in a military coup, the country's third coup since independence.'

Duke and I burst out laughing. Nothing had worked right on this job and this was the last straw! We stifled our laughter to hear the remainder of the broadcast. The newsreader described a chaotic picture, 'The situation is still not clear but heavy shooting and explosions were reported at about 4 a.m. coming from the direction of State House and the Army's military headquarters. The firing went on for four hours and continues sporadically. A spokesman for the coup leaders calling himself Corporal Gborie has issued a statement on the Sierra Leone Broadcasting Station, the SLBS, now apparently under control of the coup leaders, which said, "The Tejan Kabbah government has been removed from power. I am just an ordinary man and also the spokesman for the coup".'

We burst out laughing again. 'Who's Corporal Gborie, d'you think?' Duke asked.

'An ordinary man!' I laughed. It was like being in a film, a comedy at that. Only this was real. We sobered up and considered our position.

'No wonder Ken sounded worried,' Duke said and we both grinned again. He was probably in a real state. He was running short of food, no money and nothing to defend himself with. Fred had one of the Chinese AKs and we had the others.

At 10 a.m., we were sitting by the HF radio waiting for his call from Freetown. The set remained silent. We took turns trying to raise him, calling and re-tuning the frequency several times, but there was no reply. We looked at each other. This was no longer a joke. My passport and my plane ticket home were in Cape House.

With Ken gone, we felt more cut off than merely being at the end of a bumpy 200km road. We were desperate for news and spent the rest of the day tuned in to the BBC World News. Gradually, a picture of complete chaos began to emerge.

By midday, we learned, 'The coup began early this morning when four pickup trucks carrying about twenty heavily armed soldiers in civilian clothing drove up to Freetown's Pademba Road Prison. An explosion followed, evidently from anti-tank rockets used to blow open the steel gates. The soldiers then freed hundreds of prisoners, including nine soldiers on trial for previous coup attempts against President Kabbah. The shooting has continued all morning and other soldiers burned down the Treasury building.'

We wondered if there was any effective opposition to the coup, and what had happened to the civil government. Our question was answered later in the afternoon, when we heard that President Kabbah had fled directly to Conakry in Guinea, which was about an hour's flying time from Freetown, west along the Gold Coast. The fighting was still going in Freetown, and the newscaster had a surprising piece of detail, presumably from someone with a satellite phone, 'The Connaught Hospital reports five dead, including two civilians, and twenty-one injured, but there is reason to believe these figures will rise.'

Neither of us had any doubt about it. We had both spent long enough in Africa to know that once the fragile restraints of government control were broken, whether it was a dictatorship or democracy, the people were capable of unspeakable violence. Normally the rampaging started once the real fighting was finished. I found out soon enough that we were not wrong about the violence, but we were wrong about the Sierra Leone people.

Corporal Gborie featured again, accusing Kabbah of 'crying down' the Army. 'We want democracy,' he said, an earnest ring to his voice. 'But not this democracy.' Plainly, the Army had not been impressed with Sierra Leone's first genuine election in February '96 and tentative steps towards a modern democracy. 'Enough is enough!' said Gborie. 'We have to build our nation.' He then said Kabbah and his government had been removed because Kabbah had introduced tribalism, a remark which I did not fully understand until the following day.

'Can't get much more tribal than some of these folk around here,' remarked Duke. The local tribes in the uplands were so poor and dependent on scraping a meagre existence for their families from their 'slash-and-burn' smallholdings in the forest that it was normal to see men walking along the road completely naked, with just a parang* swinging from their hands. In the bush, ages-old animism was still more powerful than a recent dusting of Christianity or Islam – the sacrifice of virgins at the lake nearby had not been banned for long – and Paramount Chiefs were just exactly what their name implied, making Sierra Leone as tribal as any place I had ever seen in Africa.

Later that evening, another spokesman emerged from the unseen chaos down in Freetown, this time a rank or so higher. Captain Paul Thomas, who declared that, 'Private radio stations have been closed down and all foreign troops are to stay put.'

This was not surprising, since the coup forces had seized the State radio station and probably closed down others as soon as they could work through to them all. I assumed the reference to the foreign troops meant embassy guards like the US marines I had seen at Lumley Beach my first night, only a week before.

We got no further clues that evening about the real meaning behind Gborie's remark. We sat by the HF set and divided our time between trying to raise Ken in Cape House, every hour on the hour, and tuning in again to the BBC Africa Focus news or the Pan African News Agency hoping for more concrete information about what was happening in Freetown. However, there was no answer from Ken and the World Service bulletins merely went into that frustrating cycle of repetition, saying the same things

---

* Parang, or panga: a long blade, maybe 2ft long, often made from a truck spring, beaten flat and sharpened. Typical jungle agricultural tool.

over and over again. We talked about the events of the day, about what was going on in Freetown and what might have happened to Ken and Fred, trying to speculate their every action and where it left us, stuck out in the boondocks in Yara. We looked at it from every direction and got nowhere. Finally we gave up about nine o'clock and went to bed.

Monday 26 May

I was up early at 4.30 a.m., woken as usual by the skinny cockerel scratching and crowing in the baked earth of the compound, fixed myself a brew and was back on the HF set for the early morning news. I should have known better of course. For getting up early, I was rewarded by another repetition of yesterday's reports. However, by 10 a.m., there was some real news. Corporal Gborie was quoted again, saying that Nigerian forces were now cooperating with the coup leaders and he called on the Nigerian and Guinean forces to stay out of the fighting.

I wondered why Nigerian soldiers were in Sierra Leone at all and though Duke was not sure of all the details he had heard that the arrangement arose from membership of ECOWAS, the Economic Community of West African States. Elections were planned in Liberia in July and Kabbah had used the ECOWAS agreement to monitor these as an excuse to have Nigerian soldiers stationed in Sierra Leone, as part of the ECOWAS Monitoring Group, called ECOMOG. Duke thought there were about 300 Nigerians in Freetown.

I wondered if this had been another desperate attempt by Kabbah to balance the power of the dissidents in the Army and prevent a coup. If so, it had failed. At midday, we heard another statement from Captain Thomas, who had now replaced Corporal Gborie – evidently too ordinary a man to represent the coup leaders – as the coup spokesman and declared that all Sierra Leone's air, land and sea borders were closed until further notice. This was obviously for effect as the Sierra Leone Army was not remotely capable of stopping people crossing land borders in the jungle, where in any case the RUF rebels were in control; nor could their navy prevent small boats from leaving the coast. It had long been a fact, even in 'normal' times, that the majority of Sierra Leone's gold and diamonds were smuggled over the borders. Maybe this announcement had more to do with the news that Nigeria had reacted very swiftly and flown more troops straight into Lungi airport which, with troops from neighbouring Guinea as well, they had seized and now controlled. Optimistically, Captain Thomas repeated the call for all foreign troops to return to their 'bases', presumably a euphemistic reference for Nigerians to go back to Lagos and Guinean soldiers to Conakry.

With the Nigerian and Guinean ECOMOG forces occupying the airport and facing angry Sierra Leone coup troops, our chances of leaving the country by air had suddenly vanished. Even if there were flights from Lungi, the only way of getting to the airport would be to creep through the soldiers' positions, and they were bound to be very nervous and extremely trigger happy. Nor was I cheered by Captain Thomas's statement that, 'A designated head of state would brief everyone in due course!'

Meantime, we heard that soldiers were driving round in stolen cars looting everywhere, the Bank of Sierra Leone had been robbed, blown up by rocket attacks sending banknotes floating into the air in the streets around, then set on fire, and the centre of Freetown had been gutted. The hundreds of prisoners from Pademba Road Prison who had been set free at the start of the coup on Sunday morning had by now been given military uniforms and weapons and claimed they were the Army, 'as the Army should have been'.

This seemed to be a common theme of the coup announcements. Finally, the coup leader himself issued a statement. Up a rank again from Captain Thomas, Major Johnny Paul Koroma made it clear that the army hard-liners had acted before Kabbah's civil government could neutralise the Army's power.

'As custodians of state security and defenders of the constitution we have decided to overthrow the Sierra Leone People's Party government because of their failure to consolidate the claims achieved by the brokers of peace.'

This implied the cease-fire agreement between the government and the RUF rebels which had led to the foreign mercenaries leaving the country. The rebels had broken their side of the agreement and started terrorising the people again but Koroma quickly made it clear that he was not criticising Kabbah for being unable to stop this. Quite the opposite. To our surprise, he announced that he had asked the Nigerian government to release Corporal Foday Sankoh, who was the leader of the RUF rebels, from Lagos where he was being held under house arrest. Far from the Army trying to defeat the RUF, the coup leaders were calling on the RUF rebels to join them.

Koroma continued by complaining that the soldiers were not being paid enough, which may have been true as there were rumours that their rice ration had been cut by 50 per cent, but the real reason for the coup seemed buried in Corporal Gborie's remark about tribalism. Koroma repeated this, accusing Kabbah's government of being 'nurtured on tribal and sectional conflict'. He then explained what he meant: 'The activities of the Kamajors will be banned! They have been paid out too much, while our own soldiers' pay was cut. We are the national Army! Not the Kamajors!'

Suddenly I understood what they meant by tribalism. The Kamajors' strength and political advantage for Kabbah's civil government and Sam Norman were in their common roots with the people. This was Koroma's tribalism. The coup had overturned Kabbah before he could set up an alternative power block with the Kamajors to neutralise and counterbalance the Army. Sankoh's rebels were rootless criminals, the antithesis of the Kamajors, which explained why Koroma had called for the RUF to join his side in the coup.

It struck me suddenly too that the coup leaders must have known that foreigners were planning to train and fight with the Kamajors. And they probably knew who. Us. I pulled out the copy of the letter of authority signed by Sam Norman from my shirt pocket. It was not so much worthless now, with the new regime, as actually dangerous, since it linked us directly to the Kamajors, and, given that they had taken over the military headquarters in Cockerill Barracks in Freetown, they probably had a copy of this letter anyway. We had heard nothing about any resistance to the coup, so we assumed that Fred's mate Sam

Norman was now the *ex*-Minister of Defence and we guessed he had gone into hiding with Kabbah. All the same, I kept the letter.

'If someone was paying a load of money to the Kamajors, we never got to see any of it,' Duke remarked grumpily. As if on cue, we heard Fred calling us on the radio. Immediately, Duke seized the mike and asked, 'Where are you? What's the situation?'

'Don't worry,' said Fred. 'I'm okay!' His voice was distorted through the radio, reception was poor, and he sounded very strange, as if he was unable to say what he wanted. Duke asked him several times to say what he was doing, and where, but Fred just asked about us and avoided answering, as if he was being prevented by someone, and then abruptly went off the air.

Duke looked at me and said, 'Sounded as if someone was stopping him talking.' He paused, then added, 'D'you think he's been captured?'

'I agree, he sounded very odd, but how can you tell?' I shrugged. He could have been in Cape House, using the HF set there, and he had sounded as if someone had been holding a gun to his head. Maybe the coup leaders had already tried to find the foreigner training the Kamajors; maybe they had taken over Cape House and arrested Fred and Ken. If so, then why had they not made Ken answer our calls? Had he got away, or was he hurt? Or, Fred might have been with his diamond-dealing contacts who had HF sets too, so he could have been in Kono. Whatever, it was worrying: Fred was normally so positive and outgoing. The problem was that there were so many possibilities.

We made a brew and reviewed our situation. It was not good. We were stuck in Yara, and decidedly no longer flavour of the month with the Army who, if they did not know who had been working with Norman to train the Kamajors now, would soon enough find out. We had always been on the other side to the RUF rebels but now they were allied to the Army as well. We had no idea where Fred was, or Ken, and suspected that both had been grabbed by the coup leaders. They might have been languishing in Pademba Road Prison. In any case, they were out of contact and no help to us. I had left my passport in Cape House in Freetown so Murdo could change my flight. With Lungi airport surrounded by troops, I no longer believed that my ticket would be worth very much, but I needed my passport. Duke had his passport with him in Yara. We had a Chinese AK and five magazines each, fifty dollars in the Cape International petty cash box, all that was left after we had paid for Fred's calf. I had about $100 of my own, and at least it was all in small denominations.

Our options were simple. There was no one left to keep us in Yara, even the mine workforce had thinned out, so either we left Sierra Leone by driving north to the border and crossing into Guinea – which meant a very long journey through the mountains round to the capital, Conakry – or we could drive back into Freetown. Both ideas lacked appeal.

As we discussed what to do, we stayed close to the radio to catch the latest news. The looting and pillage of Freetown was in full swing. Soldiers had 'commandeered' vehicles belonging to a variety of aid missions, from the United Nations, religious missionary foundations, the Red Cross, ASSP, Farmco, North Central Agricultural Project, and Sierra Leone official cars, and they were on the rampage. They had 'liberated' the World Food Programme's warehouse full of rice; they were busy robbing houses in the richer areas, especially Freetown's rich Lebanese community; two Americans had been wounded when their home was looted, and the American Embassy had been hit by three rockets and strafed with automatic fire.

A typical list of important people had denounced the coup. The American Ambassador in Freetown, John Leigh Hirsch, somewhat understated the case when he said, 'This is totally uncalled for! These people are out to line their pockets and the country is now in a difficult situation. All the aid, and the job I have been doing here to bring economic development to Sierra Leone, are now on hold until this matter is resolved!' The United Nations Secretary General, Kofi Annan, chose the grander, more theoretical approach and said, 'The United Nations firmly upholds the principle that governments democratically elected shall not be overthrown by force. The United Nations continues to stand ready to assist the people of Sierra Leone in their quest for a society grounded in democracy, in the rule of law, with respect for human rights, and in the pursuit of peace and national reconciliation.' These fine words fell on deaf ears in Freetown where the soldiers were busy wrecking the place, and I doubted very much that the UN was quite as ready to send troops as Mr Kofi Annan suggested. We could expect no help there. Evidently, the civilian population thought so too, because they had all gone to ground. So did we. Late that evening, after a report from the Connaught Hospital which put the death toll in the fighting at a conservative fifteen, with forty injured, we went to bed.

Tuesday 27 May

Next morning, the cockerel woke us at five o'clock again and we carried straight on discussing our options where we had left off. Duke had his passport; he had already been in the jungle three months, but he was badly run down with malaria and the last thing he wanted was to be arrested if we drove to Freetown. The Paramount Chief, who was also the local witch doctor, had been talking about driving down to the coast in the smart new 4×4 which Nick Worrel had given him, but he changed his mind saying he had another hard day's work fattening the goat for sacrifice to the spirits of the lake. I reflected this was probably a good thing as polished wide-rim aluminium wheels and a 100-watt mega-bass audio system were certainly *de rigueur* for local hoods in Brixton or Harlem but might look a tad incongruous in the frontline African context of Sierra Leone two days after a coup and attract the unwelcome attention of rebels en route. However, my passport was still in Cape House; I was curious about seeing the coup; and I decided I must drive myself to Freetown.

'Why don't you stay here,' I suggested to Duke. 'I'll take a Landrover and go down. I want my passport back.'

He nodded without argument. His skin was grey with malaria.

'If you don't hear from me in forty-eight hours' time then assume something's happened to me. Go north, to Guinea.'

He agreed and watched me get ready, already looking quite alone sitting at the HF set listening to more news bulletins.

I took my small green daysack with a spare shirt and socks, some washing things, my hundred dollars, and the Chinese AK with five full magazines which I put on the floor behind my feet, hidden under some rags. As I let out the clutch in the compound, a mine worker jumped in the back of the pickup. I let him stay. He might be useful.

I drove very alert for trouble. There were more road blocks than usual, maybe twenty in all, but in the three hours to Makeni I saw only one or two soldiers at each, sitting as if there was nothing in the world to worry about in the shade of trees at the side of the road. It was not until after Makeni that I saw real evidence of any change. Typically, there was no check for miles after leaving the dusty, mud huts of the town and I was beginning to wonder if all the soldiers had gone into Freetown when, abruptly round a corner, I came across an unusually large crowd of people and soldiers hanging about in a clearing hacked out from the jungle beside the road. Armed with AKs, three soldiers wandered into the road waving their hands lazily for me to stop. I was cheerful and friendly and handed over packets of cigarettes and a few dollars. The man in the back helped in a way, diverting the soldiers' attention, but his chatting only meant it took more time to break away before I could ease off down the road.

Only a few miles on in the sweltering tropical air, which seemed trapped between the trees each side of the potholed road, I drove into another road block. Again there was a crowd of people by the road. This time, two soldiers carried RPGs and behind them were others in a mixture of dress, army trousers with torn, ragged shirts and dark glasses. I recognised them as RUF rebels, Foday Sankoh's mob whom Koroma had asked to join the coup. The soldiers who wandered out to stop me had a certain edge in their manner, more awkward and persistent as they looked inside the Landrover. Smiling broadly, a picture of bonhomie, I chatted them up, but watched their every move carefully, especially the rebels behind, suppressing my impatience. If I irritated them, they might search the Landrover, they would find the Chinese AK, and I was in serious trouble.

To my horror, several of them decided to jump in the back and I found myself taking rebels in to loot Freetown. This was helpful getting through the next road blocks, as they were a ticket through, but I did not know what was really going on in Freetown. If there was any opposition to the coup, I would certainly find myself under attack and be on the wrong side.

At the same time, the traffic built up coming the other way, leaving Freetown. Ancient battered trucks and Jeeps groaned along the bumpy road laden to the gunwales with household goods piled high on the back, mostly television sets, sofas, beds, chairs, sideboards, pots, pans and tables – even the cars had things lashed to their roofs with rope tied through the open windows – and there were loads of soldiers dangling off the sides or hanging out of the windows, festooned with weapons of all sorts, like AKs, PKMs,* bulbous RPG rockets poking up in the air and belts of ammunition slung about their necks. They were all cheerful – not surprisingly as they had just spent the last two days looting everything they could find.

The closer I got to Freetown, the more vehicles I saw, almost in convoys one after the other, all laden with loot. At the same time, I began to notice more and more rebels walking along the side of the road into town, well-armed with AKs and RPGs, but dirty, often in rags, many of them seriously tribal and wild-looking from months in the forests, their long tousled black hair stuck through with 'juju'† charms of leaves, pieces of wood, bits of mirror or God knows what else. Evidently Major Johnny Paul Koroma's appeal for the RUF to join the Army was being answered in style, and the rebels were keen to get into Freetown as soon as possible before the soldiers looted the place clean and left nothing for them.

I reached the outskirts of Freetown at about three o'clock, tired after the long journey and sweating in the hot cab of the Landrover. The soldiers at the road blocks had become even more difficult. The road was nearly choked with vehicles and rebels making their way into town. It was time to decant the rebels in the

---

* PKM (Pulemet Kalashnikov-M), Russian platoon machine gun, 50/100/200- or 250-round linked belts of 7.62×39mm AK rounds in a box magazine, weight 8.9kg, length 116cm, effective range 1,000m.
† Juju, or Jombobla, is a secret magic power, which translates directly from the Mende language as 'remover of pubic hair'. It is a cult of terror and sexual assault, in which Jombobla gangs take the pubic hairs of their rape victims as empowering fetishes and talismans.

back. I stopped the Landrover and told them the ride was over.

'No man!' They laughed at me. 'You take us all the way!'

I forced a laugh and told them, 'Company rules! More than my job's worth to be seen carrying unauthorised personnel. Sorry, lads, but you'll have to step down.' I softened this blow by doshing out handfuls of cigarette packets and reminding them I had saved them one hell of a walk. The miner from Yara helped tip the balance before it crossed their minds simply to rob me and take the Landrover themselves. Reluctantly, they climbed out and I accelerated smartly away waving cheerfully.

I decided to get away from all these lunatics as soon as possible and turned off the main road into the back streets. These desperately poor shanty areas were also crowded with people, but they were civilians, mostly men and young boys in filthy slacks and torn shirts or vests milling about with an air of uncertainty and expectancy. I drove slowly, careful not to antagonise them, not knowing if they blamed the whites for the violence. They watched me pass curiously as there were very few other cars on the streets. So far, they were not aggressive. I glimpsed women and little children lurking furtively behind half-open doors, or just faces in windows, which suggested that many of the people were staying out of trouble at home while the soldiers and rebels pillaged the town.

My problem was finding the way to Cape House when I had only been there twice before. When we left town the previous Thursday with the 4-ton truck and Mike North, we had come through back streets and I tried to retrace my steps. I got lost several times, ending up in a mess of ramshackle corrugated tin huts with garbage everywhere, and wrestled the old Landrover around to find my way back.

There was no option but to go through the centre to reach Spur Road, out towards the sea, and I found myself in scenes of total chaos. Armed soldiers and rebels were everywhere, shouting, running about, in and out of looted shops through smashed windows, especially after radios or TVs, and many of the buildings and shops were smoking or on fire. Cars were burning in the roads which were a mess of barricades, rubble and rocks scattered about. Shopping streets were strewn with glass and goods littered out over the road from looted stores. Cars and pickups drove at high speed up and down the road loaded with heavily armed soldiers, swerving in and out of the wreckage, hooting horns. They shouted at each other and fired bursts of automatic in the air. When this happened, people running about in the street dodged into the shops nearest them through smashed windows or doors, or ducked down behind broken-down or burnt-out cars stranded in the road.

I drove slowly through all this, weaving in and out of the mess, hoping no one would notice me, which I admit was pretty unlikely as I saw no other white people out on the streets. However, I guess they were so busy robbing everything they had no time for me in the old Landrover which they could see was empty anyway. All the same, I adjusted the position of the Chinese AK at my feet so I could grab it just in case. I reached for it once when some shooting broke out between two groups of soldiers stealing from the shops in Kissy Street and I thought for a moment they were attacking me.

I nearly made it through the middle without being stopped. Then, at the end of Kissy Street, a Sierra Leone officer, surrounded by a crowd of soldiers, swung his AK at me and waved me down, pointing straight at me. For a moment, I thought of trying to make a getaway, but there was no side street handy to turn into and evasive manoeuvres in an old Landrover are slower than turning the *Titanic*. I pulled up by the officer. His soldiers gathered round the front and he walked over to my window, looked in at me, and for a long moment he peered all around inside. I waited, very on edge, ready for anything.

Then he looked at me again and said, 'Don't worry! You're okay!'

He waved me on quite regally and, hugely relieved, I drove away. I recognised where I was now, and was feeling rather pleased with myself when, just as I was passing Cockerill Barracks at the top of the hill very close to Spur Road, a couple of Jeeps came roaring out of the barracks stuffed with soldiers, AKs and RPGs bristling in all directions, and someone fired a long burst of automatic at me, cracking over the roof of my Landrover. I ducked, cursing, as they swung wildly in front of me and accelerated away down the road shouting with laughter.

I was furious but it would have been insane to have got involved and I carried on down Spur Road to Cape House. I had thought about how I should approach the house, suspicious what the coup leaders might do about Cape International, but after the chaos I had seen it seemed unlikely that there was a single soldier in Sierra Leone with discipline enough to sit in ambush in the house on the off-chance an expat might come back, when all that mayhem was tempting him to go downtown for his share in the rape and pillage. I slowed up as I approached the entrance but I could see no one about and turned in at the drive.

The place was wrecked. The Nissan and Murdo's Mercedes in the drive were full of bullet holes, their tyres flat; the drive was littered with rocks and bits of slates off the roof; the big bullet-proof ground floor windows had been blown in with RPG rockets; the white walls were pock-marked with bullet holes and the double front doors were hanging open, shot through with holes too. I pulled up, cut the engine, grabbed the AK and hopped out to make an inspection.

A hot, oppressive tropical silence hung over the place; noises from the town centre were distant and sporadic, so my steps sounded loud as I walked under the portico and slipped quickly through the front door into the hall. Still no one about. I looked round. Whoever had attacked the house had shot it up big time, inside and out. Bullet holes marked the white walls and ceiling and the marble floors were covered with rubbish, stones and empty cases. I nipped up the stairs to the first floor. The place had always been sparsely furnished, with a few beds and those dreadful sixties sofa chairs, but they had ransacked it completely, taking all the bedding, and fired whole magazines all over the shop.

In Murdo's office, his table was kicked over, papers were scattered across the floor, the telephone was gone and the HF set had been ripped out, leaving bare wires trailing from the socket in the wall. I rooted about among the papers looking for my passport, but there was no sign of it. Nor any sign of Ken or his girlfriend. I looked round at the desolation, wondering what to do next. There was no point staying there so I went back downstairs and out into the hot sun.

The garden boy was standing waiting for me by the Landrover. He had been hiding in his hut in the garden and heard the Landrover come in.

'I got the radio here, boss,' he said, and showed me a cardboard box which contained one of the new Motorolas I had brought into the country and a new HF set. 'I took this box just when the soldiers arrived and hid in the garden.' I thanked him and put it in the Landrover. At least, now I could use it to get in touch with Duke.

'What happened?' I asked gesturing at the house behind me.

'The soldiers came early in the morning,' the man replied, plainly still frightened. I guessed shortly after Ken's first early call on the Sunday morning to us in Yara. 'They attacked the house and took everything.'

Johnny Koroma must have known of the links between Sam Norman and Cape International. Judging by the time it had happened, so early in the first hours of the coup, the attack on Cape House looked very much as if it had been a planned element in those first important actions at the beginning of the coup.

'And Ken?'

'Mister Ken hid in the roof, with his girl. They fired their rifles into the roof but he was okay. They never found him.' This was better news.

'So where did he go?'

'He's gone off with the girl, to stay at her house. I can show you?'

We got in the Landrover and he guided me through the town avoiding the worst areas in the centre where the looting was going on, to a rough, shanty area down by the estuary, not far from the Hotel Mammy Yoko near the sea where the streets were unsurfaced and full of potholes. Refuse lay in heaps all about and most of the houses were shacks made of corrugated tin and wood. We parked in the dusty street outside a single-storey flat-roofed house, badly built of concrete blocks with broken glass cemented onto the tops of the walls, which looked more solid, if not exactly better quality, than the rest but was still dirty and smelled. I banged on the door.

Ken opened the door, huge of course, but he had a hunted look in his face. He wore a vest, grotesquely patterned baggy trousers, and mountain-cross trainers which was all he had had on when the attack started on the house. Trapped inside while the soldiers were firing rockets at the windows and shooting the door to bits, Ken and Sonya had raced for the attic. He had pulled the ceiling trapdoor open, yanked down the ladder, shoved her up ahead of him into the roof space and just managed to shut the trap door as the soldiers burst into the rooms below.

'When they started shooting through the ceilings, we had to stand on the rafters, man!' said Ken, the girl beside him nodding as he spoke. 'Or they'd have killed us!' I could see he was badly shaken by the whole experience. The ponytail was still there, and the little goatee beard on the end of his massive chin, but without the rambo-style vest, army fatigues or wrap-around dark glasses, he did not look fierce at all. They were both convinced the soldiers had known they were in the attic and had tried to kill them by firing through the ceiling.

This sounded unlikely to me, and I felt that all the shouting about killing the foreigners and their hookers – including specific abuse about Ken's girl, so she claimed – simply confirmed that the coup leaders knew very well that Cape International and Sam Norman were in cahoots and they wanted to catch us all. If they had really known the two were in the attic, they would have winkled them out with grenades, shot them to pieces up there, or just torched the whole house. I kept these thoughts to myself, stood up to go and on the way out I asked Ken if he was going to come with me.

'No, mate,' he said looking sideways. 'I would do, only I got to look after her.' He gestured vaguely behind him at the skinny black hooker who was watching us both intently.

'What's she got to do with it?'

'Well, Sonya, she's my woman,' he replied a shade defensively.

'Ken, for Christ's sake,' I whispered. 'She lives here, she's a night fighter. Forget her!'

'I gotta look after her,' he repeated, sheepish but unmoving.

'Are you sure about this?'

He nodded.

I looked at him for a moment, then shrugged, 'Okay, it's up to you. But will you come with me to find the British High Commission? See if we can find out what's going on?' And we both needed new passports. Ken's had been taken from Cape House along with all his other possessions.

He agreed and we set out together in the Landrover again to Spur Road. Following the garden boy's advice, twisting and turning through the back streets we found the British High Commission on the top of the hill in Spur Road. The building was modern, concrete and glass, quite smart-looking in a small yard behind a high wall with 8 foot high square steel-barred security gates. This was a standard design for the Foreign Office, specifically for countries like this one where there was a strong chance of rioting, to withstand attack. The guard house by the gate had bulletproof glass windows which looked into the street, and the guard, a local man, came out rather reluctantly to talk to us through the gate to see what we wanted.

'I want to speak to one of the staff,' I said. I could see several vehicles in the yard, but there was plenty of room and I added, 'And will you open the gates so I can bring my Landrover in? It'll get stolen if I leave it here in the street.' A lot of vehicles were cruising up and down the road, crammed with soldiers and rebels, and there were others milling about by the sides of the road, AKs hanging off their shoulders, staring curiously at Ken and me standing alone outside the gates.

The man shook his head unhelpfully, 'No.'

'Listen, I'm a British citizen. Can I come in?'

'No, sah, not possible. What d'you want here?' He stood there obstinately and would not budge. I had had a long, hot tiring day, the rebels on the other side of the road were beginning to show interest in this argument of ours and I resented being treated like some sort of enemy at the High Commission. As a British citizen, and I suppose from my years in the Army, I looked on this place as almost belonging to me. In the SAS, I had worked in buildings like this for the Foreign Office. At the very least, I felt it belonged more to me than to this local bloke on the gate. 'Just go and get someone from the staff,' I snapped at him.

Grumbling, he shambled off to the High Commission building

in the yard and reappeared several minutes later with a short, plump white man with a shiny pink face and heavy sweat stains on his shirt, who said, 'I'm Dai Harris. What's all the fuss about?'

I explained, pointing at the rebels over the road. 'I need to bring this 'Rover in or those guys will steal it.'

'You can't bring it in,' said Harris bluntly.

'Well, I'm not leaving it out here, with that lot over there.' Several were ambling over in our direction. They were not aggressive but I was sure they would have stolen my car in seconds if we had left it, like they were stealing everything else. Then Ken and I would have been really stuck.

I tried everything to make Harris see this, but he flatly refused to help, almost as if it was a real cheek even to ask him. I understood all his reasons, given the circumstances, especially with Ken standing there beside me massive in his jive bunny outfit. If he let me inside, then he believed he would likely enough have everyone else wanting to come in, but there was absolutely no feel-good factor or upside in what he had to say. I had just spent hours driving from Yara in the baking sun and, perhaps naively, I had fondly dreamed that I might be offered a cup of tea and the chance of a nice chat to hear what the High Commission thought of the coup.

'This isn't an ordinary situation!' I reminded him. 'There's been a coup and there's mayhem going on down in the town! That's why we're here, to get new passports as ours have been stolen.'

'That's not the point,' he said stubbornly. He looked with distaste at my sweat-stained safari-style clothes and at Ken, with his ponytail, goatee and shades, standing huge in his baggy pyjama trousers patterned in a revolting sea-blue, black and yellow.

Harris really irritated me, but we both needed the passports. I said, 'Well, with this chaos going on, I'm armed, and I can't leave this weapon hidden in the car, or they'll take it and the car.'

'Well, you certainly can't come in here with weapons,' said Harris in bureaucratic tones, striding off back to the Commission building.

Seething, I parked the Landrover right in front of the gates, almost scraping the sides on the steel so it could be seen from the inside. We kept a wary eye on the soldiers and rebels in the road, and waited in the afternoon heat. After a few moments Harris came out again across the yard to speak to us through the gates and said curtly, 'You can't park there!'

'You won't let me come in, and now I can't park here either!'

'You'll have to move it,' he snapped. 'Here are some forms.' He thrust a couple of forms through the steel gates at us and ordered importantly, 'Return them with twenty dollars and you can have your passports.' Then he walked off again.

I looked at Ken. He shrugged. I re-parked the old Landrover, this time with its nose just over the gates at the side, right against the wall, and left the garden boy in the back with instructions to shout for help if the rebels came over. The local gate guard reluctantly let us through the gates and we crossed the yard into the Commission.

'All right, you can fill in the forms here,' said Harris. 'I suppose you need photos too?'

I ignored his tone, just determined to get the thing done and get outside again as quickly as possible. We both lined up for our pictures without a word. While he was waiting for the Polaroid prints to develop, he looked at our forms and, when he noticed that I had written my address as 'Hereford', he immediately changed his tone.

'Hereford? But you're originally from London, aren't you?' he asked, fishing.

'Yes, but I was in the Army there.'

'Ah, I know some guys from Hereford,' he said rather pleased with himself.

'Really?' I said without enthusiasm. I have found half the people in the world want to tell you they know all about the SAS, and the other half pretend they were in it. However, it turned out Dai Harris had been in Beirut and come across some people I knew from the Regiment there. The conversation led nowhere but the atmosphere between us lightened and he finished in a positively friendly tone by telling us to come back the next day for our passports.

The scene outside had hardly changed. The soldiers were standing about nearer to the gates vacantly watching the Landrover and the Commission, but no one had started any trouble. Ken insisted on going back to his woman but agreed to go for a drive round the town first and see what else was going on.

Everywhere I found the same scenes of chaos as earlier, with burned cars, rubbish on the streets and pickups full of armed rebels and soldiers. Once again with the help of the garden boy, we managed to avoid the worst areas, where the shops were. We drove to Lumley Beach, where I had had supper my first night in the country, and came across a British Army Landrover parked on the side of the road, complete with painted army markings, and beside it stood a tall, lean and fair-haired British Army officer, a major, crisply dressed in tropical jungle combat uniform and boots.

He was peering through a pair of rather expensive-looking compact binos across the estuary at a military barracks in the town, on the hill near the Commission.

I pulled over and went over to introduce myself for a chat. We shook hands.

'Will Scully.'

'Major Lincoln Jopp,' he introduced himself rather formally. 'You been here long?' he asked in a relaxed and easy manner which was quite the opposite to the treatment we had just received from Dai Harris in the Commission.

I said we had come from Yara and then asked, 'What's going on?'

He and a warrant officer had been running a small British Army training team for Kabbah's government, training Sierra Leone officers, and working with the Defence Attaché, Lt Colonel Andrew Gale, out of the British High Commission. I thought I should be pretty up front, given the situation, but I kept my story brief, and told him our house had been robbed and our passports stolen, so we were now stuck in Freetown till we could get new ones. He confirmed that the coup leaders had succeeded in seizing power, that Kabbah had run away to Conakry, and that the Nigerians were in control at Lungi airport. 'I'm afraid things are going to be very difficult here for quite some time. I suggest you both go to the Hotel Mammy Yoko: it's not far along this road. You'll find most of the expats are gathering there, and the aid

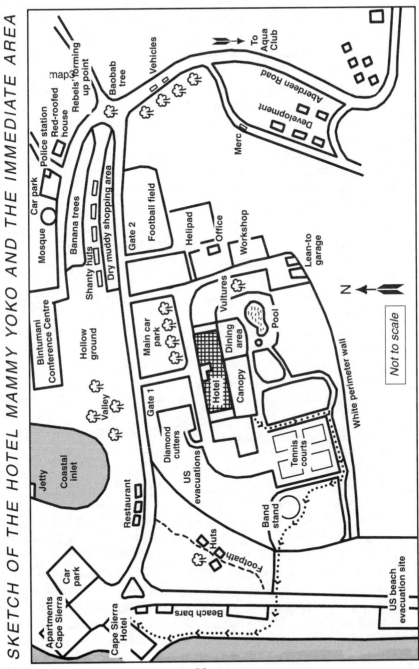

SKETCH OF THE HOTEL MAMMY YOKO AND THE IMMEDIATE AREA

agencies too. It's reasonably safe as there are about fifty Nigerian soldiers looking after it.' He said he would drop round there later for a drink and more chat.

He was friendly and easy going and restored my faith in the British. The Hotel Mammy Yoko was easy to find, not much further along the road which ran parallel to beach, and I recognised it as the place the helicopter had landed me from the airport when I arrived. Then, the roads had been quiet, secluded, part of the richer area of Freetown. Now, masses of local people were milling about on the road leading to the hotel, civilians mostly, curious to watch others turning up at the hotel seeking refuge. People who were obviously better off, in clean shirts, and slacks, some black, some Lebanese and whites, all harassed and tired in the heat, were walking in, carrying bulging suitcases or bags which they had to put down from time to time as they were so heavy. A variety of cars, many of them big luxurious 4×4s, weaved slowly through the people all over the road.

The hotel car park was packed. We left the Landrover on the side of a slip road with the garden boy, and walked to the hotel. A solid queue of people, all clutching bits of luggage, stretched from the hotel entrance uphill past the hotel, through the white perimeter wall, up some steps to the helicopter landing pad, altogether about 100m, and another two hundred massed around the pad itself where two big, blue and white Mi-17s were parked, their blades drooping to the ground as if exhausted in the heat. The small hut by the top of the steps which the Russian pilots used as an office was besieged. I guessed they were making a fortune ferrying people out of Sierra Leone.

Everyone wanted to leave. Rich local people, Europeans of all sorts, Americans, Asians and a lot of Lebanese shouted and jostled, most with families, women hustling their children around them, babies crying. I asked an American in the queue for the helipad where the Mi-17 was going.

'Conakry,' he said. It made sense. Lungi airport was held by the Nigerians but closed to regular international flights and the Guinean capital was only an hour's flying time away.

'How much?'

'At least 150 dollars a seat.'

56

And rising, I thought. I wondered how we would get out. I had less than fifty dollars and Ken was broke.

We pushed through the crowds into the hotel lobby which was filled with more people, while more still were arriving. I stood in the entrance looking for Beth Dunne, as Lincoln Jopp had said she had got out of the town unharmed and was in the Mammy Yoko. Knots of people clustered all over the lobby. A crowd of Lebanese had already taken over a table and easy chairs in the centre of the lobby and established what seemed to be a business centre, and several aid agencies had set up positions on other tables – or just chairs – like exhibitors at some mad convention centre, enjoying maximum interest from the public. It seemed to be everyone for himself and I sensed that panic was not far beneath the surface.

I could not see Beth in the crowds and decided to go over and register myself with one of the aid agencies as I had no money to pay for a bed or food, let alone get out of the country.

'I've got no money or papers,' I cold the man at the CARE desk.

'Okay,' he said, matter-of-factly, as I was just one of hundreds turning up at the hotel in the same boat. 'Just sign here and we'll find you somewhere to sleep.'

As I was doing this, I saw Beth in the middle of a group of people, near the Merlin desk. This was great, as she might have some cash from Murdo and some other news as well. She was pleased to see us and offered at once to book us a room in the hotel.

'I've got a credit card. I hope they've got something left,' she said. 'There are only 162 beds in this hotel and . . .' she waved a hand at the people crowding the lobby. Outside, people were still walking down the road with their belongings. Fortunately, there was a twin-bed room available – No. 217 on the back of the hotel – and we took it.

'What d'you want to do?' I asked Ken.

'I'll go back and stay with Sonya,' he replied.

'You sure? It's a bit dicey over there. Maybe you should move up here?'

'What about Sonya?'

57

I hesitated, but said, 'It's nothing personal, Ken, but I'm not keen on all of us in the same room!' I told him as well that, until we knew otherwise, we were actually still working for Murdo and it would not help to have Ken's night fighter in the same room. I think Ken had decided that with the country turned upside down by the coup the job for Murdo was over, as far as he was concerned. He wanted to stay with Sonya and I agreed to drive him back to her house.

We backed the Landrover out of the car park, which was stuffed with cars, and drove back another circuitous route through the side streets to Sonya's house. I dropped off Ken and came back as soon as I could. The light was fading and I did not want to be out on the streets at night. I had got away without too much trouble so far, but there was a curfew after dark and I thought the chances of being shot by drunk rebels and soldiers was high.

At the hotel, Beth and other aid agency workers from Red Cross, Farmco, *Médecins sans Frontières* and NCAP were setting up various HF radios and satcoms, occupying a little side room which the hotel manager had given them to use behind the hotel telephone exchange and the reception desks in the lobby.

I wanted to get through to Duke so Beth introduced me and let them assume I was an aid worker. Sensibly, she realised my true role in Sierra Leone was definitely not p-c with aid agency workers, so I talked casually about work in Bosnia and they asked no questions. Most agency workers had fled from their Freetown offices or bases with whatever they could bring. Many, like the UN and the International Federation, had already been robbed of vehicles and communications equipment on Sunday and Monday. There was a hotchpotch of radio gear. Some had brought sets without aerials, others had aerials, others still had connection cables, and I added my box of Motorola gear from the Landrover. We put it all on the floor in the side room and I gave them a hand trying to cobble some of the bits together. Soon we had an *ad hoc* communications 'centre', with a mess of cables running through the window to the aerials outside on the grass. This took all evening, but eventually we got a couple of sets working and the room hummed with a satisfying buzz of static as messages started reaching out from Sierra Leone to the world.

Lincoln Jopp turned up later and we repaired to the bar for a beer. We swapped stories around our mutual military background and got on well. I told him about the gold mine up country, saying that I had been in the Army too, in Hereford, and was armed, and I briefly mentioned the plan to train the Kamajors who seemed to have been so much a reason for the coup. Lincoln was unfazed by any of this and gave me a lot of detail about what had been going on in Sierra Leone, and the coup. He was in touch with the High Commission on the other side of the estuary and confirmed that the international community had taken President Kabbah's side, as the properly elected democratic civilian government. The United States, all the Western countries, the nearby West African Countries, and others in Africa like Zimbabwe, had condemned the coup and refused to recognise Koroma's announcement that an Armed Forces Revolutionary Council, the AFRC, was now the rightful government of the country. However, Koroma's regime was the power behind the violence and since Britain had always had the most influence in Sierra Leone, the British High Commissioner, Peter Penfold, had taken the lead in negotiations with the AFRC to find a peaceful solution. He had tried to set up meetings with the other principal players like the UN Special Envoy and especially the Nigerians: the Nigerian High Commissioner, Mr Chidi Abubakar, and the senior Nigerian Army officer, Brigadier Okojöko, who was commanding all the Nigerian ECOMOG troops in the country. Penfold had quickly found that the coup leaders and the Nigerian troops hated each other so much the coup leaders refused to meet in the Nigerian High Commission and the Nigerians rather understandably refused to go to the AFRC headquarters for fear they would be arrested or even killed. Penfold set up the meetings on neutral ground in his own Residence instead, but the talks began in an atmosphere which exactly reflected the mayhem on the streets in Freetown. Koroma's men representing the AFRC were violent and aggressive and the proceedings nearly degenerated into a gunfight with the Nigerians on more than one occasion.

'Nigeria has a bit of a neck banging on about the overthrow of democracy!' I said, and we both laughed. The Nigerian military dictatorship under General Abacha had seized power themselves from an elected civil government.

Lincoln smiled, 'They'll cast themselves as saviours of democracy now, with their troops here in Sierra Leone, and doubtless they're hoping to come up smelling of roses and be welcomed back again in the Commonwealth.'

'Is Sierra Leone in the Commonwealth?' I asked.

'Yes. In fact, Johnny Paul Koroma was once a cadet at the Royal Military Academy at Sandhurst, in the same platoon as a friend of mine, Caspar Hobbs,' Lincoln said pensively, no doubt recalling his own time at the British Army's famous officer training college. He told me how Koroma and the other cadets had attended an instruction class on that most basic of infantry tactics, the Platoon Attack, during which the Coldstream Guards staff sergeant, a splendid figure immaculate in starched uniform and peaked hat, had said, 'So, gentlemen, Prisoner Handling Techniques in the Consolidation Phase of the attack! What do we do with prisoners taken during the fighting?' He paused to allow this important question to sink in and give everyone a moment to recall an earlier lecture about the Geneva Convention on how to treat prisoners with proper humanity, when he noticed Koroma looking genuinely puzzled and snapped, 'Officer Cadet Koroma! What is the answer?'

Koroma retorted, 'I strangle them like chickens straight away!'

In Sierra Leone, Koroma's solution had been equally brusque. Before he was sent to Sandhurst for officers' training in Britain, Koroma was a corporal and when he heard that the platoon officer and others were plotting against him, he shot the officer.

The mayhem I had seen in Freetown exactly matched Koroma's inhuman attitude. 'I hope the soldiers and RUF don't come over here,' I observed. The cream of Freetown, anyway the richest, were gathering in the Hotel Mammy Yoko, their numbers growing hourly. Lincoln nodded, 'I agree. They'd have a field day, but the area here is protected by some of the ECOMOG Nigerian troops. There are about 200 of them all round the area, including the lot down at Aberdeen Bridge. I don't know how good they are, but so far the rebels have stayed away.'

Wednesday 28 May

I finally got through to Duke at nine the following morning, from one of the sets we had stuck together in the little side room behind Reception. I told him what had been going on in Freetown, that Ken was okay, that Cape House had been shot to bits, our passports and everything else stolen, that we were trying to get new passports but there was no sign of Fred and the place was in chaos. 'You'd best stay where you are,' I told him and agreed to call up again at 4 p.m. and keep him up to date.

The Mi-17s had started evacuation lifts early that morning, at seven, from the helipad topside of the hotel and the heavy beating of their enormous blades reminded me that I needed my passport. I walked down the stairs, made my way out through people lying all over the hotel lobby, covered with coats or sheets where they had spent the night, got into the old Landrover and drove into town. The Nigerian soldiers at the hotel entrance to the car park were bossily keeping back a crowd in the road and there were more loitering about by Aberdeen Bridge. All wore full combat uniforms, with helmets covered with bits of leaves and twigs stuck in the camouflage netting, like a modern military version of the rebels' own exotic hairstyles with their pieces of mirror or Jombobla plaits of pubic hair.

The streets were fairly clear though a lot of people were sitting about with radios glued to their ears. I had seen this before elsewhere in Africa and noticed the numbers listening avidly for news seemed to be in direct proportion to the seriousness of the political situation. There were few rebels or soldiers – they were presumably still in bed recovering from another night of drunken debauchery – and I reached the British High Commission quite easily. Dai Harris was in better spirits than when we first met and wanted to chat again, but there was no reason to delay. The crowd of soldiers or rebels was still outside the Commission, hanging about on the road and lounging in the shade of trees, their weapons lying about in the dust, but there was now an edge in the atmosphere. I suppose that, after several nights of rape and pillage, the feeling that violence is about to happen again at any moment is inevitable but my antennae were twitching. I quickly paid twenty US dollars for my new shiny maroon passport, another twenty for Ken's temporary one as he was a New Zealander, and drove straight to Sonya's house in the shanty town. Ken let me in and appeared more detached from events than even the night before, happy for me to leave him in Sonya's house out of it all. As usual, she was surly – I never saw her smile at all – and though I tried, I couldn't persuade him to leave her and join me in the Hotel Mammy Yoko. The situation in Free-town was still chaotic. Even with our passports I could not see quite how we were going to get out, and I had a feeling I was going to need some help.

I drove back to the Hotel Mammy Yoko. The sun was by now high overhead and the streets smelled of rotting rubbish, refuse and burning. I passed rows of wrecked shops; several burned-out and blackened torched cars blocked the middle of the roads.

Crowds of people were still gathered in the road to the hotel, mostly refugees seeking shelter from the mayhem in town and local people just standing about watching. As I drove up, a Jeep full of rebels in red T-shirts and soldiers armed to the teeth as usual with AKs and RPGs drove slowly past through the crowd, watching everyone as they passed, and staring intently at the hotel. It looked very much to me as if they were more than just curious. I wondered how long it would take before they got bored with pillaging the town and started looking at the richer alternatives.

When I reached the hotel entrance, I was pleased to see that the Nigerian soldiers had consolidated their control point at the entrance to the hotel. If the rebels were beginning to take an interest in the place, perhaps this was a good thing, but they were certainly taking their time to check everyone coming in, unless of course a few dollars changed hands. I squeezed the Landrover into the car park and decided to investigate the helicopter option. Lincoln had told me the British and Americans were already planning evacuations, but this was not confirmed and it made sense to know the alternatives.

The mêlée of people, luggage and screaming children in a chain was there as before, shuffling slowly and impatiently from the hotel front door up the steps to the helipad to the Mi-17s which were lifting them out about twenty-five at a time, and charging extra cash for luggage – the price of people's most valuable personal effects which was all they could carry with them. The Lebanese in the hotel lobby had set up an impromptu travel office and were organising tickets. Two helicopters were coming in and out about every half hour or so and at $150 a seat the Russian aircrews were making a fortune. I wandered over to the little office by the landing pad. There was complete pandemonium. On the outside, a throng of maybe 200 people clustered round the door, with everyone shoving and jostling each other to get inside. Pushing through with difficulty, I found at least fifteen people had squashed themselves into a small waiting room big enough for just about three, all shouting and waving fistfuls of cash for a seat. A vast black Sierra Leone stood at the door, trying to keep some sort of order and, when I had worked my way closer to the front, I glimpsed two Russians in a tiny office, one trying to keep some record of passengers in books on a desk, and the other, skinny with grey hair, pacing up and down behind shouting into a telephone in Russian.

I shouted at him, 'What's the chances of getting on the choppers?'

He shrugged, 'We've got the next seven lifts block-booked, and then these . . .' He waved his hand at the seething, shouting mass of people in the hot little room.

'I'm not going to get anywhere here,' I muttered to myself and wriggled out into the warm fresh air and sunshine.

Back in the hotel, I went to the telephone exchange behind Reception. Everyone wanted to make calls, so instead of going to my room to make the call and queuing up behind all the others trying the same thing, I sat in the exchange and made friends with the girl working there. I bought her a couple of Cokes, chatted her up, talked about the chaos in the hotel which by that time must have had more than 500 people in it – excluding all those fighting for seats on the helis – and more coming in all the time. I persuaded her to keep ringing a number Beth had given me for Murdo in England.

Outside in the lobby, the Lebanese group round the tables in the middle were constantly on the only telephone there, running their *ad hoc* business centre, juggling with all the balls in the air, managing or saving their Sierra Leone businesses, phoning Beirut and profiteering from the situation at the same time by booking charter flights to evacuate other refugees at 'special rates'.

Finally, after several hours, I got through to Murdo. I told him what had happened. 'I've found Ken, and Beth, here in Freetown, and Duke is still up in Yara.' I told him about Cape House, the passports, and the HF set.

'Well done!' Murdo shouted. The line was not good, but Murdo plunged on. He was obviously embarrassed about being stuck in London while his project in Sierra Leone had taken a mortal body blow and he felt responsible for the people left scattered around the country. The only person who could help him was me, so he went straight to the point and said, 'You remember that conversation we had in Freetown before I left? When we talked about how to run the project?'

'Yes.' I saw at once where he was going.

'Well, you're on the wages you recommended for this job.'

'You mean $8,000 a month?' I asked, to be sure there was no confusion.

'Yeah, and we'll share the profits from any projects that we generate together in Sierra Leone.'

This was more like it. Being paid to sort real problems in this kind of atmosphere was what I liked. I still had no money in my hand to get things done but I felt better already! 'Okay, I'll go to work then,' I told him and added, 'You need to know there's no sign of Fred.'

'He's in Kono with the Canadian diamond dealer,' Murdo replied. I was not surprised. Kono was a town in the centre of the Sierra Leone diamond mining area, southeast of Yara and about

280km east of Freetown. 'He got through to me eventually on the phone. There are about twenty-five of them up there, so he should be okay.'

He was referring to many former Executive Outcomes mercenaries who were protecting diamond mines for the Branch Energy mining company. When the Sierra Leone government contracted mercenaries from Executive Outcomes to fight the RUF rebels, who naturally wanted to grab the Kono diamond mines for themselves, they had no foreign currency to pay the South African company. So they offered Executive Outcomes land concessions in the diamond mines instead. Executive Outcomes used Branch Energy, a South African-linked company, and took a remarkable division of shares which indicated how desperate the government was to defeat the RUF at that time, and which was quite probably another powerful motive for Johnny Koroma and the other coup leaders to seize power and redress the balance: Branch Energy was given no less than sixty per cent of the diamonds, with only thirty per cent to the Sierra Leone government and ten per cent to the public. Of course, not all the mercenaries had left Sierra Leone in February '97, under the terms of the cease-fire with the RUF. Many had gone on to work for Branch Energy protecting their investments in the Kono diamond mines. Fred was up there in the compound they had built for themselves, a far stronger and decidedly more up-market version of the 'fort' we had lived in at Yara.

'What's the situation like in that region?'

'Fine,' I told him. I had met a diamond manager called Martin Greenwood in the bar of the hotel who had been caught in Freetown when the coup broke on Sunday. A blunt, pragmatic Yorkshireman with a booming voice, he said there had been some sporadic scrapping with the rebels in the area round Kono, but with twenty-five well-armed South African expat mercenaries in a group together guarding the compound in Kono, Fred was probably in the safest place in Sierra Leone.

Murdo seemed to think that Fred and the others in Kono wanted to get out of Sierra Leone. They were certainly strong enough to hold off the occasional attack by disorganised rebels, but as the coup looked like consolidating its grip, sooner or later

Johnny Koroma and the RUF would turn their attention to taking control of Kono and the diamond mines again. At that point, Branch Energy and its expat security men would not be in favour, especially as Koroma and the RUF knew perfectly well that Branch Energy was in fact Executive Outcomes, which had defeated them in the fighting in '96.

Talking this over with Murdo, I mentioned the two Mi-17 helicopters shuttling people from the hotel to Conakry, and Murdo asked if it was feasible to charter one of them to fly to Kono and evacuate the entire Executive Outcomes team out to Guinea to the north?

'They're booked solid,' I replied. 'But I'll see if they can do it.' This was a long route, right across Sierra Leone, but there were Russian miners in Kono too, which might encourage the pilots to look on the scheme more favourably. Martin Greenwood seemed to think that the Russian embassy was looking for a way to evacuate its citizens from Kono and might be keen to persuade the Russian pilots to fly there, especially if we were paying. I reminded Murdo that I was broke.

'Where's the cash coming from?' I asked. 'These guys are creaming it in and they'll want paying. A lot!' I told him the pilots were taking at least $150 a seat just for an hour's flight to Conakry. The journey to Kono and Guinea was at least three times as long, one-way, definitely more dangerous – especially as the pilots could not guarantee the safety of the landing site in Kono – and the opportunity cost against ferrying lucrative loads of desperate evacuees from the Hotel Mammy Yoko to Guinea put the cost of the Kono flight at something around US $40–50,000.

'What about fixing a loan from Roger Crooks?' Murdo suggested.

'Who?'

'The hotel manager. See if he'll agree to advance you some cash to guarantee payment for the heli, and I'll arrange a bank transfer to wherever he wants.' Murdo knew Roger quite well, so that would help, but I wondered if he would have sufficient ready cash in the circumstances to loan me enough to convince the Russian pilots, even if he agreed to help a total stranger walking into his office from the chaos of the hotel lobby.

I found Roger Crooks in his office behind Reception. He was from Mississippi, medium build, in his fifties, with the face of a man who knew the world and a slow southern drawl. He had worked for a long time in Red Adair's oilfield firefighting team and become a close personal friend of a rich American industrialist called Oscar Wyatt who had big oilfield investments in his multi-billion dollar company Coastal Incorporated. They were partners in the Mammy Yoko. Roger had been running the hotel for years, and there was nothing much he did not know about Sierra Leone or West Africa.

I introduced myself. I was quite prepared to find that he did not know Murdo, but fortunately he did, so I told him about the plan to fly Fred and the other expats out of Kono to Guinea using one of the Russian helis.

He grinned and said, 'Fred there too? That guy's sure a character!'

Fred's reputation was, as usual, larger than life but Murdo and Roger had apparently had some difference of opinion so I had to start from scratch with Roger and make my own relationship. I asked, 'Is there any possibility we could set up a system, say with bank guarantees in the States or Europe? Murdo will transfer money so you could advance me cash to hire this chopper?'

'Sure,' Roger responded positively straight away, which was really good of him considering I was a total stranger and at a time when his hotel was invaded by hundreds of people, his resources were stretched to breaking point and the threat of complete anarchy was growing more worrying by the hour. True, he probably felt safer than most of them. At that moment, he did not imagine he would have to leave Sierra Leone himself. However, we were interrupted and he had to go off to deal with problems. Everyone was demanding service and he was incredibly busy.

I hung around his office and it took a couple more times before I finally managed to pin him down for long enough to get the details of the bank account Murdo should transfer money into. Roger had accounts in Europe, in Paribas in Antwerp, but he preferred we use the Northern Trust Bank in Houston, Texas, as he felt they would react faster for the hotel in Sierra Leone. He was very helpful. 'As soon as my bank tells me they've cleared the funds,' he said. 'Then I'll give you the cash.'

I spent hours on the phone that day, sitting in the telephone exchange, buying more Cokes for the girl there, calling Murdo in England, each call taking about an hour to connect. I passed on the details of Roger's bank in the US and urged him to transfer the money as soon as possible. 'These Russian helis are full right now,' I warned him. 'With all the people here falling over each other to give them cash for seats to Conakry, there's no way they'll accept a deal with me unless I've got the readies in hand.'

'Don't worry!' Murdo assured me. 'I'll fix it straight away.'

I hoped he would. I was skint and, quite apart from trying to charter the Russian heli, I felt responsible for Beth and Ken too, but I could do nothing without cash.

During the course of the day, I heard that the British High Commission was planning an evacuation of all British and European citizens the following day, Thursday 29 May. The British High Commission had been trying to contact all British passport holders and tell them to go to the Mammy Yoko, some by telephone, others on VHF sets – which was not a huge success as the sets were too old and broke down – and through regular broadcasts on the BBC World Service. They had someone going round the hotel making lists of those who turned up and I saw Lincoln Jopp again too. He explained that KLM and Sabena had refused to fly into Lungi any more so the High Commission was planning to charter a jet instead. He said Beth Dunne had been told by her agency, Merlin, to go out with the British and asked me if I was going out too. I explained I was trying to sort the heli for the people in Kono and would go on that. We all felt fairly safe still in the hotel as the Nigerian troops around us had created a sort of *cordon sanitaire* keeping the rebels and rioting soldiers at bay, but occasionally, a vehicle full of sobels* drove slowly past

---

* 'Sobels' was the name coined from *so*ldiers and re*bels* to describe disaffected soldiers who took to looting, banditry and indiscriminate killing, often with the RUF rebels. In the coup, both groups amounted to the same thing: violent criminals, including those like Johnny Paul Koroma himself and others released from the Pademba Road Prison.

the hotel for a good look, and it was plain Beth's job with the aid agency was finished in Sierra Leone for the time being.

I could do nothing more till Murdo confirmed the money transfer so I decided to go out and see what was happening in the town with Stuart Friedmann, a British photo-journalist – there were several journalists in the hotel. We swapped stories of working in Africa – I mentioned my experience in Rwanda when I had been working for Associated Press as their East African correspondent in Kigali. In the same sort of chaos as we were seeing in Freetown, I had decided I needed to make my name with a good story from the front line in the jungle of Zaire. Unfortunately, I was arrested by rebels and it took me a full month to get back, fortunately unharmed.

'I hope nothing of the sort happens to us!' Stuart laughed. He was doing a piece on orphans in Sierra Leone and wanted me to go with him, for moral support, and lent me one of his cameras to clinch the deal, so we were equally keen to get some good footage or stills of events in Freetown. We went on foot to find a taxi. The Nigerians at the entrance were now making life impossible for people coming into the car park and I was worried that they would not let me bring the Landrover back in at all. Also, I felt that a taxi would be less conspicuous.

We chose the least villainous-looking of the taxi drivers lounging about by roadside stalls in front of the shanty huts up the road from the hotel, and agreed a price for a couple of hours' work. We bundled all Stuart's gear into the battered and stinking yellow taxi and trundled off towards the centre of town. We told the driver to stop from time to time, to take general shots of looted and burned shops, and one set with a body we found lying at the side of the road against a background of wrecked cars. We managed some pictures of rebels wandering along a street near the seafront in their red T-shirts which seemed to have become a sort of 'uniform'. Stuart's gear was not set up for covert photography, where a camera can be hidden inside a shoulder bag so you can take pictures without your subject knowing the slightest thing about it, so we took great care to keep the camera as much out of sight as possible in the shadows inside the back of the car.

When he saw what we were doing, the taxi driver began to

complain nervously, but we shut him up with the promise of a few more dollars. He was right to be concerned and I was keeping a very wary eye out in all directions for trouble, looking down each street as we passed. We turned into a street and saw a Landrover stuffed with rebels ahead of us, all toting AKs and RPGs as usual. I warned Stuart to be very careful.

'Keep your camera low!' I snapped.

Stuart looked startled. He was unused to covert photography and looked decidedly suspicious as he took pictures through the front windscreen while we drove slowly along behind the Landrover. I noticed the rebels beginning to take an interest in us, peering inside our taxi, and suddenly the Landrover slammed on its brakes. The rebels leaped out and one pointed his RPG at us.

'Just sit quiet,' I told Stuart as the rebels ran round the taxi screaming and shouting. The situation was getting rapidly out of control. Moving with deliberate slowness, I eased my own camera beneath my legs. Stuart hurriedly pushed his gear into a grip on the floor beneath his feet but it was too late. Several of the rebels dancing round the car began firing bursts in the air, and suddenly one reached forward with his AK47 and fired a burst through the window on my side of the car. The bullets ripped through the pillar between front and back windows and tore holes in the roof.

'Christ!' Stuart shouted, ducking to the floor.

The driver flung himself sideways onto the passenger seat, terrified and screaming.

We were lucky. No one was hurt, but these lunatics were ready to kill us without a second's thought.

'Gimme! Gimme!' The rebel screamed incoherently at Stuart as the others danced round our car. Drunk on alcohol and ganja, it was hard to say whether they were more excited about us taking photographs – which is always banned in the circumstances – or just the sight of Stuart's really expensive camera.

'Do as he says,' I said quietly to Stuart. There was no chance of driving off and I had no intention of taking a serious beating or worse for the sake of some cameras. Stuart hesitated. This gear was the tools of his trade but it was too late.

Furious, the rebel reached in, grabbed the camera by the lens and held it up triumphantly. Another seized the grip bag. Two others, not wanting to be left out, pointed at our watches and took those too.

Stuart's face collapsed. He watched in horror as the rebels shared out his camera, lenses and accessories, hooting and cheering at each other. They were so delighted with themselves that they forgot about us as suddenly as they had robbed us and danced back to their Landrover. Still hollering, laughing and threatening us with their rifles, they clambered in and drove off.

I pulled out the camera I had hidden under my legs, nipped out of the taxi and took a couple of photos of them disappearing, but Stuart sat in the back of the taxi in shock. 'That's over four thousand pounds of gear . . .' he said, his voice trailing off. He turned to look at me in supplication, as if I might wave a wand and reverse the whole scene.

I gave him back his camera and said, 'Let's go back to the hotel.' I could see he was badly frightened by the experience and devastated by the theft of his equipment. His confidence had gone and there was no point even going on to take notes for an article. Dejected, he slumped back into the taxi and I persuaded the driver to take us back to the Mammy Yoko. I saw Stuart a couple of times in the hotel later, but I don't think he went out again. Maybe he should have known that photo-journalism in these countries is risky at the best of times but I felt sorry for him losing all that gear.

When I got back, Roger said he had heard nothing from his bank, so I spent another hour in the telephone exchange trying to call Murdo.

'Murdo!' I shouted down the line when I finally got through again. 'Is the money in yet?'

'Yes,' he shouted back.

'Well, there's no sign of it here! And time's running out.' Someone from the British High Commission had been going round the hotel sticking posters advising British passport holders there would be an evacuation the next day. Roger kept pulling them down, happy to cooperate as far as he could but irritated that no one had asked his permission. 'The British evacuation is going tomorrow,' I shouted down the line. 'If I don't have the money I've no hope of getting this Russian chopper for the guys in Kono.'

He assured me he was dealing with it, and then said, 'Can you try to find Mike North and Mike Phillips?'

'Yeah,' I said without enthusiasm, remembering how antagonistic the Gold Prospect Mining Company manager had been. Mike Phillips was his office administration assistant, another British citizen.

'We should offer them the chance to get out too. They've been in touch somehow with Nick Worrel in Cornwall and he says they're hiding in a house in Freetown somewhere, camping in the cellar, scared to death of being found by the sobels.'

'Okay, fine,' I assured him. 'That's what I'm here for. Where are they?'

'Well, they're in a house along the coast in Goderich.' Murdo sounded vague. 'It's not their house. They were terrified of being attacked in their own houses, because everyone knew there were expats living there, so they're hiding with a friend. He's black, a Sierra Leone.'

'What's the address?'

He gave me possibly the most vague and hopelessly incomplete address I have ever heard. 'It's a big place, with a blue painted gate and the letters "FHS" on it.'

'Is that all?' I asked in amazement.

'Erm, yes.'

'At least tell me where to start looking?' I asked in desperation. 'What part of Freetown?'

'I'm not sure,' said Murdo defensively. 'Nick didn't know exactly, but he thinks it's along the coast somewhere.'

I stamped out of the telephone exchange feeling that things were getting away from me. Murdo still had not transferred the money and finding North and Phillips would be like looking for the proverbial needle in a haystack.

I decided to get on with it at once. I had nothing else I could do there and I still had a few dollars, enough to pay for a taxi.

I walked up the drive past the trees and shrubs around the car park, pushed my way out past the Nigerians and the crowd around the entrance in the road and up the road again to the huts.

There was no sign of the first taxi driver, who was presumably recovering from shock somewhere. I picked another and told him what I was looking for.

'You ain't got no address, man?'

'Just a blue gate with FHS on it,' I repeated shortly.

He shook his head slowly. 'Rich folks?' he asked. 'Maybe along Lumley Beach and Goderich Beach. Yeah. I know where to go look.'

We cruised off down the coast towards Lumley Beach at a leisurely tropical pace, bouncing over potholes and ruts in the road, turning off left and right under palm trees hanging lazily in the heat when he suggested a likely avenue to search. I got tired swivelling my head back and forth as we drove down endless residential roads lined with villas and houses set back behind garden walls, hedges and fences. I could have made a study of house gates of modern Sierra Leone – all colours, designs, shapes and sizes, wood, metal, spiked, riveted, cast iron, topped with barbed wire or just tacked together with string and nails – but we saw nothing with FHS on it.

Very few people were about. They were hiding out of sight and trouble, like North and Phillips, and we saw very few soldiers. The taxi driver refused to go all the way to Goderich Beach as there was a large army barracks to pass en route and he was frightened we would be attacked. After the incident with Stuart earlier, he had a point. So we searched Lumley as best we could and after an hour I was hot, tired and impatient. I told him to go back to the Mammy Yoko.

It was about four o'clock so I went to the 'comms centre' we had set up the previous night and tried to raise Duke on the HF set. After some trouble finding the frequency, and ages calling for someone to answer the radio in the compound, a voice replied, ''Allo?'

'Hallo? Is that the GPMC compound?'

''Allo?'

'Can I speak to Duke?'

''Allo?'

I wiped sweat from my eyes, took a deep breath and repeated, 'Can I speak to Duke?'

Finally, the voice said, 'Mister Dook, he is not here.'

'Where is he?'

'Mister Dook, he has gone. To Guinea.'

'You sure?'

'Yes. I am sure. Mister Dook, he has gone to Guinea.'

I seemed to have reached the bottom of that particular conversation and switched off. Duke had obviously decided that his best option was to drive out north across the Guinea border and round through the mountains and jungle to Conakry by road. This was a long way, maybe 450km, but he would avoid being caught up in the violence around Freetown. In fact, lawlessness had reached out rapidly to touch even remote areas and he was already in trouble when I called. However, he was out of touch and there was nothing further I could do for him.

By the time I finished my call to Yara, the light was fading, curfew had started so the sobels could loot in the town all night and there was nothing more I could do outside the hotel. I found Martin Greenwood in the lobby and he said the most intelligent thing I had heard all day, 'How about a beer?'

The bar was filled with people talking about what was going on. Most of them had had some terrible experiences in the town, and once they reached the refuge of the hotel they had no intention of leaving. Their only source of information was listening to others' stories and the place was alive with the buzz of conversations in a hotchpotch of languages. Several Lebanese had been murdered, the Sabena ground staff women had been raped in front of the men and fifty homes of British citizens in Freetown had been looted. One family of three said they had hidden under the veranda of the house while the rebels looted and robbed inside. The boy, Anthony, aged only fifteen, said they had raped several women they had caught. He heard them shouting that the ordinary people had been having too good a time at the Army's expense and now it was their turn.

'Not surprising the civilians want out,' I said.

'There've been two evacuations today,' Martin said, sipping his cold *Elephant* beer.

'In addition to the Russian choppers which have been going all day?'

'Yes, the UN took out a load of all their workers and dependants on a ship appropriately called the *Salvation* and the Lebanese flew out about three hundred women and children. I've heard they both included maybe sixty British people.'

'You going on the British evacuation?'

He shook his head. 'My work is here. Can't see any point in leaving.'

'The lure of diamonds?' I grinned at him.

He shrugged and said, 'We're safe enough in the hotel. With all them Nigerian soldiers around us.'

Thursday 29 May

First thing in the morning, I was back in the little room behind Reception on the phone to Murdo. I came straight to the point and demanded, 'Where's the cash?'

'I've transferred it,' Murdo's voice came back, distorted by the bad line.

'Well, nothing has got through to Roger's bank in Houston,' I said. I told him the British were chartering a Tri-Star and all the British citizens were going to be evacuated later that day. 'If I'm staying here, I want to know that you're going to get that money through!'

'I've got some through,' said Murdo back-tracking. He explained that the wealthy Canadian industrialist Fred was looking after had agreed to put up some of the money, but not all of it. Rather understandably, he did not want to pay for everyone's seat on the Russian helicopter just because he was a rich man.

'What about Executive Outcomes?' I demanded.

'They're being difficult,' Murdo admitted. 'They only want to pay when they're out.' I understood why. Executive Outcomes had lost a chunk of money when they quit Sierra Leone so, not surprisingly, they were extremely reluctant to forward any money to Murdo before the helicopter actually turned up in Kono and flew them out. In spite of this, Murdo was trying to work a deal with EO to avoid exposing his own funds, whereby EO transferred the money instead. His logic was plain enough. He was only brokering the heli, whereas the people who would take the seats were EO men, including Fred in a way as he had been with EO in the early days. Executive Outcomes saw it differently. They had people looking after the Branch Energy mines, but there were others who might take seats in the Russian chopper: the Russian miners, British miners from Martin Greenwood's project, and Fred who was with the Canadian diamond dealer. Murdo wanted the Canadian and EO to pay for the heli before committing his own money for the flight, while EO refused to pay the full sum till they had been evacuated, and the Canadian had no intention of forking out for everyone. In the mercenary world, no one trusted anyone else.

I reminded him of the reality, 'The Russians aren't likely to fly over there unless they get paid first.'

The argument went back and forth, and later EO's Tim Spicer, the ex-Scots Guards colonel well known for his doomed efforts to raise a mercenary force in Papua New Guinea, joined battle with Murdo and between them they both ended up billing Martin Greenwood for his miners' seats on the helicopter. While these two groups fought out their tired, all-too-predictable rivalries about dividing up the faloose, I was left facing reality in Freetown.

'Murdo, just tell me what's going on,' I said finally.

'The Canadian promised me that his company has transferred some money. I can't guarantee it, but that's what he said.'

Exasperated, I put the phone down and went back to Roger in his office who shook his head and said, 'Nope. No sign.'

I pulled a face. I was helpless to negotiate a final deal with the Russians – or do much else – till I could show them the cash. Roger saw the expression on my face and added, 'Okay. Here's what I'll do. I'll trust you that Murdo has got some money through. I must be mad, but I know you've got nothing at all, so I'll give you some cash as an advance.'

He was extremely generous. In the conditions of chaos in his hotel, let alone the mayhem in Freetown outside, he still found time to take this risk and we drew up an IOU on a piece of paper by which he advanced me $5,000 of the total $22,000 he would give when Murdo's money transfer got through. However, he could only give me US$2,000, and the rest in Leones. With rampant inflation in Sierra Leone, the exchange rate was 850 Leones to one dollar and he methodically counted out 2,550,000 Leones onto the table in grubby, soiled small-denomination

50- and 100-Leone notes. We packed them into 'bricks,' I thanked him profusely and shovelled them into my green daysack like a bank robber.

Solvent at last, I went back to the Russians at the helipad and tried to persuade them to do the lift from Kono. I fought my way into their little office through the crowds and was at my most persuasive with the thin, grey-haired Russian inside. 'We'll pick up your Russian miners too,' I added, playing the nationalistic card.

'No! I can't do anything today,' he said, waving his hand at the mob crowding up to the helicopters. Our conversation was drowned out for several moments while one of the Mi-17s lifted off and climbed away over the hotel. 'We're full up with more Lebanese; forty Italians want taking to Conakry and the British to Lungi. Maybe you see me tonight and we make agreement?'

Even the promise of a large cash payment would not budge him. As I thought, they were making so much money on the easy, quick ride to Lungi or Conakry that there was little incentive to fly to Kono and then further up to Guinea. I pushed out into the sunshine again. English voices among the groups waiting for lifts confirmed his excuses. The British High Commission and the German Mission in Freetown had arranged for British and other European Community citizens to be flown by the Russians to Lungi where their charter was expected to turn up in the afternoon and fly them straight to the United Kingdom.

I ran down the slope beside the chain of women and children waiting on the steps up to the helipad. Options were closing in fast, and I was beginning to feel time was slipping away. I went up the stairs two at a time to my room to get some of the cash from my daysack and then found the taxi driver up the road who had taken me the day before to find the house with FHS on the gate.

He was sitting in his taxi, the doors wide open to let the air through against the heat and shrugged, 'Okay, man. Looking for the same place?' Plainly, he thought I was wasting my time, but as long as he got paid, one day was as good as another.

He drove agonisingly slowly as before, and I began to learn the ins and outs of the Lumley Beach area quite well, but there was no sign of any blue gates with letters on them and he flatly refused to go past the army barracks along Goderich Beach. Every time we saw vehicles with rebels or soldiers, we turned off at once down a side street. This time I saw a couple of bodies lying in the road which told me the looters were moving out from the centre of town into these richer areas. The sun beat down on the roof turning the taxi into a tin oven, and after two more long, sweaty hours searching alleys and tracks through residential districts off the main potholed tarmac coast road, I told him to go back to the Mammy Yoko.

By the time I got back all the British evacuees had gone and another option was closed off. I went for a cold Coke in the telephone exchange and chatted to the girl while she tried to get another line to Murdo. I was brief. I told him Roger had gone out on a limb and loaned me some cash which I had signed for against Murdo's company Cape International. Murdo did not sound too happy at that, but I told him Beth had gone with the British evacuation which meant that Ken and I, North and Phillips plus all their various women wherever they were, were therefore marooned and that he had better get the money transferred at once.

I grabbed something to eat in the bar and later met Lincoln briefly in the lobby. He said the British evacuation had taken 395 people, including 250 Brits, from Lungi airport in a Corsair 747 chartered from Paris and was due to land at Stansted late that night. He was off back to help the British High Commissioner in his negotiations with the coup leaders, who had only agreed to let the British evacuation take place under threat of British military intervention. 'Peter Penfold's been bullying and bluffing them all week,' said Lincoln. 'There's just a chance they might call a halt to the rioting, but it's a slim hope. Trouble is that more RUF have been coming into Freetown every day from up country. Koroma's lot are bad enough, but the rebels are out of anyone's control.'

This matched what I had been seeing out on the streets. I decided to have another try at finding North and Phillips. I had my doubts that Penfold's negotiations would change much in Freetown, the situation was getting worse and North and Phillips should have been with all the other expats taking shelter in the Mammy Yoko. In town, the house belonging to the IMF's representative had been looted six times, more Lebanese had turned up with stories of rape and several more had been murdered. The sobels released from prison, like Koroma himself, went for revenge to the houses where they had been caught stealing before and specially targeted the rich Lebanese. At least in the hotel there was some safety in numbers whereas, alone in their house, North and Phillips increasingly risked being found, robbed and beaten up. Their women would be assaulted and maybe lose their lives.

There was time for another look for them before dark, so I found another taxi driver and rattled off up the coast again in the late-afternoon sun. In streets where dogs lay flat out asleep in the shadows and nothing moved except palms waving gently in the sea breeze, it was hard to believe the country had fallen apart. Then we passed two men padding along in the dust with a body slung in a hammock between two poles on their shoulders. Disgusted and fed up with this fruitless driving about, I told the driver to go back to the hotel.

We saw a truck full of rebels driving slowly down the road which ran topside of the Mammy Yoko past the big baobab tree and their looks must have been as much from hunger as greed. All Freetown's shops and usual services had been closed, looted or burned out for the past five days and the rebels were moving out to the suburbs to find food as much as goods to steal. I was pleased when we turned into the road by the shanty huts. I paid off the driver and forced my way through the crowd at the entrance to the hotel which seemed bigger than ever. The Nigerian soldiers were arrogant, shouting at people to stay back, and they harassed everyone, especially those going out on the choppers at the side of the hotel, asking, 'Have you got something for me?' or blatantly, 'Can I have your watch?' My watch had already been stolen by the rebels but, as usual, the Nigerians prevented me from coming back into the hotel until I slipped them a handful of Leones. Still, without them the hotel would have been invaded by locals, with the rebels close behind.

I went up the steps to see the Russians again at their helipad by the football pitch. The Mi-17s had been busy flying in and out all day but now they were parked, engines quiet, long blades drooping like palm fronds and the ends tied down for the night. To my surprise, the Russians agreed to fly to Kono the following day and I went at once to call Murdo again.

'How much is it going to cost?' he asked.

'We're going to sort it out in the morning,' I replied. I could tell he did not like that but he switched to another issue and said, 'There's someone else I'd like you to find.'

My heart sank.

Murdo carried blithely on. 'There's a guy I do some business with in Sierra Leone and I've bumped into him here in London. He says his girlfriend is stuck in Freetown.' He ran a trucking business, importing secondhand vehicles abroad for aid agencies, but Murdo wanted to use them for military purposes on his project with Sam Norman and the Kamajors.

'Like to give me a clue where she is, Murdo?'

'I can do better than that,' he said. 'I've arranged for a local guy to take you to her. He'll be outside the hotel tomorrow morning.'

'There are lots of locals outside the hotel,' I told him with studied understatement. 'Several hundreds actually.'

'He'll have a newspaper on his head.'

'A newspaper?'

'Yeah. No problem.'

Friday 30 May

I woke early, dressed quickly and went down to the helipad to fix the deal with the Russians. Oddly, the steps up to the helipad were empty of people, several Nigerian soldiers sat in the sun on the slope by the white perimeter wall doing nothing and the helipad itself was deserted. The crowds round the little hut had gone and inside just a few papers lay about on the floor in the dust. Getting up in my room, I had heard the noise of the Mi-17s start up as usual and take off with the first lift for Conakry, but now there was nothing. The Russians had gone. For good. My options were closing in.

I had some breakfast with Martin Greenwood who sympathised and then I got on the phone to Murdo again. After the usual delay I told him, 'No chance of that heli for Kono. It's gone, and it's not coming back. It's gone to Guinea. If you want to help Fred and the others in Kono, you'll have to go to Guinea yourself, and try to organise something from there.'

Murdo agreed and said he would fix himself a flight straight away.

With another person to look after, I reckoned I had better find Phillips and North as soon as possible. There were hundreds of people milling around in the lobby and in the drive outside the hotel as I left. They were all getting ready for the American evacuation. By good chance, the American aircraft carrier USS *Kearsarge*, commanded by Captain Michael Wittkamp, had been on duty off the coast of the Congo where it had been poised to assist the emergency evacuation of Kinshasa. That crisis had passed over and the ship was on its way back to the Mediterranean when the Sierra Leone coup occurred. With 2,000 US

83

marines aboard and prepared for exactly this sort of operation, the *Kearsarge* was ideally placed and the Americans ordered her to turn back to Freetown. Now the Marines were due into the Hotel Mammy Yoko by helicopter that morning, though for reasons of operational secrecy no one knew precisely when. In a perfect world, I might have been able to gather all the people I was responsible for together at the hotel and perhaps get them away with the Americans but they were scattered all round Freetown. Ken refused to come to the hotel and I had no idea where the rest were hiding.

In fine contrast, more hundreds of locals were hanging around outside the hotel on the road and among the trees in the hollow ground on the opposite side of the road. They sensed something was going to happen at the hotel and there was a buzz of excited chatter. I shoved past the Nigerians holding them back from their barrier at the top of the drive, through the crowds, and found another taxi.

This time I concentrated on the houses on the coast side of the road, as the bigger places faced the sea. However, Lumley and Goderich were not on nice straight seafronts like St Leonards or Eastbourne in England. Lush tropical trees in gardens and along the roads concealed clusters of houses which were dotted about in a confusing pattern of small inlets cutting inland between beaches, and it was hard to keep a sense of direction. This search was no more successful than the previous efforts and once again the taxi driver refused to drive past the army barracks. Maybe he was right, seeing a couple of bodies on the main coast road not far from the soldiers' checkpoint outside their camp probably put him off for sure, but I was now convinced that the house with FHS on blue gates was beyond this barracks.

Driving about on unsurfaced dusty tracks full of craters and ruts took longer than I had hoped so by the time I got back the American evacuation had gone. The US Marines had performed a slick, text-book operation. Preparations had been made through the previous afternoon with US citizens in the hotel organising evacuees and the Marines had turned up suddenly out of the blue morning sky in big transport helicopters which landed inside the hotel grounds downside of the six-floor pink hotel. Big grey

CH-53 Sea Stallions* and medium transport CH-46 Sea Knights†
with twin rotors had come sweeping in to land, blowing up the
dust and flattening the grass with the downdraft from their rotors.
US marines in full combat gear armed with M-16s,‡ M-249s§ and
M-60** machine guns had jumped out and run to secure the area,
setting up defensive positions and keeping everyone back from the
helicopters. High in the sky above, smaller choppers – ground-
attack AH-1 Super Cobras†† – had floated like wasps on top-
cover duty, to protect the operation on the ground. These Super
Cobras are nothing more than an incredible weapons platform,
with missiles and rapid-fire .30 calibre cannon which can chew
ground, troops and armour with devastating accuracy.

Roger told me the marines had been polite but absolutely firm

---

* CH-53E Super Sea Stallion, the Navy's version of the Jolly Green Giant,
commonly called 'Echoes'. A heavy-lift cargo mover of a MEU, 32,000lb
external slung load or fifty-five fully equipped marines. Inside, it can carry
three jeeps, or two 105mm howitzers, with a range of 450 nautical miles,
cruising speed 130 knots, maximum speed 165 knots.

† CH-46 Sea Knight, the Navy's version of the Chinook. Workhorse of the US
services, designed in 1967 and still valuable. Can carry twenty-five fully
equipped marines, or 4,200lb of cargo. Range, the limiting factor, is 75
nautical miles, maximum speed 145 knots.

‡ M16A2 rifle, 5.56mm calibre high velocity US assault rifle manufactured by
Colt Industries, twenty- or thirty-round box magazine, weight 2.9kg, cyclic
rate 650–850rpm, maximum range 550m; easy to fire, easy to clean; small
calibre means light rounds so more can be carried. Success in Vietnam and
acceptance by other forces since have led to some three million being
produced.

§ M249s – The 'Minimi' 5.56mm squad machine gun, weight 6.36kg, effective
range 900m with a useful 1,000 rounds per minute high rate of fire.

** M60E3 GPMG (general purpose machine gun), calibre 7.62mm NATO
round, weight 10.4kg, effective range 900m, cyclic rate 550rpm; basically a
copy of the German WWII MG42, a useful platoon 'workhorse' which saw
extensive use in Vietnam.

†† AH-1T/W Super Cobra assault helicopter, this is a 4-foot wide fuselage,
narrow-profile weapons platform, firing an arsenal of 2.75in folding-fin aerial
rockets, 5in 'Zuni' rockets, TOW anti-tank missiles, AIM-9L Sidewinder
missiles, or Sidearm anti-radiation missiles, fuel-air bombs, and a 20mm
Gatling gun; at speeds of up to 170 knots for up to three hours (the AH-1W is
faster, carries more and stays up longer).

and would let no one through their cordon except past their evacuation control point which was set up by the hotel. With the assistance of coordinator Anne Wright, who had turned up with a clipboard and organised all the US citizens, they had put every-one in an orderly queue, checked their American passports, hustled them into ' sticks',* given them all orange life-preservers and sound-protective headgear to wear, even for the short ten-minute trip to the aircraft carrier, and moved them smartly one stick after another onto the choppers. Ground-to-air radios had blared as officers at the evacuation control passed information to operations control high above in a command heli and back to the ship while the big transport helicopters had come in a deafening procession one after the other, like huge grey birds beating the air with their blades, landing, loading all the people, lifting off and climbing rapidly away over the beach. After nearly two hours, over 1,000 men, women and children, mostly Americans with 200 British and a few other expatriates, had been whisked out of the chaos of Freetown to safety on the USS *Kearsarge*. When the last marines in the guard force had been pulled through the open doors of a hovering CH-53 by their combat webbing, and the chopper lifted, turned and thudded away to sea, silence and heat had descended on the Mammy Yoko once more.

Tension in the crowds hanging about outside the hotel had been racked up another notch by this evacuation. There were more than ever out in the road, and they all knew the significance of the American move. The civilian population had been unim-pressed by demands broadcast all week by the coup leaders that they go back to work, even less by one statement which urged all the school students just to carry on and sit their exams as if nothing was happening. Now the locals saw the expats and the rich leaving, like the proverbial rats, these being the very people who had urged Sierra Leone towards the democratic institutions which had so dramatically failed, while all the time behind them

---

* A 'stick' is a discrete number of people travelling in a military aircraft; e.g., the Russians were taking 'sticks' of twenty-five in their Mi-17 while the Americans organised people in 'sticks' of seventeen, one for the Ch-46s, two for the CH-53s.

the violence in the town washed ever closer to the enclave of the Mammy Yoko.

I went out to the road at the front of the hotel to find Murdo's contact. Hundreds were there, and it seemed to me that most of them had newspapers on their heads, shading themselves from the sun. In fact, they had all sorts of things on their heads since this was how the locals carried things about. Worse, with all the excitement of the US helicopter evacuation they all kept moving about and it was impossible to keep track of the men I had counted as I looked for my contact.

I stayed an hour or more, standing prominently by the entrance but apart from the Nigerians, but I did not see anyone who looked like the person Murdo had described, nor did any of the locals there come up to me. I was not having much success with all this searching and stamped back into the hotel in disgust.

'No bloody good,' I told Murdo flatly when the girl in the exchange finally got through. I had been worried he had already left his flat for the airport and his flight to Conakry. 'I've been all over the place looking for Mike North and there was no sign of that bloke with the newspaper on his head. They all had papers on their heads.'

Murdo insisted the man had been there. I was amazed how sure he was considering he was in London and giving me these instructions through a third party as well. 'Okay, I'll have another look later, but meantime you need to know that the Marines came in this morning and took off about 1,000 people. That means we have had five emergency evacuations so far – the British, American, United Nations, Lebanese and the Italians – and there are no more planned as far as I know.' I had asked Roger and Lincoln.

There was a pause and Murdo asked, 'What are you going to do?'

'I'll have to sort something by boat,' I replied. I had been thinking about this carefully while we drove about looking for the house with the blue gates and 'FHS' on them. 'Conakry is only about seventy nautical miles from Freetown, easily within reach of a motor boat if I can find one in reasonable nick.' I reckoned it would take us about seven to ten hours and it was a good move for Murdo to get himself to Conakry to meet us.

'Okay, but sounds a bit dodgy to me,' said Murdo, with a fighter pilot's suspicion of the sea in an open boat full of locals.

'Well, I haven't got any option now,' I told him.

'This chap outside might be some help,' Murdo said. Maybe it was the static on the line, but it sounded awfully as if he was trying to be optimistic.

'If he's turned up,' I grunted. Murdo's plans seemed to lack some essential definition, but I promised him I would go out for another look.

As I walked up the drive past the tropical green shrubs and trees round the car park, I heard screaming and noise coming along the road. A truck filled with rebels in red and fluorescent pink T-shirts was coming fast down the road past the hotel scattering locals in all directions as it drove through the crowd. Waving their AKs at the Nigerians, they jeered and catcalled as they roared defiantly past. One or two Nigerians shook their fists but most just watched sullenly and I wondered how much longer their confidence, or arrogance, would hold up. With all the evacuations going on from the Mammy Yoko, they, like the locals in the crowd outside, were beginning to wonder what might happen if the rebels came for them.

More rebels drove past, one lot in a stolen 4×4 with 'UN' emblazoned on the side, in the two hours I spent searching the crowd outside on the road for my contact. Gradually I got to recognise those who obviously had nothing to do with me. Finally, I noticed a slim Sierra Leone in shorts and a T-shirt with a short curly beard loitering about on the edge of the road. He carried a folded newspaper in his hand which he occasionally brushed around his neck or over the top of his head, much as though he was batting off flies in the hot afternoon. The weather had turned very close and gathering dark clouds threatened rain. This was not exactly holding a paper over his head, but at this stage anyone would do.

I approached him, asked him if he was there to meet an expat, and gave my name.

His face split in a broad smile, he nodded and said his name was Alfa Barr. 'I have a Mercedes,' he said. 'And I am a very good driver. I will show you where to find the girl.'

'Okay, but first let's see if we can find some other people,' I said to him. Big drops of rain had started to spatter on the ground and I saw an opportunity to get past the sobels' barracks on the way to Goderich Beach and find the house with the blue gates. He agreed and led me up the road to an old creamy white Mercedes 380 parked on the side of the road by the stalls.

As we drove through Lumley Beach, the storm hit us and we continued in near darkness through a torrential downpour which battered on the roof of the car, bounced off the tarmac and blanketed the trees and houses in grey curtains of rain. When Alfa Barr mentioned the sobels' checkpoint, I assured him there would be no problem. They had peered at me the last time in the taxi, probably wondering what I was doing driving about so much in their area, so I had some packets of Lucky Strike handy, but this time the rain was in our favour.

Sure enough, we saw no one at all at the checkpoint outside the camp, which was deluged with floods running alongside the road, and we sailed past unhindered. I hoped the rain would keep up as this was the only road along the coast.

I had almost given up hope of ever finding North and Phillips when, right down the end of Goderich Beach on a side road, we spotted the letters 'FHS' on the blue gates of a big villa backing onto the sea in a small inlet. The house was set in extensive grounds and enormous, built in a grandiose, stuccoed and taste-less 1970s African style of the sort to gladden the hearts of the likes of Idi Amin or President Mobuto. I hopped out of the car, opened the gates and ran to a porch while Alfa Barr parked the white Mercedes. For long minutes, I banged on the door and shouted till a local Sierra Leone, the owner, finally opened up. Behind him in the shadows of the hall was the tall lean figure of Mike North, his pistol ready in his hand.

He led me into a large room at the back of the house where they were all gathered in the gloom while the rain beat down steadily outside. Mike Phillips was there, and their women, local Sierra Leones with several friends.

I had taken too long to find them, and I was sure they could have used the phone to help themselves. They knew the telephone number of the British High Commission which was still occupied, trying to negotiate with the coup leaders, and they could have taken the broadcasting advice on radio more seriously, for all British passport holders and other expatriates to make their way to the Hotel Mammy Yoko. I told them that there had been five evacuations already while I had been trying to find them, which meant I would have to take them all out by sea. Mike North grudgingly approved my plan to hire a boat to take everyone to Conakry. He knew from all his years along this coast that this was a regular route used by as many gold or diamond smugglers as fishermen.

'Good, so let's get back to the hotel,' I said.

Mike North shook his head, 'No, we might get stopped by the sobels down the road.'

'You're going to have to leave this place sometime,' I told him, losing patience. 'You might as well make it now as any time, so you'll all be in the same place for the boat trip I'm setting up.'

'What about sending the boat round to pick us up from the back of the house?' All the big houses in Goderich backed on to the sea, and this one was off a tiny estuary.

I shook my head. 'To be honest, I probably won't be able to find this place from the sea. There's hundreds of houses along this coastline and they all look the same.' It was a miracle I had found the place at all. 'I'd be out there in the dark, or at dawn, and probably get lost.'

He looked unhelpful, so I reminded him: 'Besides, I just took two days trying to find you here, and I don't want to spend another two floating about trying to locate the place again from the sea.'

There was no thanks. He just said, 'What if I build a bonfire?'

Nice idea, I thought, but totally unrealistic. Exasperated, I replied, 'I could spend hours and hours fiddling about trying to see a bonfire hidden down this estuary, which is way south of Freetown when we really want to be going north to Guinea. Why can't you come to the hotel like everyone else?'

Mike North refused. I could see Mike Phillips wanted to come with me, but at the same time he did not want to leave his boss and ended up siding with him.

'Well, there are rebels all over the place,' I warned them. 'And you're next.'

Phillips looked badly worried. I told them frankly that tensions were very finely balanced out on the streets; rebels were looting houses and raping women in other parts of the town and working their way gradually out from the centre towards Lumley and Goderich. When I had first started looking for the house, there had been few rebels about, but now I had been stopped several times and seen more bodies lying in the roads. 'I'm not sure I'll be able to come back for you. I will make every effort but I can't promise anything.'

'We'll take our chances,' said North obstinately, dominating the people with him.

I was not impressed, but I didn't want to waste any more time and walked out. I had to find a boat.

The rain had eased off when Alfa Barr drove me back to the hotel and we were stopped at the sobels' checkpoint on the road outside the camp. The soldier wandered over to stop us, vaguely waving his AK in our direction, but it was still drizzling and his heart was not in it. Cheerfully, I handed him a couple of packets of cigarettes and he waved us through. This was no weather for robbing and murder.

I called Murdo for the last time. He would be out of touch on his way to Conakry the next day and was delighted to hear I had found Mike North. 'I'll be there tomorrow, or certainly by Sunday,' he said. 'So if you arrange to get there on Monday, I'll be waiting for you all in the old port.'

There was no daylight left to go looking for a boat so I arranged to see Alfa Barr first thing the following day. Later, in the bar after supper, Roger's deputy manager Steve Lawson told me that he had seen Lincoln earlier during the afternoon in his Landrover on the way from his apartment in the annex of the Hotel Cape Sierra a few hundred yards down the road. 'Apparently, the Indians left today,' he said. 'About a hundred of them in a private charter to Abidjan. They're the sixth evacuation to go.' As each one left, my options narrowed, but counting the evacuations had become a game for the long-term expats. It was clear Steve and Roger felt safe in their hotel, protected by the Nigerian ECOMOG soldiers, but I had seen Africa in chaos before, in Zaire and Rwanda, and did not share their optimism. After the departure of the Americans and the UN, the British High Commissioner and the Nigerian High Commissioner were left on their own trying to negotiate a return to order, which must have been like trying to catch soap in a bloody bath. The AFRC never sent the same people, so Penfold and Abubakar had to suffer a tirade of aggressive nonsense from each new self-important rebel officer till any progress could be made. By this time, the Corporal Gbories and captains of this world had been elbowed to one side and a Colonel Anderson was representing Johnny Paul Koroma and the other coup leaders. However, Penfold's problem was that whatever was painfully agreed with Anderson was then impossible to endorse with the rest of the AFRC who were presumably all out on the streets, raping, looting and murdering.

Inside the Mammy Yoko, the numbers rose continually as hundreds more people evaded the sobels cruising the roads nearby to find sanctuary in the hotel. Many Americans, French, Germans, more Italians and dozens of British families had struggled in. The High Commission had failed to contact all British passport holders about the British evacuation as their warden system had broken down with bad communications and many of the families had been out of touch for days hiding from the rebels in cellars or under houses. By evening, there were hundreds again in the hotel and the lobby was full. Luggage lay everywhere; men argued or sat about exhausted; young girls went about with eyes red from weeping, and a woman in the lobby had an epileptic fit. I hoped I could find a boat the following day.

Saturday 31 May

I spent all morning with Alfa Barr. The storm clouds had cleared during the night and we set off from the hotel in his old Mercedes in glorious sunshine, the sort that gives you complete confidence in your plans for the new day. We started at the Aqua Club, which was a mooring on the inlet not far from the hotel, and found a number of locals hanging about on the jetty who were paid to look after the yachts and motor boats in the water. One or two boats might have been suitable but they were not for hire, even with the power of the Leones and dollars in my daysack. In spite of the sun, which made the trees and even the houses sparkle after the downpour, this was not a promising start to the day.

'Got any ideas?' I asked Alfa Barr.

'Yep,' he said. 'I know someone who might help, in Kissy.'

He hesitated and I said, 'What's the problem?'

'It's on the other side of Freetown.' The suburb was about 15km from the Hotel Mammy Yoko on Cape Sierra but I had little choice.

Alfa Barr used side roads as best he could. We were too early for the rebels but passed more evidence of the anarchy and saw several bodies lying in the gutter on the way. Kissy was a hotchpotch of colonial buildings sliding into the Sierra Leone River. Narrow streets, potholes, painted shop signs, bits of neon, a maze of telephone wires draped from house to house: all chaotic enough in good times, but now most of the shops had been looted, some burned out and the reeking smell of charred rubbish hung on the warm morning air.

Alfa Barr drove downhill to the port area, more stinking than the rest because the rain had washed so much garbage from above downhill to the quaysides which were littered with filth. Sewage, plastic bags and bottles floated among the boats in the mud-grey water. The Sierra Leone River estuary was about 2 or 3km wide at this point and I wondered what was happening on the other side at Lungi airport where there was still a stand-off between the Nigerians and the coup forces.

Alfa Barr took me to a hut on a quayside where we found an old man in dirty shorts and T-shirt who owned a pirogue, a 30 foot-long wooden boat with an outboard engine, like those which ferried people across the estuary to Tagrin for the airport. Some were brave enough to make the much longer journey to Guinea. The old man wiped his calloused hands on his shorts and padded barefoot across the dock to show us his boat. I got in to inspect it as best I could. It was long enough to accommodate us all, and there was space for some stores and spare cans of fuel. There was a chunk of concrete in the back to make the front rise up over the waves and it was powered by a car engine with a long drive shaft to the propeller.

'How much?' I asked the elderly local.

'To Conakry?' he confirmed, and to let me know this was the exception which raised the price.

I nodded.

With half an eye on Alfa Barr, who knew prices, he said, 'Six hundred dollars.'

I had some negotiating to do. I needed four places for Ken, the two night fighters and me, but if I could winkle Mike North's group out of the house with the blue gates miles away the other side of Freetown we would be eight with their women too. Alfa Barr, the old man and I haggled around the base price of the boat and the cost per person if others came too and ended up with US$500 for the boat and up to five people, plus another $100 per person for the other three if they turned up. Alfa Barr would get another $200 so the whole deal would cost about $1,000.

'Okay,' I said. I had the money and I had no time for a long debate. A group of rebels had appeared further along the dock-side, mad in clothes they had stolen from shops. One wore several colourfully patterned women's skirts, one over the other, incongruous as he swung his AK47, and another several brilliant

T-shirts over combat trousers. They began to take an interest in us, chattering to each other and pointing.

'We need to get some fuel,' Alfa Barr told me, watching the rebels nervously.

The old boat owner shrugged, 'No fuel. All stolen.'

I glanced up the street at the rebels and said, 'You know where we can find some?'

Alfa Barr nodded vigorously, keen to leave before the rebels came over.

However, fuel in Freetown was at a premium. The coup was seven days old and the civilian population had gone to ground in face of the continuing violence. The AFRC had called on people to go back to work as usual, but with increasing numbers of Foday Sankoh's RUF rebels coming into Freetown to celebrate victory with an orgy of looting after years ostracised in the jungle, the situation was far from normal and everyone stayed at home. The civilians had gone on strike leaving the soldiers and RUF to wreck the place.

Alfa Barr drove me to six gas stations but there were long queues at each, locals arguing and shouting with soldiers who had taken over the fuel distribution and hiked the prices to absurd levels. We risked being robbed by them in any case. By mid-morning, groups of sobels were back on the streets on the lookout for loot and we were stopped frequently. They crowded round, checking inside to see what we had to steal, but we had carefully cleaned the car out and I had stuffed my green daysack under my seat. Each time Alfa Barr and I chatted them up through the open windows, and bribed our way past with handfuls of Leones and packets of Lucky Strike. I sensed that this would become increasingly difficult as the day wore on.

Once again, Alfa Barr proved useful. We drove to a scruffy, run-down garage which was deserted and shut. We parked and walked round the back to a store where Alfa Barr found a local Sierra Leone who had salted away a stock of fuel in a filthy old tank in a corrugated tin lockup behind his house. Alfa Barr knew the man and negotiated twenty gallons at US$5 each. In Sierra Leone, this was high, but it was worth it in the circumstances.

The man siphoned our fuel into the Mercedes and some cans

and we drove back to the old man with the pirogue at Kissy who was still sitting in his shack on the dock. He gave the impression his whole life had passed by just sitting there. I only gave him two gallons and fifty dollars. This was enough to get him and his boat up in the morning and round to the Aqua Club in the coastal inlet opposite the hotel, but not so much that he would take the money and never bother turning up.

I explained the plan: 'We're taking people from the Hotel Mammy Yoko to Conakry on Monday morning, so you'll have to drive the boat all the way round Freetown to Aberdeen at dawn.' He agreed and I told him I would meet him at the jetty. I planned to go south along the coast with Alfa Barr to Goderich Beach to find Mike North and Mike Phillips with their women at six o'clock and bring them back to the hotel. Then I would go straight to the jetty to meet the boatman in the pirogue, after which I would send Alfa Barr back to fetch Ken, the two hookers and North's party. All this meant we had to start in the dark as I wanted everyone in the boat ready to set out by seven o'clock. We had a ten-hour journey, depending on currents, and I wanted to complete the trip in daylight.

The old boatman seemed unconcerned by any of this. He said he knew the coast to Guinea well, on smuggling trips, and tried to impress us with talk of river estuaries spilling from the mountains into the sea, sandbanks, mangrove swamps and treacherous tidal currents. 'We stay well out to sea,' he admitted finally. 'Maybe twenty miles. Maybe more.' I wondered how the others would cope.

The boat sorted, I got Alfa Barr to take me to find other necessities for our trip, including some fresh food which was wrapped in leaves for protection and plastic containers for water. Near the hardware store, we stopped in a narrow street while a crowd of locals ran past, four in a line with their arms out, like a shelf, holding the blood-drenched body of someone who was either dead or seriously wounded. A mêlée of others jogged along around them shouting and crying. Given the shaking ride and the din, I doubted this impromptu human ambulance would reach the Connaught Hospital with its patient alive. Alfa Barr shook his head sadly. 'This is the third coup in five years,' he said. 'But the world is truly gone mad this time.'

Finally, we took the food, water containers and the remaining fuel back to cache in his house. By this time, he had persuaded me to let him come with us in the pirogue to Guinea. I was not keen to overload the boat, in case of heavy seas, but he had been genuinely helpful and agreeing to bring him along secured the confidence that he would look after the fuel and stop it being stolen.

We had done well so far, especially to avoid rebels when we had the fuel and stores in the Mercedes. I said, 'Let's go and find the girlfriend of this partner of yours.'

He drove me to a really run-down shanty slum of tin or wood huts not far from Sonya's house where Ken was staying and stopped the Mercedes in the dust. Rotting refuse lay about everywhere. The entire neighbourhood lay stinking, dusty and depressed under the beating tropical sun. The 'house' where the girl lived was nothing more than a tin-roofed shack made of mud about 12 feet square, inside which several elderly local men and women squatted on the earth floor. From the way Murdo had described his British business contact, I thought his girlfriend was a European who had been hiding out with this family, so I asked, 'Where is Didi?'

'She is not here,' said a wrinkled old man in a dirty old vest. 'She has took her things and gone off on the ferry boat to get away from Freetown.'

One of the women ran off up a track between the huts while I was standing in the doorway. She reappeared a few moments later. She had a telephone in her shack and had somehow got in touch with Didi. 'I've told her to come back and that you're here,' she said, looking at me a certain way. She had assumed I was the rich guy who was going to spirit her friend away from Sierra Leone.

'When?' I asked without enthusiasm.

'She will be here very soon,' the woman lied.

The shack was filthy so Alfa Barr and I sat in his Mercedes for more than an hour in the heat, with the windows and front doors open. Then the first woman came dabbing along the street in the dust with another tall, skinny local girl in a tight tube-top and miniskirt and two things were immediately clear to me. First, I was being landed with another night fighter to look after, and, second, Didi was a local, not a European as Murdo had led me to think, with only Sierra Leone papers if she had any at all. It dawned on me that, listening to Murdo and Ken, I had let both the British and American evacuations go by just to find myself saddled with a couple of local hookers.

She stuck her head in the window of the Mercedes, much as if she was at work, and gave me a wide toothsome smile. She had a lovely body but, to tell the truth, she was no oil painting. 'Get in the back,' I told her shortly. It seemed I was doomed to collecting up all the mullocks* of Freetown.

I got Alfa to drive round to Sonya's house and shouted for Ken as I banged on the door. This time I was going to stand no more nonsense about Ken staying there. They had to come into the hotel and wait there till we left in the boat. They needed no persuading. That day, rebels had come through the shanty area raiding houses nearby and they were thankful to see me.

In the Mammy Yoko, I went in search of Steve Lawson, Roger's deputy manager. He was a chubby Englishman in his mid-forties and helpful. 'Have you got a spare room?' I asked desperately. The idea of sharing mine with Ken and two hookers was out of the question. Apart from getting little sleep and the fact that Sonya was the surliest and most depressingly morose individual I had met for years, this would hardly rate as good family behaviour with my wife back home.

'Yes,' he said grinning at the trio behind me. Ken, 17 stone and hugely muscled in his multi-coloured pyjama trousers, stood there with these two skinny local tarts in tight miniskirts like extras off a B-movie Hollywood set. 'You're lucky,' he said to me still grinning. 'We were helping out with another evacuation this morning and I've a few empty rooms to spare.'

At short notice, the French Honorary Consul and the British High Commission had contacted the French government to ask if

---

* Mullock, a rock containing no gold, or the rock refuse left after extracting gold, so, colloquially, rubbish.

they could help take off the hundreds of expatriates who had arrived at the Mammy Yoko even in the twenty-four hours since the American evacuation to the USS *Kearsarge*. The French kept a corvette permanently on station off the West African coast, to support their military bases in Libreville, Abidjan and Dakar, and with only three hours' notice they had diverted the *Jean Moulin*, named after a famous French resistance fighter of the Second World War, to Freetown. That morning, three individuals in the French Navy had appeared in a large inflatable dinghy and stepped onto the beach dressed as if for a day's sunbathing, in crisp, white shirts, shorts and snappy tropical socks. The officer produced a small laptop computer linked in real time to his ship and from there patched immediately to a computer database in France to check the nationalities of evacuees. Waiting on the beach were 255 European Community citizens with their families, including more than 150 British passport holders. In a short couple of hours, with the assistance of Roger Crooks, Steve Lawson, Lincoln and others from the British High Commission, this slimline, high-tech operation had transferred them all to the ship.

'It was typical minimalist French stuff,' said Steve. 'None the less welcome, but a bit of a contrast to hundreds of US Marines swooping down on us in choppers and full combat gear.'

Judging by the numbers still filling the lobby, it was hard to believe there had been another evacuation, and more people were coming in all the time. British, Americans and other foreigners were still turning up after hiding out for days, like North and Phillips, too frightened to escape past rebels rampaging round their houses. They had missed the evacuations but followed the BBC radio broadcasts to reach the Hotel Mammy Yoko, still considered a safe enclave. No one knew how quickly that could change.

Steve kindly gave them a room opposite me, with a fine view over the front of the hotel, across the road, the coastal inlet below on the bay and towards Freetown over Aberdeen Bridge and the estuary. Sonya crawled straight onto a bed, curled up and began to cry.

'Get her to cheer up,' I told Ken on my way out. He had

insisted that she come with us to Conakry and in that state she might be a positive danger to the rest of us on the long sea journey.

'She's upset,' said Ken rather weakly, his huge arms hanging limply by his side. 'She's convinced they're out to kill her.'

'They'd get us all if they got a chance.'

'No,' Ken said stubbornly. 'She said they were shouting out the name of her family when they attacked us in Cape House.'

'How d'you know?' I demanded. I had had enough of this nonsense.

'She told me,' he replied.

'You for real, or are you buttoned up the back or something?' I asked in genuine amazement. 'Since when d'you speak Mende, for Christ's sake? Of course she told you all that, so you would be stupid enough to look after her.'

'No, she wouldn't do that,' Ken insisted.

'Rubbish,' I snapped at him and left them to it. My morale was at a low point. I had spent all day sorting our escape by boat, which had gone well, but the only people I had been able to persuade to come into the hotel were two local hookers and Ken.

The sun was going down as I came back downstairs and there was nothing more I could do. This was the time of madness, when the coup soldiers and rebels went on the rampage. In confirmation, I heard a vehicle roar past the Nigerians outside the hotel and another burst of gunfire.

I saw Lincoln later and asked him what was happening on the diplomatic front. I had been so bogged down with the details of my own boat evacuation that I had lost touch with the wider picture. He would not be drawn on the details but indicated that Peter Penfold had led some extremely tough negotiations with various Sierra Leone colonels headed by Colonel Anderson and there was a chance of a settlement. Penfold and the Nigerian, Chidi Abubakar, had bluffed Colonel Anderson with the complete fiction that the Americans and British would launch a military counterstrike against the coup, and Anderson had lied in turn with a hollow promise to obtain the agreement of Johnny Paul Koroma and the full Council to stop the violence and return to barracks. The fact was that the situation was now out of

Koroma's control. I told Lincoln I had seen more RUF rebels than ever in Freetown while I had been in town fixing our boat.

'That's why the Marines are coming off the *Kearsarge* again, and because we've counted another 200 US, British and other western expats here,' he said. 'But this will be the last chance to get out of here.'

Sunday 1 June

I got up early, met Alfa Barr outside by the shanty huts under the big baobab tree at the T-junction and we drove along the coast road to Goderich Beach to see Mike North. Another handful of Leones changed hands at the checkpoint by the barracks and we were at the big house with the blue gates by seven o'clock.

'The Americans have got one more evacuation,' I told them. 'If you come at once, we might just make it.' There was still a chance that we might not have to do the boat trip.

Mike Phillips looked hopefully at his boss, but Mike North, gaunt and strained after a week in hiding, was as uncompromising as ever.

'Out of the question,' he said authoritatively. 'They would accept Mike and me, maybe, but they won't take the women as they've only got Sierra Leone papers.'

I said I thought that the Americans might make an exception this time, owing to the increasing danger to people left behind, but the uncertainty was unacceptable to North so I told them about the boat I had arranged. As before, he tried to persuade me to pick them up from the inlet at the back of the house, but this would have been a complete waste of time and risked wrecking the whole plan if we were left out on the sea too late into the night. I flatly refused. 'I've been driving all over Freetown for days at risk from these rebels,' I reminded them bluntly. 'So, you'll come down to the Mammy Yoko on Monday morning, or you can stay here.'

They agreed.

'Okay,' I said, tired with North's obstinacy. 'Be ready, because I will be here at six thirty and we don't want to lose time.'

'What can we bring?' Mike Phillips asked sensibly.

'Just a small bag with something warm,' I replied. It might get cold if we were still at sea on Monday night. 'But don't bring great suitcases. There isn't room.'

In fact, when I got back to the hotel, the US Marines had just completed their second and last evacuation in another slick heliborne operation. Their big grey helicopters had used the same landing site downside of the hotel and lifted out 200 more expatriates, mainly American nationals. Martin Greenwood thought maybe a couple of dozen Brits had gone too and said someone from the High Commission had been in the hotel early on in the day arranging for nearly fifty other British passport holders to join a final Lebanese evacuation by ship from the port for Conakry with 300 people.

'They went this morning and that's it,' he said with grim satisfaction. 'That's the last evacuation. They've all gone. Now we're on our own.'

Trouble was, they had not all gone. I was glad of our plan to leave by boat since although nine evacuations had rescued over 3,000 people from the tragedy of Freetown, the hotel was still as full as ever. Roger reckoned the numbers were already back up to about 1,000 refugees crammed into his 162-bed hotel even after the morning's exodus, and there were bigger crowds than ever on the road trying to get in. People were camped out all over the place. Families, tiny babies, teenagers, groups of aid workers, business-men, men from the mines, airline crews, and journalists lay among their luggage trying to sleep or hung about talking despondently, and they blocked all the public rooms, the corridors, the lobby, the bar, the conference hall, and the dining room. People had even spread themselves around in the kitchens, and the cooks had given up trying to prepare meals. In fact, after a week of this, the hotel was in complete chaos and normal services had broken down. The drink had run out in the bar and there was no more food. Even if the cooks had been able to use their kitchen to cook, Roger had been unable to buy any food. Some people, including children, had not eaten for more than twenty-four hours.

For the first time in days, I felt I had done all I could. As long as the old boatman and Alfa Barr turned up the next morning, we were all set for our escape by sea the following morning, and I had time to spare. So, since Roger had been so helpful when I was strapped for cash – I simply could not have arranged the boat without his loan – I went to his office and said, 'Roger, d'you need someone to go into town and get some food?'

'Yeah,' he said wiping the sweat from his eyes with a tired gesture. He was exhausted trying to keep the hotel running. 'But no one wants to risk leaving the hotel.'

'Give me a truck, and I'll drive it to the warehouse. You make the arrangements and I'll pick up the food for you.'

He was extremely grateful and immediately went off to speak to the Lebanese in the lobby. A few faces had changed as some had gone out, but they still maintained their 'business centre' round the tables and chairs in the middle. In fact, the moment he mentioned food, they began complaining there was nothing to eat in the hotel.

Roger replied in his slow Mississippi drawl, 'Listen, boys, you open your stores and I'll get some food. I got a guy to bring it back and we'll cook it.'

The Lebanese liked this idea but they said, 'We want cash.'

Roger sighed, 'I'm accepting your credit cards for your rooms here, and yet you want me to pay you cash?'

They nodded.

'Well listen up, 'cause this is real simple,' Roger said. 'You pay me cash for being in my hotel, and I will then pay you cash for the food.'

'If you can't pay cash, you can't have the food!' responded the Lebanese. For them business was business, coup or not.

They beat round the same argument for some minutes till the logic sank in: no food, they stayed hungry, and, in spite of diplomatic talking, there was no sign the violence in town would die away. No one had any idea how long the chaos would last. Roger finally came back to me with a slim young guy with a closely trimmed beard and olive skin, typically Lebanese.

He said, 'It's all sorted. This guy will show you where the warehouse is; he'll speak to the men there to let you in.'

'And the payment?' I asked.

'It has been arranged,' said the young man smoothly. 'The warehouse belongs to my brother.' Many of the Lebanese had portable radio telephones which they were using to keep in touch with their premises in Freetown and abroad, keeping their businesses alive in spite of the anarchy.

Roger gave me the keys to a small green low-slung box-body Hyundai van. I drove and we left the hotel. Getting out of the entrance at the top of the road was even more difficult than before. The Nigerian soldiers were in positions all round the hotel on the white perimeter wall, and they had further tightened their control of the entrance off the road by the main car park. Several hundreds were now clustered outside who would have sought refuge in the hotel too if they could have found a way past the Nigerian soldiers. They shouted and jostled, impatient with the Nigerians who refused to let them in, and it was obvious that some of the soldiers were getting increasingly nervous.

As we drove up the driveway from the car park, another jeep, loaded as usual with rebels, drove past the hotel at speed, with lots of jeering and shouting at the Nigerian troops. A couple of rebels fired off bursts from their AKs. The bullets all went in the air, but one Nigerian soldier fired a few rounds back, more in panic than aimed shots, and the crowd screamed and ran for cover at the sides of the road. No one was hurt, the jeep roared off downhill and the people massed back on to the road around the hotel entrance. The rebels and soldiers were testing the Nigerians, not for the first time. The atmosphere up at the gate was growing significantly more tense. I recognised the signs. It was only a matter of time before someone was hurt.

The Nigerians let us through their barrier, shoving the people back, some using their rifles across their chests, others simply lashing out with nightsticks. We eased through the mob and I drove up the road to the T-junction under the big baobab tree on the high ground overlooking the hotel, and then turned downhill towards Aberdeen Bridge into town. The roads, bad at the best of times, were still littered with rubbish, rocks and wrecked cars. I got the young Lebanese to find a route off the main roads to avoid meeting rebels and we found the streets were deserted in the residential areas. The civilians were all staying in their homes in spite of the coup leaders' calls for them to return to work. We passed several vehicles, doors open, rebels leaning out or sitting on the roofs. They stared at us unpleasantly. Cold aggression had replaced the excited madness of the first few days' looting, although they were still finding places to rob. One lot had obviously looted a clothes shop because they looked more bizarre than ever. They were wearing everything they had stolen, with sports shorts under multi-coloured patterned girls' skirts, several bright T-shirts at once, one on top of the other in spite of the heat, and they all wore the same brand of trainers, several of them with wholly different sizes on each foot.

The warehouse was in the San Tropeter district, only a twenty-minute drive but this was quite far enough in the circumstances. It was hidden among offices down back streets, which is maybe why the looters had missed it but we had to drive back with a load of food on board at serious risk of being robbed.

The young man beat on the solid wood door for several minutes until an old Lebanese man opened the door a crack. He recognised the young man and let us in. He and his wife lived over the store on the floors above. The old Lebanese cut straight to the nub and asked us, 'Where's the money?' We told him that the deal had been fixed in the hotel and all we had to do was pick up the goods.

'No money, no stores,' the old man declared emphatically and shut the door on us.

The young Lebanese with me shrugged, as if it was absolutely nothing to do with him. We got in the van again and I drove back to the Hotel Mammy Yoko. At the crowded hotel entrance, the Nigerian soldiers were getting more and more edgy and difficult. They insisted on opening the van but they could see it was empty and I argued my way through. Inside the hotel, I found Roger and we went to see the Lebanese in the lobby.

'I've just been down there and the guy said I've got to bring cash!'

The Lebanese smiled at each other, doubtless pleased the old warehouseman was dogged as ever, but they assured me, 'It's all okay. We've made an agreement and you can go back now, pick everything up.'

I looked at them for a long moment, unsure whether to believe them or not, but we got back in the van and set out again for another twenty minutes' drive through Freetown, past the Nigerians and the crowd at the gate, through the chaos in the streets, back to the warehouse in San Tropeter.

Exactly the same thing happened again. The old Lebanese flatly refused to let us in, no matter how much the young Lebanese with me told him the deal was fixed.

'No money, no food!' he stated.

At this point, I said to them both, 'Right, I've had enough of this! Let's get on the bloody telephone and get it sorted out.' I left them to it, got a cup of coffee and sat down out of the way, thoroughly irritated. After a great deal of arguing with someone on the phone, the old man was finally persuaded to open the warehouse doors to us. He turned to me and asked, 'So, what d'you want?'

'How should I know? I don't go shopping for hotels too often!'

We got on the phone again to the hotel, this time to the *chef d'hotel*, who gave us a long list of provisions, and we filled the van to the roof till the springs groaned. Finally, on top of boxes of tins, fresh vegetables, jars, olive oil, flour, pasta, chickens, and rice, we stacked six enormous deep frozen Marlin fish.

At this stage, the young Lebanese explained he had to stay at the warehouse for a while, to sort the paperwork. A look in his face told me the real reason was that he was frightened. If the van was stopped by a bunch of rebels, they would undoubtedly rob us. All the people in the hotel had told horrendous stories of the looting; many of the Lebanese women had been raped, often in front of their families, and shootings were commonplace. A man called Kange said the rebels had shot the padlock off the gate of his house, charged in and begun shooting between his legs threatening to kill him and his family. One pointed an RPG at his head till he told them that if he fired it the blast would kill everyone in the room. He said they were all drunk or high on ganja. During my own trips round town, I had seen maybe twenty corpses lying in the road. The young Lebanese was frightened and he knew the rich Lebanese community had been specially targeted.

So I drove back to the hotel on my own, taking longer to ease over the potholes as the Hyundai was badly overloaded. I came up behind the mob at the hotel entrance and pushed slowly through the hundreds of people in the road around the barrier. This time the Nigerian soldiers were really aggressive. I'm not sure what had happened while I had been out – maybe more rebels had driven past shooting over their heads, or perhaps they were worried because the crowd in the road had grown bigger and more dangerous, or maybe it was just that they were trying to ape the efficient way the US marines had behaved. The Nigerians had watched two highly impressive military evacuations by the US Marines and they wanted to show that they were just as good soldiers. The result was that they were both aggressive and incredibly officious.

They stopped me at the barrier and one big soldier, a sergeant, waved his hand dismissively, shouting in a booming, bossy voice over the din of the people around, 'You can't come in here!'

'I've just driven out, twice!' I said, taken aback.

'No! You can't come in,' he shook his head coming round to my window, his black face gleaming under his combat helmet.

I tried to control my temper and replied, 'I've got to come in here. I've got all the food for the hotel in this truck.' I kept my voice down as I did not want the mob to know. Regular square meals were rare as hens' teeth in Freetown and they would steal the lot if they got the chance.

The Nigerian soldiers gave them the chance. The soldier at the window of my truck demanded, 'Open the back of the truck!'

I stared at him in amazement and said, 'Well, no, I really don't think it's a good idea we should open it just here.'

'Why?' he boomed arrogantly. 'What is in it?'

'I just told you. All the food for the hotel.' I looked at the mass of faces pressed around the van and knew this would be a disaster.

'Open the truck!' boomed the Nigerian soldier again.

'No,' I said. 'There are hundreds of people out there, all starving, and if we open the back we'll cause a riot!'

'Don't you say "No!" to me,' he shouted furiously, losing his temper. The other soldiers scowled, shifting their rifles uncertainly in their hands. They were all nervous and the situation had suddenly become rather volatile. It seemed insane that I could get into trouble driving a load of food into the hotel, so I backtracked and said, 'Well, what I mean is that I don't think it would be a good idea to open the back here! Why don't we bring the van inside the barrier and then you can look inside it?'

It was too late. He had worked himself into a hot lather of arrogant indignation in which any suggestion, no matter how brilliant, was pure insult and he bellowed, 'No! You do as I say!' With that, he brought up his rifle, pointed it at me and cocked it.

No contest. I climbed out of the cab, went round the back with the Nigerian soldier and opened the van doors. Immediately the crowd around surged forward with a guttural hungry roar, squashing me and the soldiers against the truck, and hands reached past me from all directions trying to grab the food in the van.

'Shut the back up and get inside!' screamed the Nigerian soldier by me in complete panic, struggling to free himself from the mêlée. Someone fired a couple of shots, which stopped the mob for a moment, and we got the back shut. I slithered down the side of the van into the cab, started up and pulled inside the barrier, while the Nigerians, all shouting like maniacs, beat the mob back with long sticks.

I drove down the slope and around the hotel to the kitchens entrance at the back, grateful for a moment of the peace and quiet there. I parked the van by the service door in the basement, walked in through the kitchens, picking my way over all the people lying about on the floors, told someone to find the head chef to say the grub was outside, and made my way up through the dining room to the rooms at the back of the Reception in the lobby. I suppose it took me about ten minutes to do all this.

The deep silence in the lobby should have warned me. The usual buzz of talk among the dozens of people camped all over the floor and people constantly shouting into telephones was gone as though switched off. Not a sound disturbed the hot afternoon as I walked into the back of the lobby. Maybe 200 people stood frozen where they were, lying on the floor among their luggage, sitting on the few chairs or boxes they had brought, or standing in groups talking, and they were all staring at the front entrance. There, by the glass doors, were three rebels, glaring round at everyone, in filthy mixed combats and civvy shirts, one in a skirt. Two carried AKs and the third carried an RPG.

They had just burst in through the front door, their eyes were wide and staring, and they were breathing hard, having run past the

Nigerian soldiers to get into the hotel. Waving his AK aggressively, one shouted, 'Where is Mister Crooks? The manager!'

No one said a word.

The rebels swung round with their AKs and the RPG threateningly, and everyone swayed back like a wave washing around the room as they found themselves looking down the barrels. I stood quite still, like everyone else. There was nothing we could do. The slightest wrong move might precipitate a violent reaction and if the rebels started shooting in the lobby, or were mad enough to fire the RPG, there would be a massacre.

'Where's the manager?' one shouted again.

No one replied.

Behind, in the hotel offices in the passage behind me, I could distinctly hear the booming voice of the colonel of the Nigerian soldiers down the corridor in an office saying, 'You are safe in our hands! We are securing the hotel!' I assumed he was speaking to Roger Crooks. He was obviously completely unaware of what was happening in the lobby.

Fortunately the three mad-looking rebels over by the front door never heard these bold words. Abruptly they spun around, shoved out through the glass doors and vanished into the hotel grounds. Inside, there was a huge sigh of relief. Slowly, people started talking again, in a state of shock. Suddenly, they had seen that their blind faith in the Nigerian soldiers was misplaced, and they might be in as much danger here as anywhere else in Freetown.

I went to find Roger. I wanted to tell him that eventually I had got the food back and used the intercom at the front desk to speak to him in his office. He invited me in at once and I found him in the middle of a tense meeting with the Nigerian Colonel, another Nigerian who turned out to be the Nigerian Consul, Martin Greenwood, the Yorkshire diamond mine manager, Roger's deputy manager Steve Lawson, an American called Marshall and Colin Glass, an official from the British High Commission. The atmosphere was tense, so I told Roger about the food and made to leave.

'Join us, Will,' Roger said, waving his hand for me to stay. 'You heard the rebels broke in?'

'I was in the lobby.'

The Nigerian colonel butted in with, 'Don't worry! You are all safe!'

Someone asked him, 'How did they get in, past your soldiers?'

'Don't worry!' the colonel repeated. 'It won't happen again!' He stoutly defended his troops' capacity to protect the hotel, but after a couple of minutes of this pointless to and fro, I had to interject:

'Well, if that had happened with the British Army or the Americans, we'd have shot those three dead! Before they got anywhere near the hotel. Soldiers' orders for opening fire are to stop loss of life, and letting those rebels through is putting people's lives at risk by anyone's standards.'

The colonel stared at me, but he said nothing.

'The soldiers should have done something at least to stop them.'

He found his voice and answered lamely, 'We will deal with it. It will not happen again!'

'Well, what guarantee have you got?'

Steve Lawson, a reasonable man, comfortably built in his mid-forties, but maybe desperate for some reassurance of safety, said placatingly, 'The colonel has promised it won't happen again.'

'Let's put it this way,' I said, changing tack from theoretical talk of the future to practical considerations for the present. 'Don't you think we should make some plans of our own? To defend the hotel?'

'Why? We've got the Nigerians.'

'Okay, but how stupid are we going to look if more rebels break in again, and we haven't done anything?'

It struck me that all of them had blithely assumed that the rebels and rioting Sierra Leone soldiers outside could not touch them inside the hotel, and that they were in no danger. They had heard countless stories of the violence in the town, about the looting, beatings, rapes and murders, but all that was outside the Mammy Yoko. Most of them left in the hotel after the French, British and American evacuations had gone were long-term expats who probably assumed they could lie safe in the hotel until the violence blew over and then go home. Until the three rebels stormed into the lobby. Suddenly, the risks were clear. Much as Samuel Johnson put it, when a man knows he is to be hanged . . . it concentrates his mind wonderfully.

'Regardless of what the Nigerian soldiers are going to do, shouldn't we have some plan? If the Nigerians do keep them out, then fine, but what if they don't? Shouldn't we have a plan to defend ourselves?'

The colonel bridled, 'You don't need to do that!'

I shrugged: 'With all due respect, I think we do.'

Roger had been listening closely, saying little, making up his mind. This was his hotel and his responsibility. He spoke up: 'Will, over to you. You make us a plan.'

The meeting broke up with the Nigerian colonel blustering out, followed by his consul. When everyone had gone, I turned to Roger and quietly told him about my military background. 'I spent a long time with the Special Air Service in the British Army,' I said. 'So I'm not going to come up with some crazy scheme.'

That may sound like a total contradiction in terms to some people sitting in the comfort of their armchairs and eager to carp or find fault, but Roger was pleased of my help at that moment. He called Steve and Martin back to start working out what we were going to do.

'I'm going to leave it all to you guys with Will,' Roger said, and Steve and Martin volunteered at once to help.

'I've just brought in a load of food,' I told them. 'So let's get the kitchens cleared so we can eat.'

I went to the Lebanese 'business centre' around the chairs and table in the middle of the lobby and spoke to the leaders there. Without giving them the opportunity to raise questions, something the Lebanese seem to love doing, I told them that I needed volunteers to help me organise a plan. The rebels bursting in had focused their minds too and they immediately agreed to join forces. Within minutes, I had about ten men as assistants, or marshals, some of whom I had got to know during the previous few days, and the Lebanese found nearly two dozen Lebanese chefs and cooks who normally ran their own restaurants in Freetown. Next, we went to the kitchens and moved everyone out to other places. A few grumbled till I told them this was so we could make a meal. Most of the 1,000 refugees in the hotel had not eaten for at least two days. I left them and went off to explore the hotel. Walking quickly up and down stairs and along corridors, I poked my nose into the rooms on every floor, working from the basement to the ground floor and the six floors above to the roof, assessing what space and facilities we had available. This recce of the hotel was to prove valuable sooner than I thought. As I went round, I worked out the numbers of the refugees, the space available, what was required, and how to bring some order into the chaos. I also worked out what they should all do in an emergency if the hotel was attacked.

When I got back to the lobby, I found Martin, Steve and the marshals and went through my plan. We opened up a series of large conference rooms Steve had shown me, enrolled the Lebanese marshals, and began shifting all the people dossing in the dining room, the kitchens and lobby into these other more spacious rooms. I made it clear that the conference rooms were designated as sleeping areas now and arranged the groups so they had space to sleep properly. Our problem was that everyone had staggered into the hotel with their belongings, many exhausted and traumatised, and just dropped down on any bit of empty floor they could find. However, reorganising them was easier than I had thought it would be once we told them the kitchens were being cleared for the cooks. The prospect of a decent meal really cheered them up.

I designated certain rooms or areas for each group's luggage, so the sleeping areas and public rooms were no longer cluttered with suitcases, boxes and bags, and I allocated toilets to specific groups too, giving them responsibility for keeping them clean and working. The stand-off between the rebels and the Nigerians was getting more like a siege, and none of us had any idea how long this would go on. Keeping the hotel's sanitary and washing facilities in order, especially in the heat, was essential.

I left the marshals working on all this, gradually reorganising the hundreds of people, and turned my attention to an emergency plan. During my trip round the hotel, I went up on the roof, to see if it would be suitable for a helicopter evacuation, but it was covered with a mess of square air conditioning pipes running the

15 March 1996: newly elected President Ahmed Tejan Kabbah waves to voters in the Sierra Leone capital Freetown. (*Associated Press*)

8 June 1997: Johnny Paul Koroma speaks to reporters about his self-proclaimed military government. (*AP*)

The Hotel Mammy Yoko before the attack of 2 June 1997. (*Dorian Taylor*)

Nigerian soldiers deployed around the hotel, protecting the civilians taking shelter there awaiting evacuation. (*Popperfoto/Reuter*)

A soldier of the RUF (Revolutionary United Front) shows off for the cameras in the centre of Freetown after the 25 May coup. (*Popperfoto*)

One of Koroma's bodyguards sporting an RPG launcher plus two additional rockets. (*Popperfoto/Reuter*)

Combined rebel and army forces display an array of weapons including a heavy machine gun of the type used in the attack on the Mammy Yoko. (*Popperfoto/Reuter*)

One of many rebel road blocks keeping a grip on the capital the day before the hotel came under fire. (*Popperfoto/Reuter*)

A Nigerian soldier points his rifle at Sierra Leone civilians clamouring to take refuge in the Mammy Yoko. (*Popperfoto/Reuter*)

A fatally wounded Nigerian soldier lies in the hotel's basement. (*Reuters Television Library*)

On the roof of the Mammy Yoko early on in the attack, looking for the best firing position. Note the drainage hole in the buttress wall – these were used later as firing ports when the battle intensified. (*Reuters Television Library*)

Taking command of the Nigerian defence force and redeploying them into effective firing positions. (*Reuters Television Library*)

Major Lincoln Jopp after receiving shrapnel wounds, making his way downstairs for further treatment. (*Reuters Television Library*)

A rebel soldier lies dead in the street as stunned civilians look on. (*AP*)

Over a thousand people wait in line to be evacuated from Freetown on 3 June as a US marine aboard an armoured personnel carrier stands guard. (*Popperfoto*)

Evacuees cross the deck of the USS *Kearsarge* after arriving by marine transport helicopter. (*AP*)

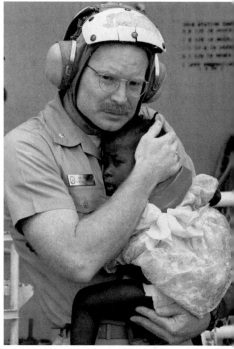

A US serviceman holds an orphaned baby evacuated from Freetown. (*AP*)

length of the building, and a big rusted metal air-con machine beside a large concrete water tower in the middle. Instead, I chose the same place the Americans had used for their evacuation, on open grass in the grounds near the hotel at the sea end. Actually, I really had no idea where help could come from, though the Nigerians over at Lungi airport were our closest allies. At least this area was down the slope from the main road above the hotel and more or less out of view of the rebels behind tall trees and bushes if they forced their way through the barrier at the top of the drive where the Nigerian soldiers were keeping the ever-increasing mob at bay.

Back in Roger's office, Steve and I set to writing instructions for the emergency plan, to inform everyone in the hotel what we wanted them to do. He sat at his computer and I paced about dictating the instructions. I started with great diplomacy, saying, 'We have some very capable Nigerian troops from ECOMOG who are protecting the hotel.' Steve glanced at me sideways, grinning. I continued, 'However, in the event of an emergency or to evacuate the hotel, this is the procedure to follow.' I had identified all the new areas in the hotel which I had organised for people to rest in routinely as Block A, B, C etc, then where each group should go in an emergency, for example Area 1 in the basement, and briefed the marshals on the detail. However, I did not want to confuse the people with this and merely dictated to Steve, 'In the event of an attack or fire, all guests in the upper floors will make their way to the stair well and wait to be guided to safe areas by marshals,' I said, seeing it all happen in my mind as I spoke. 'Those on the ground floors will make their way to the foyer where their marshals will direct them.'

By now I had twenty marshals to act as guides and shepherd everyone from where they had just been told to sleep or spend the day, to the safest parts of the hotel. The basement was ideal, but with so many people to look after the second and third floors were needed too, in the corners of the hotel furthest from the entrance and the approach road topside of the hotel. They would be out of danger there if the rebels started shooting at the hotel. Finally, we wrote instructions on how the different groups should evacuate the building to the grass areas behind the hotel. We got all this on a single A4 sheet of paper which Steve photocopied and we gave handfuls to the marshals who distributed the sheets to every group in the conference rooms or slipped the sheets under the door of every bedroom. By this time, it was midnight and we had spent nearly six hours bringing some order to the Mammy Yoko.

During this time, the *chef d'hotel* and Lebanese cooks had been slaving hard to make enough food for over 1,000 people. The meal – chicken, fish stew and lots of rice – was not ready till nearly 1 a.m., but there was a tangible up-beat feel in the dining room as people ate their first decent meal for two days. In a matter of hours, the chaos of their lives had suddenly been given some structure. They had somewhere to sleep among their contacts and friends; they had eaten; there was the prospect of more food, and they knew people in the hotel had taken collective responsibility for their own safety. No longer were these a mass of individuals. I detected a genuine feeling of community spirit and cooperation. They would need all this confidence and more in the next forty-eight hours.

It was nearly two o'clock when I got to my room, and I had mixed feelings. In all the rushing round the hotel, I had not given Ken, the two hookers, Mike North, Mike Phillips and their women a moment's thought. However, as I tried to relax in my room, I began to think about my plan to get them all away by boat to Guinea. The boat was fixed, I had extra food for the trip which I had taken from the warehouse and stashed in my room, and the guy with the Mercedes was going to drive us to the rendezvous with the boat from Kissy in the morning. Everything for Guinea was set up, paid up and ready to go, but in agreeing to help Roger organise the refugees in the hotel, I had given myself a greater responsibility. I had no idea what would happen, but in the last eight hours over 1,000 people had recovered their spirit, had had their first square meal for days, and found some structure among the chaos of their lives. Many of them knew or recognised me and I felt they had come to depend on me. I was dog-tired, but before I fell asleep I realised I had given myself no option but to stay in the Hotel Mammy Yoko.

Monday 2 June

When I woke at 5.30 a.m., my choice was even clearer. I had a responsibility for the two GPMC mine workers and their families, as I was being paid by Murdo to work for GPMC, and that included Ken, the gloomy Sonya and Didi, the girlfriend of Murdo's contact in London. My plan to evacuate them by boat started with leaving the hotel at six to fetch Mike North and the others from the house with the blue gates in Goderich Beach, but now that I had taken on the job of helping all the people in the hotel, I felt I simply could not just walk out at dawn and leave them for good.

Ken was not happy about that at all. The night before, I had told him what I was thinking. 'You know the plan very well,' I had reassured him. 'I'll go and get Mike North and Phillips, I'll go to the Aqua Club with you, and I'll put you all on to the fisherman's boat coming round from Kissy. But you have to take them all to Conakry on your own. I've got to stay here. I'll follow you later.'

He was not keen. 'When's later?'

Throwing doubt on how I would get out was valid, but with all the others who were helping to manage the problems, like Roger, Steve, Martin, Lincoln Jopp and the High Commission staff, I was not alone. True, we were not a large group, but people had endlessly come up to me the previous night while we were all working to install some order in the hotel to ask me about all sorts of things, seeing me as the person 'in charge'. That touched the main issue. Against the handful I was responsible for in the boat to Conakry, I found it impossible to turn my back on all the people in the hotel.

It was a ten- to fourteen-hour journey by sea to Conakry. The

117

boatmen would take a route 30km out to sea to avoid the jagged inlets, islands and complex river deltas covered with mangrove swamps and they did this with no navigation aids at all, merely watching the swell and movement of the currents to tell where they were. I gave Ken my Silva compass to boost his confidence in the bearing they would take up the coast. I told him where to find Murdo, at the *Petits Bateaux* old port in Conakry harbour which we had arranged on our last telephone call together. Ken had been to Conakry and knew the place, so I underlined his role and insisted simply that, 'All you have to do is get on the boat this morning.'

I was thinking about all this, tired after too short a night's sleep, and shaving when there was a knock on the door. 'Come in!' I called and Didi appeared in the door looking worried. Gesturing at their room on the other side of the corridor, she asked, 'What's that noise?'

We went back into Ken's room, and looked out of the window. The clear pale grey light of dawn gave the green grass and palm trees in the hotel grounds a clean, fresh look, before the heat of the day. In Freetown, across the sparkling blue estuary, buildings on the hill glowed in the early sunlight in the area of Spur Road and the military barracks, where the square modern shape of the British High Commission was just visible over the roofs of other buildings. Lower down I could see the trees hiding the wreck of Cape House. Apart from a few wisps of smoke rising into the still air which gave away places the rebels had looted and burned, the town looked really quite clean, even attractive.

Didi's 'noise' was unmistakeably shooting. Down by Aberdeen Bridge, the sounds of single shots and bursts of automatic floated up to me, quite clear but distant, as if from another planet. My plan to get the guys on the boat to Conakry had just fallen apart.

'What is it?' Didi repeated.

It was gunfire. Ken sitting huge and despondent on the bed knew that, but to avoid panic, I said, 'People mucking about with dustbins. You stay here and I'll go down to see what's going on.'

I went back to my room, dressed quickly and ran down the stairs to the lobby to see what was happening. The lobby was clear now, with everyone sleeping where we had re-positioned them the night before, but one or two people had heard something was going on and were hanging about uncertainly in the foyer. I found several Nigerian soldiers at the front entrance who stopped me leaving the hotel. They knew what was going on but they refused to say. They were adamant. It soon became abundantly clear.

I estimated the firing was about 400 metres away to start with, but quickly enough there was a sharp urgency in the crack and thump of bullets snapping over the hotel itself. The shooting was unquestionably coming closer all the time. By six o'clock, only half an hour after we had first heard the shooting, stray rounds were smacking into the pink concrete walls of the building itself.

I saw Nigerian soldiers running back through the grounds outside and guessed that they were falling back, what the Army officially calls a 'withdrawal'. Moments later, a larger group of Nigerians in combats stumbled through the front doors pulling two others who had been wounded. They had been hit in the back and arms where large dark bloodstains glistened on their disruptive pattern uniforms. One had been shot in the head and his blood looked dark purple on his short black hair. Their fellow Nigerians unceremoniously dumped these two on the floor in the middle of the lobby and ran off outside again.

The few people standing about in the lobby stared in shock at the two wounded soldiers lying abandoned and groaning on the floor, but a couple of locals came over and, before long, several civilians were gathered round the wounded men giving them what first aid they could. As far as I knew from our work the previous night, the only medically qualified man among the refugees was a gynaecologist, but they seemed to be doing their best by committee and carried the two men away. I went up the stairs at a run to the roof to see if I could see what was happening and found about a dozen more Nigerian soldiers casually looking over the parapet in the direction of Aberdeen Bridge, their rifles resting on the top of the concrete wall, like soldiers standing ready for an attack against a castle. A few rounds were cracking overhead from the fighting in the distance.

Lincoln Jopp was on the roof. He had heard the shooting start just before dawn from his apartment in the Hotel Cape Sierra down by the sea nearby on the point and he had come up to the Hotel Mammy Yoko to get a better view from the highest place around, on the water tower in the middle of the roof. He was dressed as before in his combat uniform, every inch the Guards officer in tropical issue, and peering intently through his binoculars. I climbed up the concrete stairs inside the tower and then up the exposed iron ladder on the outside to join him and asked him what he thought was going on.

'There are Nigerian warships out to sea,' he told me. 'Destroyers, I think, and they took it into their heads to liven things up this morning with a spot of NGS.'* He pulled a face. 'They fired some starburst shells over the town just before dawn and although the High Commission think they missed Freetown altogether, it seems to have stirred up the rebels. Not surprisingly, they want to hit back at anything Nigerian. They can't get at the Nigerians holding the airport at Lungi so they're having a go at us.'

'You mean they're tired of robbing and looting in town so now they want to have a go at all the rich folk in the Mammy Yoko?'

'Probably,' said Lincoln. 'But the naval gunfire seems to have sparked it off and Koroma's boys have attacked the Nigerians at Aberdeen Bridge. I don't think they're doing very well and they're falling back here to the hotel.'

We could see several Nigerian soldiers half running, half walking down the road from the big baobab tree which spread its branches wide over the T-junction beyond the football pitch topside of the hotel. As the Nigerians reached the turn in to the hotel drive, a few rebels appeared under the tree and fired off bursts of AK. The shots were not aimed and cracked harmlessly overhead.

'I think the rebels are coming up from the bridge behind that plantation, and forming up by the house with the red roof,' Lincoln said, still looking through his binos and pointing to a banana plantation behind some scruffy huts on the left of the big baobab. The road to the Aberdeen Bridge disappeared behind the tall-leaved bananas past the red-roofed house and out of sight

---

* NGS, naval gunfire support.

downhill to the estuary. The big tree was about 400m away, and under it I could see a small knot of armed men in mixed combats and civilian shirts. Lincoln passed me his binos and I saw one or two firing off long bursts with their AKs, mad, unaimed shots full of bravado, from the hip.

When it seemed all the Nigerians had jogged safely down the road, through the car park and into the hotel, suddenly a large crowd of fifty or sixty people, all civilians, mostly men in shirts and slacks and a few women in colourful patterned dresses, appeared on the road from Aberdeen. They passed under the big baobab and came towards the hotel, chanting and singing songs. They carried banners painted with 'Peace' and 'Harmony to all Mankind' and sang lilting African songs about love and Christ.

The rebels spotted their chance and crept down the road behind them, using the parade as cover. They fired a few rounds off at the hotel from away behind the crowd but the Nigerians would not fire back directly for fear of hitting the civilians. Instead, they fired at the group under the big tree, but it was a long way off and as they never even took aim, I doubt very much if anything was hit except the leaves in the tree.

This ruse worked for a moment, till one or two of the soldiers on the main roof below us began to fire a few rounds over the heads of the crowd. The rebels thought better of it and dodged back to cover among the scruffy huts by the bananas.

In return the rebels by the tree fired a couple of RPG rockets at us. Fortunately, these burred past well over our heads. Roger Crooks, Steve and a few journalists from the crowds in the hotel had joined us on the roof, some taking film or photographs. Among them was the Nigerian colonel who decided it was time to assert his military control and retaliate with the same measure of force. He ordered one of his soldiers to prepare an RPG. 'Hit the truck!' he bellowed, pointing at the battered old vehicle stuffed with more rebels which had turned up on the T-junction under the baobab.

Lincoln and I watched this soldier fiddling about with the RPG, trying to fit the long rocket stem into the launcher shaft, all fingers and thumbs dodging about hoping to succeed by trial and error for lack of skill. Just watching him, we both knew that he had never fired a live rocket before in practice, let alone in action, for real.

The soldier was painfully aware that everyone was looking at him, which made him worse.

'Fire!' the colonel kept bellowing, pointing grandly over the parapet. 'Fire at the truck!'

Panicked by this harassment and nervous about the AK rounds pinging over his head, the soldier finally got ready to fire, put the rocket launcher over his shoulder and tentatively pointed it at the truck.

I had come down to see the view they had from the main roof and to watch more closely what they were doing. As the soldier took aim, I nipped quickly well over to one side, to avoid the backblast. The 60° cone of gases which explodes from the rear of such anti-tank rocket launchers can seriously injure and maim anyone standing in the way. It was just as well we took cover.

The Nigerian was so obviously terrified of what was going to happen when he pulled the trigger that he screwed up his eyes and the bulbous rocket began to float way off target. The colonel was shouting at him to fire, everyone was watching, the pressure was on so much that by the time he jerked the trigger, he was so far off line that the rocket took off with a roar nearly 40° off target, whirred across the road which ran downhill past the hotel and exploded through the window of a room in the Bintumani Conference Centre opposite.

In the embarrassing silence on the roof after this ignominious military effort, I distinctly heard the unruffled tones of Lincoln on the water tower informing the British High Commission on the radio that, 'No, the Bintumani is not under attack by the rebels.' The staff in the Commission had a reasonably clear view across the estuary of both hotels. 'It's just a spot of "collateral" damage from an RPG fired by the Nigerians with us. Not to worry. Just getting their eye in,' he said laconically.

I asked the man, 'Was that the first time you've fired an RPG?'

'No,' he replied, still evidently in shock. 'I'm an instructor.'

I shook my head and turned away as a few more rounds

cracked around our heads. More rebels were gathering over by the tree and the fire was gradually increasing in volume, though still very inaccurate.

The colonel was still keen to hit the rebels' truck and shouted for another rocket. I could not stand by and watch this buffoon waste another round so I stepped forward, picked up a rocket from a little pile they had put on the roof and offered to help the unfortunate soldier fire the next round. He was a bit reluctant at first. He was a soldier, dressed in the full monty: combats, helmet covered with bits of cam' netting, pouches of magazines and ammunition on his belt. He looked the part but his military pride was dented, not just by missing his target by a distance almost equal to the range of the shot, but now to find a scruffy white civilian in sweat-stained safari-style shirt and slacks offering to help him fire his own RPG.

I persisted, gently, showing him how to load the rocket neatly on the end of the launcher shaft, how to hold the pistol grip and put the launcher over his shoulder. I knelt down with him, put my arm over his to steady the launcher, on the other side to him, holding him nice and tight, instructed him how to take aim through the sights, find a good sight picture, leaned over to check the aim myself, told him to put his finger round the trigger, and whispered softly to keep him calm, 'Squeeze it gently, squeeze . . .' Suddenly, it went off.

The truck exploded. All the Nigerians cheered, clustering round to congratulate him, and he was so chuffed with his success – probably the first in his life – and his colonel's delight that he grabbed another round. He fitted it, flung the launcher over his shoulder grinning happily, and fired. He missed completely, the rocket whirring over the big tree and exploding out of sight behind. I looked at Lincoln who shrugged.

I hated seeing this waste, so I asked, 'How many RPG rounds have we got left?'

'We have got eight rockets,' answered the colonel.

'Is that all?'

'Yes,' said the colonel, looking less delighted. By this time, the rebels had fired several RPGs of their own, far over the top of the hotel, and it was plain they would not have the same shortages as us. Since we had heard that they had emptied the town's military armoury earlier in the week, it seemed more than likely they would have an unlimited supply of anything they wanted. This was ironic, since I still had the letter of authority from Sam Norman in my pocket to help myself to whatever I wanted from the same armoury.

'They're setting up a twelve point seven,'* Lincoln called down from the water tower. This was serious. I looked over the parapet and could see a knot of rebels clustered on the road between the big tree and the banana plantation around what did seem to be a heavy machine gun. I went over to the Nigerian with the RPG launcher and said shortly, 'Here, give me that, I want to use it,' and pointed at the rebels. We had no time for niceties any longer but I gave him a wink of encouragement all the same.

'No, this is my RPG!' he said.

'You've just missed, twice!' I pointed out. 'And we've only got a few rounds left!'

This was unbeatable logic. He hesitated, then gave up, letting me take the launcher from him. Without delay, I began to load a fresh rocket. AK rounds were one thing, but if the rebels got a 12.7 set up, then the odds would change dramatically.

The Nigerian soldier stood by me, as if to indicate that the RPG was still his really, but made no move to stop me. I snapped the long stem of the rocket in the launcher shaft, knelt beside the parapet with the weapon resting just in the crook of my left arm on the top of the wall to steady it, took careful aim and pulled the trigger.

The rocket took off with that satisfying RPG roar, dropped right on top of the machine gun and exploded among the rebels. It was difficult to say what damage was caused 400m away but it certainly knocked some over and scattered the rest. At least for the time being.

The Nigerians cheered and the colonel recovered his humour,

---

* DShK46 (Degtyarev-Schpagin-Kalashnikov) 12.7×108mm heavy machine gun, weight 35.5kg, effective range 1,500m, 250 linked rounds in a belt; was the standard Soviet support weapon, mounted on vehicles or wheeled carriage and fired by removing the wheels and unfolding the legs into a tripod.

delighted again. The owner of the RPG set about finding all the rockets they had for me to use, presumably enjoying the reflected glory of this success with his launcher, even if he himself was not the firer. I fired a couple more rounds, to disperse the rebels when they grouped again, conscious of our limited supplies, but it was obvious that the Nigerians had no such thoughts. The soldiers were just leaning over the parapet, taking general aim more or less in the direction of the rebels over by the bananas or the big baobab and pulling the trigger. They were really only firing to make themselves feel good and give themselves confidence in the battle. At a range of 400m, this was a complete waste of ammunition. Later on, this would be crucial.

I turned to the soldiers near me at the parapet and shouted at them, 'Don't fire unless you have a good target. Take careful aim!'

The colonel, doubtless recognising this as good military advice, took to striding up and down behind his soldiers checking them, as if he were on the range, shouting at them when he saw something he did not approve of.

'What are you doing?' he boomed at one unfortunate soldier.

'I'm firing,' the soldier replied truthfully, though not necessarily accurately.

'You haven't even got your sights up!' the colonel bellowed and whacked the man sideways on his helmet. I wondered if the colonel had been to the RMA Sandhurst too, like the rebels' coup leader, Johnny Paul Koroma.

'What are you doing?' he shouted over and over, but the way his soldiers were firing, I doubt they had any ideas of the answers.

He came over to the soldier whose RPG I had taken and, pointing at me, he shouted, 'Look at this man, a civilian! What is he doing with your rocket launcher?' For a moment I thought he was going to make me give it back, but he went on, 'Dis is how you fire de lancher! Learn from 'im!' Turning to me, he boomed, 'You teach him properly to fire the launcher!'

The colonel was obviously uncertain whether I was making a nonsense of his command or not, so this seemed a suitable compromise by which he could reassert his rank. However, this was not the time for wasting rounds training anyone. We had too few. There were probably nearly fifty rebels over at the T-junction and the volume of their AK fire was gradually growing more effective. More and more rounds were smacking into the parapet and walls of the hotel beneath us, and into the water tower, though a lot continued to crack well clear over our heads too.

I played the game a bit, and said, 'Look, Colonel, the rebels seem to be grouping again over there.'

'Oh yes? Let me have a look,' he said, and, shading his eyes to peer at the T-junction, he said, 'Yes, you are right. Can you put one in there?'

This was command by auto-suggestion and compromise. I took aim, fired and dropped another RPG rocket on the rebels, who dispersed again leaving a couple lying on the road. He beamed. 'Well done!' He then turned away to berate and tutor his soldiers again, marching up and down the parapet like one of the British officers in the farmyard at Rorke's Drift.

The rebels were now firing RPGs fairly steadily at us, but their aim was wholly erratic. Most rounds went over our heads, with only a few exploding into the floors below us. Happily the rebels were untrained. Even though they had no shortage of ammunition, they did not have the sense to work out that if they were missing us on the parapet by firing high, then all they had to do was fire deliberately low at the hotel, a big enough target by anyone's standards, and raise their aim floor by floor till they struck the parapet at the top. They had also set up a mortar somewhere behind the banana plantation, over by the red-roofed house, but fortunately these bombs too went sailing way over the hotel and landed out on the beach the other side.

The view from the roof was restricted in places by the trees and I wanted to see if I could identify the rebel positions better, so I took the RPG and left the parapet on the main roof to join Lincoln on the water tower. The first steps were inside, but halfway up I had to climb outside on to the iron ladder in full view of the rebels which prompted them to fire a furious burst in our direction. Rounds slammed into the walls or the metal sheets over the air conditioning ducts or pinged over our heads.

I fired more rockets at groups of rebels, keeping them dispersed and preventing them setting up their heavy machine guns. Then the RPG rounds ran out. I turned my attention to a soldier near

126

Lincoln and me who had a British Army GPMG.* This was an excellent weapon, very accurate properly fired, and one I was well familiar with. However, the Nigerian soldier firing it was having real trouble. He had the bipod legs open and perched on the top of the narrow breeze-block parapet wall at the top of the water tower, so that every time he fired the gun's recoil would push him back and the bipod legs fell off the wall, dropping the barrel onto the concrete.

Lincoln looked over at me and said rather desperately, 'Can you do anything with this?'

I nodded and simply took the gun from the Nigerian, saying, 'Here, let me show you.' He made no complaint. I folded the legs and clipped them under the barrel, rested the gun on the parapet, adjusted the sights to 400m – he had had them set on 800m, which made me doubt he had checked them at all – and settled down for a couple of bursts to get my range. I started firing well low, at the middle of the football pitch in front of the T-junction to get an idea of the accuracy and fall of shot on the pitch. Lincoln watched through his binos, calling out where my rounds were landing, which helped a lot, and I gradually increased my elevation till I could be sure to drop a short burst of two or three rounds on target every time. The Nigerian watched amazed, having been able to hit nothing.

It was about eight o'clock by now, and the sun was hot on our heads. Judging by the figures we could see in the shadows of the big baobab and behind the banana trees, dozens more rebels had joined the party. Putting the gun to good use for the first time, I picked on the groups I could see under the baobab and fired several short bursts in among them, scattering them to cover in shock. Until then, they had probably felt as casual about the Nigerians' accuracy as we felt about theirs. With Lincoln spotting through the binos, we could just make them out about 500m away beyond the swaying banana leaves by a small mosque opposite the

---

* L7 Series GPMG, 7.62×72mm standard NATO round, fed by disintegrating linked belt, weight 10.8kg, effective range 800m, made by Fabrique National, Belgium. First class platoon weapon on bipod, excellent on a tripod in sustained fire role. Used in many Commonwealth countries.

red-roofed house where they appeared to have set up a forward ammunition dump. They were loading up their RPG rocket grenades there, then walking back through the bananas, sneaking closer in behind the shanty huts before getting into fire positions about 300m away to shoot at us in the hotel. As each RPG was fired, Lincoln and I tracked quickly back down the fizzing trail to spot the firing point hidden in the huts, and I fired a few rounds from the gun straight on to them.

The Nigerian colonel had a bright idea. He wanted to call in an air strike. He called me to come down the stairs to a building in the trees by the hotel car park which was fitted out with diamond cutting machinery and which he had taken over as his 'field headquarters'. From here, he had been trying to keep in touch on his radios with the other Nigerian forces in Freetown, though I believe by then most of them had already been captured by the coup leaders, and with the Nigerian warships which had precipitated the rebels' attack on Aberdeen Bridge and the Hotel Mammy Yoko with pointless salvos of naval gunfire.

His problem was that since there were no Nigerian nor friendly Sierra Leone planes available, he had to try the Guinean Air Force, under the auspices of the ECOMOG force. He ordered his signaller to tune in to the frequency and I knew at once this was sheer pie in the sky. He plugged into a continuous babble of hysterical and mostly incomprehensible traffic and could hardly get a word in at all. When he finally did break in to the net, no one took any notice of him.

'Hallo! Hallo!' shouted the colonel frantically, one hand holding the radio handset glued to his ear, the other waving about in frustration. He drew breath and shouted some more at his wretched signaller to check the frequency but it was correct and he began bellowing again to break into the gibbering messages filling the airways from Guinea. It was extremely hot and close in the room and when I saw him wiping tears of frustration and sweat from his eyes, I left him to it. I went back on to the roof with the distinct impression that even if he managed by some miracle to contact the Guinean Air Force it was evens that the pilots would hit us in the hotel and not the rebels.

I climbed back up the ladder to the water tower and continued to pick off groups of rebels moving forward through the shanty huts and shortly the colonel reappeared and joined us. He looked badly out of breath, which was probably due less to the twelve flights of stairs than to taking too many tablets to control his asthma – which he had been given by one of the aid agencies before they left. I wondered if he might have a heart attack, but he recovered seeing how I was hitting the rebels. Soon, he was clambering about over the ducting, peering through his binos and calling out targets to me. He called to me from the parapet which overlooked the back above the swimming pool and garage:

'Will! Can you get that car?'

He pointed towards some derelict half-constructed houses away on the right beyond the helipad, beside the road running along the high ground topside of the hotel. I had borrowed a pair of binos from a Nigerian and could see some rebels milling around a white Mercedes 190. They appeared to be trying to use it to get around the back of the hotel, to outflank us. About six of them jumped in and the car moved off over the rough ground between the houses.

'Can you get them?' the colonel shouted at me.

I nodded. I took up a good fire position, nice and firm on the parapet, checked the range at 400m, made sure the top cover of the GPMG was horizontal, and when the car appeared in view between two houses, I squeezed off a burst of five or six rounds. The Mercedes stopped moving. I fired two more bursts into the windows and roof. No one got out.

The colonel shouted in delight, 'This is what I want!'

'This is what I do,' I replied.

He roared with laughter.

Tracking fire positions with Lincoln was a double act which was proving quite effective, but the number of rebels was growing all the time. Several trucks had arrived over by the mosque with ten or more in each.

'Lot of people out there,' I remarked to Lincoln after firing another burst at some more rebels in the shanty huts.

'Umm, yes,' he said thoughtfully. 'And they've got more ammo than us.' In the distance, by the mosque, we could both see the rebels unloading boxes from the trucks. Up by the huts in front of the banana plants, more of them were firing like crazy, with no worries about resupply, often loosing off entire thirty-round magazines of AK at the big pink hotel. This gave them confidence, and gradually they began creeping closer.

'We better keep them on the move,' I said, and fired another carefully aimed short burst at a group. When they got closer I had better results, and it was satisfying seeing them scatter but I was only too aware how little belt ammo I had. I decided to fire only at good targets and then perhaps only one or two rounds each time.

Just when we were starting to have some effect on this advance, it suddenly became obvious that the rebel reinforcements included some better trained soldiers, probably sobels – and among them someone who really knew how to fire an RPG.

A rocket whizzed past very low indeed over our heads, making us duck involuntarily. I guessed it was no more than a foot over the top of the parapet.

Annoyed, the Nigerian by me picked up the RPG launcher I had brought up, and, before I could work out where he had got the rocket from, he had loaded it, aimed in the general direction of the shanty huts and pulled the trigger. Meantime, Lincoln had moved round the other side of the tower with his binos to see if the rebels were trying to work their way around our backs, then gone to a water bag on the floor by a big air conditioning venting pipe to get a drink. The RPG backblast hit him full on and flung him sideways into the ducting pipe.

Gasping for breath, blown and crumpled on to the floor, Lincoln shouted, 'You stupid bastard!' The Nigerian looked round in astonishment that he could have been responsible. Lincoln clambered to his feet, shaken but absolutely spitting with rage, determined to inform the Nigerian personally just how responsible he really was.

'Hey! Will!' The colonel shouted up at me from the main roof below us. 'Can you put some fire along the front of the banana plantation? I think they are coming from there!'

I nodded and settled down behind the GPMG, picked up the rebels the colonel had seen moving through the leaves, and fired a couple of rounds.

I saw another rocket fizzing out towards me from the bananas. It whacked into the thin parapet wall right under me with an enormous explosion which enveloped me and carried on behind me. The barrel of my gun was blown up in the air, me still holding onto it in the shoulder, then it crashed back on to the top of the wall. I could feel the adrenaline really going now. I carried on firing, sending a couple of bursts straight along the line of the rocket to kill the rebels who had just fired the RPG.

Then I looked down at my feet. My legs and shoes were covered in bits of grey concrete and rubble. There was a big hole in the bottom of the parapet where I was standing. The rocket had blasted through the thin wall, blown it apart like dust, carrying the explosion through and behind me, right between my legs. 'Fuck me, Lincoln!' I shouted. 'That was close!'

Then I looked round. Lincoln, who had been just struggling to his feet after being hit by the backblast from the Nigerian's RPG, had been hit again and flung back into the air conditioning duct. This time, he was hurt. I ran over to him, put down the GPMG and asked, 'Are you okay?'

He groaned, 'I've been hit. I don't feel well!' In a daze, he tried to sit up and then stand. He had a big gash in his forehead, cuts all over his face and he looked a mess.

'It's just a nick.' I told him. I did not think it would help to tell him half his head seemed to be hanging off at the front. Blood was streaming down his face from his head wound and his shirt was ripped and cut. Recalling my medical training, I took him firmly and sat him down, holding him from behind with my leg over his legs to stop him trying to stand again. I reached round into his combat shirt top pocket and, sure enough, like a good soldier, I found his battle first aid shell dressing where regulations say it must be kept. Actually, British Army shell dressings are pretty useless for trauma cases – the bandages are unyielding cotton rather than soft crêpe and cause a tourniquet effect – but for a head wound it was fine. I pulled it out, scraped up the torn skin with the padding and pressed it back into place on his skull, then tied the cotton round his head in place. 'You hurt anywhere else?' I asked, looking at him sideways from behind his head as I worked.

'The back of my head,' he groaned.

A quick look showed he had all sorts of holes and cuts in the back of his head too, which looked very like shrapnel wounds but not too bad. I left them and then proceeded to check if he had anything more serious. Still sitting behind him, I told him what I was going to do, then ripped his shirt open and ran my hands over his chest and back. He had lots of light shrapnel cuts but I could find no sign of any more severe bleeding or bruising which might indicate a deep puncture or broken bones.

'Can you breathe okay?' I asked, to find out if his lungs had been pierced.

'Yes, fine,' he replied, his voice clear though he was obviously in pain.

Suddenly a round whacked a big hole straight through the wall beside my back and whirred past, spattering sharp pieces of concrete over our faces. I was still sitting directly behind Lincoln, with my back against the wall. A foot the wrong way and the bullet might have killed us both.

'I think we better get out of here!' I said. The rebels had certainly got our range, they were now at last on target and that round looked like something heavier than an AK round. Someone with experience was telling them what to do and the parapet wall round the top of the water tower was too thin to protect us.

I slung the GPMG over my shoulder and helped Lincoln down the iron ladder. As before, the rebels' fire increased when they saw us on the ladder, with bullets cracking through the air around us and snapping into the thin metal sheets of the air conditioning ducts. When we got to the main roof, we found the Nigerians were huddling together at the bottom of the water tower, inside, and some were already on their way down into the hotel. They were quitting. The rebels' new-found accuracy had driven them away from the parapet of the main roof even and they had decided to vacate the roof altogether.

I was not completely taken by surprise. At dawn, when the rebels had begun shooting at the hotel, there had been quite a crowd of Nigerians on the roof, happily firing their rifles at the few dozen rebels up by the baobab or in the banana plantation.

Then, as the numbers increased, I had seen one or two slide off
back to the stair well and disappear when the colonel had been
busy at the other end of the roof. I had even called a couple back
to the parapet myself, but as soon as my back was turned, they
sneaked away again to the empty space beneath the water tower at
the top of the stairs into the hotel or hung around under the maze
of air conditioning machinery beside it. Now, the rebels had
increased to maybe 100 or more – and still turning up by the
truckload – and their RPGs and heavy machine guns were right
on target. Suddenly, with Lincoln hit everything had become
rather serious. Seeing him blown off his feet by the RPG round,
his head bandaged and his face covered in blood, was the final
straw. The Nigerians were off like long-dogs down the stairs, and
there was nothing I could do to stop them.

Lincoln was still badly dazed.

'Thanks, Will,' he said to me and followed the Nigerians and
remaining journalists down into the hotel. I suppose I never
thought about the implications of his departure, or what it would
mean in the next hours. It was clear he needed some proper first
aid, to patch himself up and rest.

Alone, I turned back to the roof. I could have done with
some help, of course, but there was a certain pleasure in the
clarity of being left on my own. The decks were cleared, I no
longer had to worry about Nigerian soldiers not doing their job
properly on one side of the hotel and whether the rebels were
taking advantage of them in some way I could not see.
Abruptly, the responsibility was entirely mine. In a way, this
situation was clean, but at that moment I had no idea what that
implied. Immediately, I was worried that if there was no one
firing at the rebels, they would think resistance had collapsed
and come surging into the hotel. As the Nigerians left to follow
their colonel downstairs, I dodged about the central air conditioning machinery checking the front and back of the hotel.
The rebels had already crept forward along the line of derelict
huts to within 300m where they had fired the RPG at Lincoln
and me on the tower. Rounds were slicing through the top of
the parapet wall around the main roof and it was clear the
rebels had finally set up a 12.7mm heavy machine gun, or even

its big brother a 14.5mm.* It was no longer healthy to walk about the roof, even crouched over. I crawled towards the parapet on my hands and knees, dragging the GPMG along beside me with the carrying handle, taking care not to damage the long belts of linked ammunition which were slung round my neck, and kept my head beneath the level of the bottom half of the parapet, which was concrete nearly half a metre thick and stopped the heavy machine gun bullets.

My problem was the air conditioning ducts. The roof was cut in half from end to end by a large square metal duct which ran out from the machinery in the centre by the water tower, and in places much smaller vents branched off to the sides. These pipes had not bothered us earlier in the morning, when the rebels' fire had been wildly inaccurate and their bullets sang past far over our heads – we had just stepped over the ducts. But now rounds were smacking into the parapet, the water tower and through the metal sheets over the air-con machinery, and getting over the pipes was plain dangerous. Either I had to go back to the middle of the hotel, where there was a way through by the central machinery over feed pipes, or crawl round the ends of the ducting. The option of going over the bulky square duct anywhere else exposed me to stray fire even if the rebels could not see me in the middle of the roof.

Fortunately, there were square drain holes at intervals in the wall which meant I did not have to show my head over the top of the wall. As I crawled along the roof, I stopped at each hole to peer down and see what the rebels were doing, but I stayed well back from the hole, so they could not see my white face through the gap. Since they now had someone who knew how to fire the heavy machine guns, I assumed they would have binos too and must be trying to pin down exactly where the resistance was on

---

* KPV (Krupnokaliberniy Pulemet V) 14.5mm heavy machine gun, weight 48.9kg, effective range 1,100m, using 100 linked rounds in a belt. Designed round WWII anti-tank ammo, the gun has a formidable punch through armour and is widely distributed in former Warsaw Pact and Third World countries.

the roof. Little did I realise just how treacherous they would be in their efforts to eliminate me.

I crawled over the concrete to the top corner of the roof which gave the best view over the road past the front of the hotel, the shanty huts and the banana plantation, and peered through a drain hole. I was looking for the 12.7mm gun position, but I noticed instead a group of rebels creeping down the far side of the road by the huts towards the hotel car park entrance, where the Nigerians had manned the barriers. I had to stop this movement towards the hotel. I rolled on my right side, pulled the gun up to my chest, flicked open the catch under the gas piston cylinder which held the bipod legs tucked in the shut away position, opened them out, and set the gun on its legs. I rolled over on my stomach, lifted the butt into my shoulder, wriggled backwards slightly to make sure the barrel was not too close to the drain hole opening in case it was seen, and settled down behind the gun to check my aim. The barrel was too high, so I reached forward to give the nut between the bipod legs a few quick turns and adjust the height of the muzzle so it fired through the centre of the drain hole. Satisfied, I picked up the rebels' group again over my sights. I could see their heads dipping up and down behind a rusted corrugated iron sheet in a dilapidated fence by a hut. I slipped off the safety catch, took a sight picture on a bit of the sheet where I judged their bodies were in relation to the top of their heads, and squeezed the trigger briefly for a short three- or four-round burst. The GPMG is a highly effective weapon at battle range, 300m. My bullets rattled through the corrugated iron and the heads disappeared. This group had just learned a fundamental lesson of infantry tactics, which is that cover from view is never quite the same as cover from fire: just because your enemy cannot see you, never necessarily means his bullets cannot reach you. As the hours passed, I found they were not the only ones determined or foolish enough to ignore this important truth of the modern battlefield.

As soon as I stopped firing, I wriggled back from the drain hole, dropped the bipod legs and crawled along the roof. It would be tempting fate to stay at the same drain hole too long just in case they had seen where I was firing from. I had already seen how accurate they could be now with an RPG. My few rounds did produce a reaction, but even though fairly accurate it was more furious than controlled, as suddenly the top part of the parapet was ripped through by another long burst from their heavy machine gun. I lay on my back till the storm passed. Little chunks of concrete spattered down on my face as bullets tore through the parapet above my head and ripped into the water tower and metal sheets of the central air-con housing. I guess they just loaded a 250-round belt of 12.7 ammo and fired off the entire belt. Obviously, they had no problems with ammunition resupply.

I began to worry that I could not be in two places at once, that while I was on one side of the hotel, the rebels would sneak round the other. They were certainly closer all the time. When the attack had started, at dawn, the rebels had been winding themselves up under the big baobab tree a good 400m away. In the first few hours, bolstered by reinforcements, they had moved closer along the line of shanty huts to 300m, and by mid-morning, having driven the Nigerians off the roof, they were edging closer still. Maybe they did not know I was alone on the roof, but I had to make it seem that there were still several people defending the hotel with me, or they would outflank me at the back of the hotel and put in a final assault. The thought of what these lunatics would do to the families in the hotel, especially the women, did not bear thinking about, but there had been enough stories of the mayhem in Freetown to leave me in no doubt.

Almost immediately my concern was confirmed. I wriggled on my hands and knees across the concrete dragging the gun around to the corner overlooking the football pitch and helipad and peered carefully through a drain hole. I searched through the branches of the trees around the hotel which slightly obscured my view, trying to pick up movement which would give the rebels away. At once, I spotted a small group of rebels creeping around the back towards the helipad area. Amazingly, many of them were wearing brightly coloured T-shirts over combat trousers, red, white, yellow or even fluorescent orange or green, presumably all looted from the town, which made my job of seeing them much easier.

Then I lost sight of them behind the branches and had to move quickly on my hands and knees along to the next drain hole. This happened a couple of times while they jumped quickly from wall to wall and I saw them duck down out of sight behind the white perimeter wall between the hotel and the Russians' helipad. Like the others on the other side of the hotel, they thought that if they could not be seen they were safe. More than this, the slope of the ground from the road across the football pitch told me that the main group could not see what happened to these others once they reached the white wall below the helipad. I set up the gun again, as I had before, adjusted my sights on the wall, waited till I saw a couple of heads peeking over the top and fired a burst through the bricks. Once again, the heads disappeared.

Moving back and forth across the hotel became an obsession. As soon as I had shot up one group trying to get around the back of the hotel, usually at the white wall where they always went to hide as the ground was much more open on that side and alternative cover was sparse, I was back on my hands and knees dragging the GPMG across the roof to the other side, to see where the rebels had got to on that side.

Sometimes I had to stop and lie flat behind the cover of the thick bottom part of the parapet as yet another entire belt of 12.7 or 14.5mm rounds were fired off in one long burst, wrecking the wall and the air conditioning machinery in the middle of the hotel. In between, the rebels kept up a fairly steady, though completely erratic, rate of fire of smaller AK 7.62mm rounds which cracked overhead to remind me that I was safer on my hands and knees moving around the roof than risking a crouching run. In any case, running bent over is tiring. On my hands and knees I could stop at each drain hole and look down to see what was going on.

I was getting really dehydrated. The sun was very hot and right overhead; the concrete roof was baking; my clothes were drenched in sweat and I had nothing to drink. All I could think about was the rebels at the front of the hotel who were gradually closing the distance to the hotel and the ones trying to outflank me at the back. The feeling grew that I was tied to the roof or they would run at the hotel.

At regular intervals, more RPGs hit the water tower, or came through the parapet wall on the main roof. Some thudded into the hotel floors below. Smoke billowed up the walls into the air overhead making an acrid smell and spoiling my view through the drain holes. Unknown to me, Roger Crooks, Steve Lawson and Martin Greenwood were frantically busy below me fighting fires in one part of the hotel or another, and what made their task even more difficult was that one of the early RPGs had hit the water system on the roof and seriously damaged the water supply so they were almost completely dependent on fire extinguishers.

The rebels' accuracy improved all the time. They were getting on-the-job training and had all the ammunition they needed to practise, but their tactics were still bad. After shooting another group behind the white wall, it struck me I had seen none of them with radios and I realised that whoever was coordinating the attack on the hotel had no contact with the rebels he kept sending round the back. By the time they crossed the first bit of open ground by the football pitch they were out of touch with the main group by the big baobab tree, and the rebels' command never knew I was shooting them up behind the white wall.

I wondered who was controlling the rebels and soldiers behind the banana plantation over by the red-roofed house where the supply trucks and main group appeared to be gathered. Was this Johnny Paul Koroma, or Captain Thomas, or another coup leader from the RUF who was known as the Mosquito? He had made a real name for himself pillaging, raping and killing in Freetown, and was described by some of the refugees he and his men had attacked. He wore black-rimmed glasses without glass which gave him an insect-like appearance, pieces of mirror were plaited into his hair, and he was permanently high on ganja. Two women wearing dresses made of the same material as men's fatigues accompanied him everywhere, shrieking and dancing; he was convinced he could fly and was indestructible. During a calm moment at the end of another savage belt of 12.7mm I reflected that the famous examples of Napoleon and Hitler meant that even Corporal Gborie might be a formidable opponent, although the rebels were devoting less effort to tactics than to simply trying to rip the roof, and me, apart with sheer firepower.

Each time the heavy machine gun raked the roof, I imagined

this was a prelude to an attack, so as soon as the strafing stopped, I struggled onto my hands and knees again to look outside through a drain hole and see what was happening. One time, I saw a vehicle moving along the top road beyond the derelict houses where the white Mercedes I had shot up earlier still sat silent in the dust and heat. Through my binos, I saw the vehicle was a 4×4, presumably stolen from one of the aid agencies during the coup the previous week, and it was filled with more rebels and soldiers. I lay down behind my gun, waited till it came clearly into view again between two trees and stopped it dead with a burst of rounds. I saw no one get out, but I gave it another short burst. Then, I wriggled back from the drain hole and crawled back across to the other side of the roof to see what was happening at the front of the hotel.

By midday, I was tired, hot, my shirt and trousers dark with sweat and I was badly dehydrated. I was the only person firing back at the rebels and the thought kept running through my head, 'If I don't keep them pinned down, they'll overrun the hotel.' With no one to help me cover the back side of the hotel, I had to keep on scurrying on my hands and knees across the roof to check front and back, time and time again, round the air conditioning duct, peering through drain holes as I went, and firing a short burst when I picked up the bright T-shirts of rebels moving down the road or around the rear of the football pitch to the white wall behind the Mammy Yoko. By this time, the rebels at the front had taken advantage of the trees and cover along the far side of the road and advanced from the shanty huts along a piece of hollow ground with trees across the road in front of the hotel. This was opposite the place where the Nigerians had had their barrier at the top of the drive by the car park, which was only 100m from the hotel – only a matter of seconds to rush down the access road into the lobby.

Maybe the sun was getting to me, but the closer they got, the more obsessive I became about scuttling back and forth over the roof. When the long bursts of heavy machine gun fire pinned me down for a few moments and I had to lie on my back while the bullets ripped through the thinner parapet wall over my head, I became impatient, imagining they were using the time to assault the front or rush around to the kitchens entrance at the back. Soon after midday, I rolled back on my stomach after another long pasting by the 12.7mm and peered quickly through the drain hole overlooking the front. The rebels had learned to keep better hidden during the long morning, but I could still see a flash of bright clothing through the trees.

Then, I heard the unmistakeable thumping noise of a big helicopter approaching and my spirits lifted. Someone at last was on the way to lend a hand. The beat of its blades swelled to a crescendo as it suddenly rose into view over the ridge above the hotel and swung in a big lazy arc over the hotel. I twisted round and shaded my eyes against the sun. I could not make out the markings, but this was an Mi-24 Hind 'D', the Soviet Union's most famous and successful ground-attack helicopter which had terrorised the Mujahadeen in the Afghan war. It looked like something from *Star Wars*, with tandem bubble cockpits stacked up one behind the other at the front like bulging insect's eyes, short stubby wings sticking out each side from which hung racks of 57mm rockets and Spiral missiles, and a nose-mounted Gatling gun* which could fire 3,000 rounds a minute. This was a fearsome airborne weapons platform, something really good to have on your side.

The Hind circled round the hotel, flew over the beach and out to sea, then swung back inland over the hotel again. As it came in, a rocket launched from beneath one stubby wing plunged on to the grass on the beach side of the hotel, exploding among the palm trees. It was the enemy, firing at us.

Out on the roof at the end of the hotel, I was completely exposed to view from the air. I jumped up, grabbed the gun and started running down the roof towards the central air conditioning machinery and the water tower. The helicopter fired a second rocket which hit the hotel somewhere beneath the parapet, on the second floor, and shook the whole building.

'Shit!' I muttered to myself as I raced along the roof. 'This is not good at all!'

The Hind was coming in fast. Near the centre of the roof, I

---

* Gatling gun, 25mm rapid fire machine gun.

dropped to my knees again and dived under the big square air duct, wriggling out of sight, and prayed.

The Hind roared over the top of the hotel, a deafening noise of long beating blades pulling it round in another tight aggressive circle over the roof with me as the epicentre of its turn. I was its target. I rolled out from under the duct, jumped up, grabbed the gun and started sprinting towards the water tower.

The chopper completed its turn almost lazily, hanging in the air over the hotel, a cacophony of noise as it steadied to fire again, the harsh sunlight gleaming on the bulging cockpit plexiglass. I was almost at the stair well when I heard a third rocket whoosh towards the hotel. Another colossal explosion shook the building, this time at the front of the water tower, and the hot blast blew me down the stairs to the first landing, ripping the belt of ammo off the GPMG as it clattered on the concrete steps. Behind me and all around, a hail of steel flechettes rattled viciously on the air conditioning ducts like heavy tropical rain.

I picked myself up, whipped around and saw the helicopter framed in the opening from the stair well still hanging over the roof, as if checking to see if I was still alive. Furious, I lifted the GPMG into a firing position with the butt on a low concrete wall by the stairs and began firing. After a short burst, the link ran out and I suddenly remembered that Russian Mi-24s are heavily armoured, all along the belly, under the fuel tanks and around the cockpits to protect the pilots. I was stupidly wasting my precious ammunition. I brought the gun down.

Being on the roof was out of the question while the Hind was there. Careful to stay out of sight hidden behind ducting, I took the opportunity to rest, grateful of the shade for a change, and watched it circle the hotel. The Hind Mi-24 was a savage and highly effective ground-attack device and I reflected that the person coordinating the rebels' attack on the ground had found himself a battle winner. I could do little except perhaps try to shoot the tail rotor, which is the only vulnerable part. But I had too little ammunition. I scooped up the broken belt of link off the floor, cleared the GPMG, flicked the end of the belt back over the feed tray, dropped the top cover back down, smacked it flat, and cocked the weapon. I slipped the safety catch to 'Safe' and glanced out of the stair well. The Hind was still banking round the hotel. I had no idea what the rebels were doing. No one was firing at them, but I could not go on the roof. In a panic, I ran down the stairs for the first time in hours.

On the top floor, I sprinted along the corridor and chose a room I thought would give me a view over the front. If I could not get at the rebels from the roof, I needed to move from room to room on the top floor of the hotel. I kicked in the door, smashing it open with the heavy butt of the gun, and ran over to the window. The view was obscured by trees which from the roof above I could just see over. I ran out along the corridor and kicked in another door. Same again. Panicking about the rebels outside while the minutes ticked past, I tried several more rooms and apartments, kicking the doors open one after the other and working my way round to see if there was at least a view over the back. The rooms were all empty, but none of them offered a view.

Judging where the trees might be thin enough to see through, I ran down the stairs three at a time to the second floor. Thick smoke filled the corridor. The hotel was badly on fire after the Hind Mi-24 rocket attack. Martin Greenwood and Steve Lawson were shouting and organising a team of volunteers, many of them Lebanese, to put out the flames. We said a brief 'Hallo!' to each other as I ran past, but they were desperate to control the fire and I was equally desperate to find out what the rebels were doing. If either of us failed, everyone in the hotel would be in serious trouble.

I kicked my way through double doors into a room overlooking the topside of the hotel, over the front where the road ran past with a view to the shanty huts on the opposite side to the beach. To my relief, I found that from here the rise of the hill above the hotel, towards the big baobab and the banana plantation, meant that I was able to see under the branches and between the trunks of the big trees which had obscured the view from the floors higher up. All this had perhaps not taken more than a few minutes since I had been blasted off the roof by the Hind, which I could still hear beating round above the hotel, but quite a group of rebels had gathered behind the wall on the hotel perimeter beyond the car park. I fired a couple of bursts at them, hitting a few and scattering the rest to cover. Then I pulled back from the window, ran out into the corridor to another room I guessed would give me a view over the back, kicked in the door and looked carefully out of the window. More rebels were moving about behind the white wall. I fired another burst.

At least I was in the shade as I ran back and forth between rooms. I battered my way into other rooms, to avoid always firing from the same places, because the rebels kept up a constant patter of return fire at the windows, but whereas on the roof I could see out as I crawled on my hands and knees along the parapet by looking through the drain holes as I passed, I was blind as I moved between rooms on the second floor. The rebels were now far too close to the hotel. I realised it was only a matter of time before they wound themselves up to an attack. And I was seriously short of linked ammunition for the gun.

I ran back up to the roof. I had taken a load of loose 7.62mm bullets off the Nigerians but at the time I had had neither the link nor the time to make them into a belt for the gun. Now, I had no option. I had to fetch the spent link the gun had spat out the right hand side of the feed tray at each drain hole where I had fired at the rebels. At the top of the stair well, I stopped to check that the Hind had really gone. Helicopters can approach a target in almost total silence and appear very suddenly if the pilot flies in low out of sight of the people he is going to attack, so I listened intently for the distant sound of beating blades the other side of the hill above the hotel and crawled as fast as I could out on to the roof. I dragged the gun with me, just in case, and set about picking up the link scattered about at the drain holes. Without these little black pieces of metal which linked the bullets into a belt, the GPMG was useless. As I worked, a few more RPG rockets exploded and AK rounds continued to spatter on the pink walls of the hotel and smack into the metal air conditioning ducts. I wished I had as much ammunition as them. Running out altogether did not bear thinking about. After filling my shirt pockets with handfuls from several drain holes, I crawled back to the central air conditioning machinery and the stair well.

I ran downstairs to the second floor again, along the corridor and into one of the rooms at the front. I put the gun down on its bipod legs, sat down and began to link rounds. When I had increased the belt on the gun by another thirty or so, I went to the window to check activity outside.

A colossal explosion at the window knocked me off my feet into the room onto my back. A roasting blast swept over me, shards of glass blew everywhere and the room caught fire immediately. In a moment of clarity in the noise and heat as I lay on my back, I guessed an RPG rocket had struck the wall between rooms, so I had got some of the blast, like Lincoln on the roof, but fortunately not all of it. Flashover had occurred very quickly and flames were racing up the walls. The room was filling with choking, acrid smoke and I could not breathe. I struggled to my feet, grabbed the gun and staggered to the back of the room to get out. The explosion had slammed the door shut. I reached out for the handle. It was already red hot, impossible to touch. Panicking, I smashed at the door with the heavy metal butt plate of the GPMG, hefting the twenty-four pound gun and ten pounds of linked ammunition like a two-pound sledge hammer in desperation. I smashed the door to bits and burst out of the room into the corridor.

'You all right, Will?' shouted Martin. He and Steve Lawson were already there, ready to put out the fire. Every time a rocket or missile hit the hotel, they ran to see if a fire had started and put it out. They had been busy at this all day and were covered in soot, filthy and tired, but they had been winning so far.

It was good to see them, even briefly, as they were the only support I had seen for hours, but they gave me strange looks as I passed. I was fortunately not much cut by the glass from the windows but I was covered in Lincoln's dried blood from hours before on the water tower, my trousers were torn and wrecked from crawling and dragging myself about the concrete roof, I was soaked in my own sweat, and blackened with smoke dust from this last explosion. I thanked them for their help and ran back up ten flights of stairs to the roof again, for more link.

As I was dodging about at the top of the stair well trying to look out on all sides to make sure the chopper was nowhere to be seen and locate another good firing position, I found five Nigerian soldiers tucked away out of sight in a little room under the water tower. They had chosen one of the safest places in the whole hotel, surrounded by concrete walls supporting the water tank, and had done nothing all day. We stared at each other in the darkness. Their eyes big, they sat on the floor, their legs hunched up, and said nothing.

'Give me all your rounds,' I snapped. Maybe they felt embarrassment they had done nothing to help, but I doubt it and anyway I did not care. I went round each of them without further ado to gather every last round of 7.62mm ball ammunition they had. They emptied their FN magazines onto the floor. I gave them some link and told them bluntly but firmly to link the rounds to make a belt. I watched them a moment to see they were doing it right, then I went out onto the roof.

The rebels at the front of the hotel were still gathering in the hollow ground the other side of the road. They were trying to keep their heads below the level of the white perimeter wall but I managed to put a couple of bursts among two bigger groups who looked as if they were forming up and scattered them again. I picked up the link ejected from the gun, put it in my pockets so I could make up the belt with the Nigerians' loose ammo, and had just turned to crawl across to the back of the hotel when the parapet above my head fell apart under another hail of big 12.7mm rounds. They fired a whole belt again and I lay on my back till the attack had finished.

Then I ran back down the stairs again to the second floor and found another two Nigerian soldiers had come to sit in the stair well, so I took their ammunition too. I had not seen anyone else in the hotel, apart from Martin and Steve and their firefighting volunteers, and I suppose these two had decided the stair well in the centre of the hotel was safer than most places. The rebels had been firing RPGs on and off all day and never really let up with AK and belts of heavy machine gun fire. I jogged to a room on the topside of the hotel, and saw, inevitably, another cluster of dark shapes sneaking along behind the white wall to outflank me around the back of the hotel. This time they had crept quite close to the office by the helicopter pad. I waited till they paused, far too tightly bunched, and fired a burst through the wall, dropping them all.

A couple of RPGs slammed into the hotel again, but I had kept well back from the open window in the shadows inside the room and fortunately they had not seen which room I was in. My problem was that although I could see under the branches of the trees around the hotel, the best place to see what was happening was always the roof, so I ran back up the stairs to the roof again. I crawled out to check the rebels in front of the hotel in the hollow ground as the height of the hotel gave me the best angle on them from the roof. I had no sooner fired a couple of bursts at this group when their 12.7mm opened up again, hitting the parapet right above me with a furious long burst and hundreds of lesser AK rounds.

This was not the first time the rebels had caught me with a blast of heavy machine gun fire when I had got back to the roof, almost as if they knew when I was up there. I was really careful keeping back from the drain holes and I was sure they could not easily see the muzzle of the GPMG at all, so it seemed more than just good luck that they pasted the parapet just at the moment I was up there. Dehydrated, tired and wound up so tight, I was almost ready to believe these lunatics might have the supernatural powers their leader Mosquito and his mad women acolytes claimed. I pushed this ridiculous idea out of my mind and ran down the stairs again. As I got pinned down each time I went on the roof, I had to continue running down to the second floor and dash from room to room firing as I went to stop them feeling they could assault the hotel. In reality, I knew well-trained troops would have attacked at any time. In fact, they probably would have run in long before, but so far these sobels were put off by my all-too-infrequent bursts of fire at them, and I had no option but to carry on. I worked on and on at them, breaking up groups in the hollow or behind the white wall to stop them gathering enough courage for an attack.

As soon as I could, I wriggled off the roof keeping as low as possible, dragging the gun and my belt of link with me, and ran down the stairs again. Another explanation for these furious storms of fire at the hotel was that the rebels had built up enough confidence to try an attack, and each time I wanted to see if there was any movement closer to the front. The groups in the hollow were not much more than 100m from the front entrance which would take them moments to cross. The idea that the rebels were already in the hotel became fixed in my mind and I raced down the stairs.

I saw absolutely no one in the corridors as I passed each of the six floors down. Martin Greenwood and Steve Lawson and their crew, even the Nigerian soldiers in the stair well, had all disappeared. Everyone had gone, leaving me holding the hotel, to pin down the rebels while they escaped out the back towards the sea. I reached the lobby, cautiously peering round as I emerged from the stairs for the first time since the attack had started. It was deserted, except for papers and other mess on the floor. I looked through the big plate glass windows outside, but there was no one in the drive. I ran into the offices behind Reception. The doors were open, but silent. The conference room was desolate, empty of people and with only a few suitcases lying abandoned. 'Shit!' I said to myself. 'They've bloody left me!'

I ran along the corridor into the corner of the hotel furthest from the action and burst into a store room. I stopped dead and stared round at a roomful of people, mostly sitting hunched up against the wall, some trying to sleep stretched out on the floor, some standing. They all stared back in panic, their eyes huge and white in the gloom of the room after the bright afternoon sunlight outside. For a long moment I tried to work out what on earth they were all doing stuck in this room, some with white sheets over their heads which looked bizarre, and then it dawned on me that they were obediently doing what I had organised for them the night before. When the shooting had started at dawn, Roger, Steve, Martin, all the 'marshals' and others had ushered every single person in the hotel into their emergency safety positions which I had designated for them, and that was where they had remained all day, listening to the explosions and firing above them in the hotel. I suppose they had been terrified when they heard me running about in the corridors and banging doors looking for someone, probably thinking they had only moments to live before a crowd of rebels charged in to rob and kill them. Judging by the looks on their faces, they thought I was a rebel anyway. Blackened by smoke and filth, with a bloody face, my clothes dark with sweat and torn, my gun slung over one shoulder with a long belt of ammunition, I probably looked like one.

Once again, the feeling grew in my mind that the rebels would take advantage of my absence from the roof where I could hold them at bay, so I left them hiding in their rooms and went back up the stairs as fast as I could. The climb seemed to be longer every time. I was tired. The hotel was hot, the GPMG and the ammunition belt weighed over 30lb, and by 2 p.m. it felt like 60lb. I had been on the go for eight hours, alone for six of them.

At the top, I grabbed a length of belt from the Nigerians hiding under the water tower. They had linked everything they had, so this was the last of the ammunition unless I could find some more downstairs. As usual, I stood by the air conditioning machinery, plugged with bullet holes and blackened from the Hind Mi-24 missile attack, and checked the roof before leaving cover. Nothing stirred in the baking hot sun. I crawled out on my hands and knees again, dragging the gun along beside me. The concrete was almost unbearably hot; my knees kept landing on sharp little pieces of concrete shot away from the parapet; the metal ducting was roasting when I put my hands on it.

At the parapet, I took care again to keep well back from the drain hole and fired a burst at the rebels in the hollow. I had not been there for more than a few moments when the rebels seemed to open up with everything they had. At least one, probably two, 12.7 or 14.5mm heavy machine guns battered the pink wall, demolishing the top part of the parapet, and a rain of smaller AK cracked and whistled overhead.

Instinctively, I ducked my head down and pulled back from the drain hole and rolled sideways away behind the protection of the thicker lower part of the parapet. In a terrible cacophony of noise, the upper part appeared to be coming apart like dust, scattering small chunks of concrete all over me and the roof. They kept on and on, using belt after belt.

Then there was a pause. I rolled back, pushed the gun towards the drain hole to my side, took aim on some dark figures in the hollow behind the white wall at the front and squeezed off a rapid burst. This made me feel better. If the rebels were trying to pin me

148

down while they attacked, I hoped that would make them think twice.

To my horror, these few rounds were answered with an even greater storm of heavy machine gun fire from the rebel positions on the high ground. Shocked by the thunderous racket on the walls and metal ducting behind me, I rolled back again and lay on my back staring into the blue sky above. Suddenly, my situation seemed utterly hopeless. I imagined the machine gun fire relentlessly ripping its way down through the wall to me and tearing my body apart as I lay on the hot concrete. All round the roof, bullets were pinging off the metal ducts and walls, ricocheting in all directions, and I was terrified of being hit by these as much as by the 12.7mms smashing down the wall behind. Basically, I was shitting myself.

I wanted to get up and run, off the roof, but the weight of fire was too much. It would have been suicidal. Slowly, I curled up in a foetal position on my side, pulled the gun in close and put my hands over my head. I knew it was pointless, but I could not help myself and it seemed the only thing to do at that moment. The adrenaline and tension in my stomach made me feel sick. My arse tightened spasmodically as I flinched at each crescendo of gunfire around me. This was crisis. I had a real moment with myself. I hated it, and I heard myself swearing aloud, over and over and over. This was terror. Pure and simple. Hot waves of it washed over me, but my thoughts worked with astonishing clarity. Curled up, I fought each surge of panic rising from the depths of my stomach. I told myself I had to hold it together. I had a job to do. All the people down in the hotel depended on me. The logic was utterly clear. I had to do what I had to do. I could not, I would not stay where I was.

I detected a slight pause in the rebels' firing. Probably they had run clean through the belts of 12.7mm link. Abruptly, angry, I rolled back in front of the drain hole, rammed the gun into my shoulder, found a target in the hollow, behind a tree and shot them. Without waiting, I rolled back out of sight, wriggled to the next drain hole further along, and repeated the action. The 12.7mm started up again, thrashing the parapet, but in between long thudding bursts I slowly crawled on my stomach back across the roof, dragging the gun, its bipod legs folded, sliding under the metal ducting or rolling as fast as I could over the top if the gap under was too small. I stopped at the drain holes as I wriggled past to fire a few rounds if I saw any rebels, just to let them know I was still bloody well alive and kicking.

Finally, I reached the air conditioning machinery, wriggled snake-like over the pipes into relative cover, and drew breath. I was exhausted. I just could not work out how they knew every time I got on the roof, but the weight of fire was so great I had to go downstairs.

I ran all the way down to the lobby, just to see if the rebels had in fact begun their final assault. As before, there was no movement outside the entrance or in the drive up to the barrier past the car park. I felt better at that and turned back up the stairs to the second floor again, to see what was happening at the back of the hotel. There was no movement towards the white wall. Only some big black birds stirred in the oppressive mid-afternoon heat, lazily swooping and circling down to land in a large tree by the hotel workshops. They were vultures. I focused the binos on the tree and realised the branches were thick with them. The big birds sat with timeless patience right over the white wall where I had been shooting groups of rebels trying to sneak round the back of the hotel. The bodies had been lying in the heat all day and a couple of hundred vultures had congregated in the tree waiting for the shooting to stop. Disgustingly, the tree looked quite black and more circled in the sky above. In Africa, humans could be as much part of the food chain as any other animal.

I became aware something odd had happened. There was an eerie silence outside. The rebels had stopped even their sporadic firing of AKs at the hotel. I had to see what was happening, which meant getting back on the roof. Wearily, I climbed back up the stairs with the gun and checked from the central water tower out over the roof again. I could hear no distant beating rotors, and there was still no shooting. All the same, I took no chances and crawled quickly over the roof to the front side and peered cautiously through a drain hole. Using the binos, for a while I saw nothing out of the ordinary because I was looking too close, where the rebels had crept to within 100–150m of the hotel just beyond the white perimeter wall.

Then I picked up movement on the other side of the banana plantation, beside the mosque about 400m away near the house with the red roof. Presumably thinking themselves out of sight of the hotel behind the banana leaves, the rebels were busy executing a young local. They dragged him kicking and screaming into the middle of the road, flung him face up on the tarmac and several rebels sat on his hands and legs. Sounds of shrieking and chanting carried towards me in the hotel on the still, hot air. One, a leader, stood over the victim brandishing a knife. He knelt down and I could see him slashing and cutting. He reached down with his hands and pulled violently back and upwards. He was clutching the man's heart in his hands, still attached to the thick corded veins and arteries, still beating. In some crude animist ceremony, the man was being shown his own heart, alive. The knife flashed down again severing the bloody organ and the leader held it up over his head.

I opened fire, put a burst in among them and shot the lot.

There was no longer any doubt what my fate would be if I let them get into the hotel, and I had seen enough of Africa in Cameroon, Chad, Zaire and Rwanda to know that a good many of the refugees in the hotel below me would suffer the same fate. These lunatics wanted to kill us for the sheer hell of it, without a moment's thought. The intense gunfire, my own moment of panic, and now this repulsive execution in the road, had left me feeling quite detached. I crawled back across the roof and jogged down the twelve flights of stairs again to the lobby to see if the rebels had tried to come in yet.

I cannot remember how many times I went up and down the stairs. Sometimes I saw Nigerian soldiers and took every bit of their 7.62mm NATO ammunition. Each time I fired from a hotel room it was not long before RPGs began to explode on the walls, and every time I went up to the roof the heavy machine guns opened up. I knew the rebels were really close. Each time, I assumed the way I attracted their fire wherever I went, like a magnet, was because they were preparing to assault. Frantically I kept trying to see what they were doing beneath me as they crept closer. I was tired, but completely lucid. I just wanted to cover both sides of the hotel, but the options, like my ammunition, were reducing to nothing fast.

Back on the roof in the unrelenting heat of the afternoon, lying on my back again while the rebels pasted the walls and parapet over my head with more thudding belts of heavy machine gun fire and with absolutely no idea what more I could do to stop them getting into the hotel so they could kill us, I resigned myself to dying there. I gazed into the vault of blue sky high above me and wondered what my wife Veronica and my two boys Maxwell and Daniel were doing back in Hereford. I did not think I would see them again. I just lay there and thought, 'Sorry, darling, I've fucked up this time.'

This short conversation with myself confirmed a state of extreme detachment which had been growing in my mind through these hot, dangerous hours. There was nothing further that could happen to me short of death itself, so nothing that happened till then mattered any longer. Perhaps this is the body's ultimate way of protecting itself, so one can do whatever is necessary, take whatever decisions may be needed for continued survival, no matter how extreme they might appear in normal life. I had two 36 grenades* I had taken from the Nigerians. I felt them in my pockets and decided that, if the rebels came for me up the stairs, I would slow them down with the grenades and then jump over the roof onto the canopy over the dining area behind the hotel. This was a long way down but it might help soften my fall. I had no intention of falling into the rebels' hands.

I rolled over to peer out through a drain hole and caught sight of another vehicle, an aid agency 4×4, coming along the road from the town. The rebels inside were easy to see, armed with AKs and RPGs as usual. More reinforcements. I gripped the gun again, watching carefully as the 4×4 came into view and disappeared again behind the half-finished houses where I had shot up the white Mercedes. I waited till I had a longer moment as it drove past the big trees lining the road approaching the baobab

---

* British Army 36 Grenade, 4 second delay, weight 0.7kg, made of cast iron, egg-shaped, grooved to fragment on detonation. Range 23m on soft ground to 200+m on hard ground.

and then opened up, stopping it in its tracks. I looked along the barrel and counted six others I had stopped, plus the Mercedes which was still sitting silent in the heat beside the derelict housing development.

Once more, the 12.7mm started up and made life untenable on the roof. In a slight lull, I crawled off the roof again and ran down the stairs. This time, there were a couple of Lebanese near the reception desk. They had noticed the heavy firing at the roof and were also checking to see if rebels were trying to get in. One, whom I had seen before, called me over and said quietly, 'We've caught him. This man.'

This made no sense. I tried to focus on what he was telling me and said, 'What man?'

'The man who's been talking to the rebels.'

'What d'you mean?' I felt suddenly cold.

As we talked, he led me quickly along corridors to the back of the hotel, on the sea side, where some of the 1,000-plus refugees were waiting in their emergency locations. Men sat hunched up, their backs to the walls; many of the women rocked smaller children cuddled in their arms; young girls cried silently trying to comfort each other; and people lay about unable to sleep among bags and suitcases on the floor. They were everywhere and I sensed an air of desperation. The balance of their lives was out of their control. They knew they were in danger – most had experienced the rebels' violence; everyone had heard the stories – but they could do nothing but sit and wait. Their fate was being decided by others, and it struck me the detachment I felt was denied to them because they were inactive. This detachment, or state of Nirvana, is sought by so many in life and it is 'on offer' through gurus or spiritualists in group discussions, meetings or silent meditation all over the world (usually the fad of rich urban dwellers) and yet for most people it is nothing more than a hopeless Holy Grail – often no more than a cynical con to relieve them of their money. All the time it is easily within everyone's grasp: through action – determined, committed action. I know it is easy for me to say that, as fighting is what I do well, but all around me that day people sat doing nothing in the hotel passages, not even helping to put out fires, and that inertia put them

153

at the other end of the scale. Waiting, inactive and passive, these refugees had already made themselves victims of the world, and the suffering they endured through extreme nervous strain was etched on every face.

The Lebanese led me into a big room filled with well over a hundred Lebanese. Oddly, most of them had white sheets over their heads, like Arab headdresses.

'What's going on?' I demanded. After so long on the roof under fire, my temper was short and I did not think I was going to like what the Lebanese was trying to tell me.

'These people have done a deal,' the Lebanese told me. He looked very embarrassed as if he hated to be associated with them.

'What deal?'

A group of Lebanese came down the corridor roughly pushing a big man in front of them. He was well over six foot, fat from over-indulgence, maybe 17 stone, dark hair, swarthy and arrogant.

'We heard him,' said the Lebanese with me, gesturing at the big man. 'He's one of us but he's disgusting. He was talking to the rebels and we overheard him.'

Before the coup, a good many local soldiers moonlighted as guards for the rich Lebanese, guarding their compounds and houses, using radio telephones which they kept after the violence started when they joined the rebels. Gradually, the explanation of the furious gunfire I had suffered every time I went on the roof became clear, and the RPGs fired at the hotel when I was on the second floor were explained.

'This man told them when you went up on the roof,' said the Lebanese, eliminating every chance of misunderstanding. 'As soon as one of his gang heard your gun firing on the roof, he called the rebel commander on his radio telephone to say you were up there again.'

And the rebels had opened up with everything they had to kill me. I was not impressed.

'What's all this about white sheets?' I demanded.

'The rebels agreed with him that if he told them where you were so they could kill you and then come into the hotel to rob and loot everyone, they would let all those with white sheets over their heads go free.'

The big Lebanese just looked down his nose at me and shrugged arrogantly. 'You can do nothing about me,' he sneered dismissively. He was a rich man used to getting his own way all the time. He manipulated people, paid them off, made deals without a shred of moral consideration. He was utterly selfish, a man without humanity. This callousness for all the other people in the hotel, over 1,000 of them and many his fellow Lebanese – this even more than his putting me personally at risk suddenly infuriated me. Hot rage rushed up my neck and I hit him as hard as I could with the heavy butt of my gun, swinging it in a fast circle into his face. He collapsed, bloodied and screaming. Then I turned away and ran back upstairs, more determined than ever to stop the rebels coming into the hotel.

I think the other Lebanese shot him. They were furious that he had been so ready to hand them all to the rebels. I suspect that if he had been prepared to do that to them at that time in the Mammy Yoko there was probably also a past history of his behaviour well-known among the Lebanese community.

I had been missing off the roof for maybe a quarter of an hour in the basement with the Lebanese, so I took the stairs two at a time, lugging the gun slung round my neck. I paused for a quick look for any rebels in the drive through the glass windows of the lobby, but the palms hung still in the heat and nothing stirred. I turned to the stair well and lurched up the twelve flights to the roof, slowing to a steady plod, completely out of breath at the sixth floor. I ran across the roof to the parapet, crouched over to save time, and dropped to my stomach to look through the nearest drain hole over the front of the hotel. I had been downstairs out of the battle for too long.

There were rebels in their colourful T-shirts toting AKs and RPGs everywhere in front of the hotel, all over the road less than 100m from the building and dozens coming down from the big baobab on the high ground beyond the bananas. More were emerging from the shanty huts and the hollow opposite the hotel where they had been hiding, chanting and whooping with delight. A large group of women in a mixture of colourful fabrics and combats were ululating, singing and screeching, waving their arms over their heads as they sashayed down the road towards the hotel entrance. The rebels were on their way to pillage the hotel. They thought they had won.

Grimly, thinking of the betrayal downstairs, I tucked the butt of the GPMG hard into my shoulder, gripped the narrow neck of it with my left hand and the pistol grip with my right, twisted to lock the gun tight, took aim on the densest group on the road and fired a long burst. I dropped a lot of them, raking the burst up the road through the crowd, the bullets ricocheting through them off the tarmac. They scattered, screaming, back to cover in the hollow and behind the shanty huts. I was back.

I crawled further up the roof to the top end of the hotel and fired another burst at more of them trying to creep around the back again. Dozens of vultures in the big tree fluttered slightly at the noise but settled down again on the branches to watch the tangle of bodies behind the white wall in grim, silent anticipation.

All of a sudden, there was a strange silence. The shouting died away and even the erratic fire the rebels had returned at me stopped, as though everyone had finally succumbed in the heat.

The vehicle at the junction was moving so slowly, I almost did not see it. From under the broad shady branches of the big baobab, a white Landcruiser seemed to materialise in the harsh sunlight shimmering off the hot tarmac. I peered down at it through the drain hole over the barrel of my GPMG and found myself unable to focus properly. It was by this time past four o'clock; I was tired; I was dehydrated; the gun barrel was hot and the Landcruiser inched down the road in a haze. I wondered what new trick the rebels were trying to work on me now? I blinked, rubbed the sweat out of my eyes and tried to focus the Landcruiser's front windscreen in my sights. I put the foresight on the place where the driver would be and tightened my grip ready to fire a burst. I began to squeeze the trigger. I could not allow the rebels closer to the hotel. Something flickered in my sight picture. I relaxed my trigger finger a fraction and looked again. A tiny flag was fluttering on the roof of the car. I recognised the Red Cross.

I could not believe it. At last, after so long, my detachment from all hope began to fade, just a bit. Here was a chance of survival which I had abandoned hours before. The familiar flag of the International Committee of the Red Cross became clearer as I watched the Landcruiser move terribly slowly past the main car park and turn into the drive. It disappeared from my view under the palm trees towards the foyer entrance.

I waited another ten minutes on the roof. I did not trust the rebels and wanted to see if they took advantage of the Red Cross to sneak forward. However, there was no more shooting and no movement. I pulled back from the drain hole, picked up the gun, made my way crouched over back across the air conditioning ducts to the stair well and jogged down the stairs to see what was going on.

For the first time, I went right down to the basement and was immediately struck by the contrast. I had spent all day on my own on the roof or dashing up and downstairs to various floors in the hotel and I had seen only a handful of men, like Martin, Steve and a few Lebanese firefighting, but all the time the basement had been stuffed with literally hundreds and hundreds of people, mostly local Sierra Leones. The roof had certainly been hot under the broiling sun, but the atmosphere in those cellar rooms was close, chokingly stale and unbearable.

It was bedlam, but there was an air of anticipation that had been entirely absent when I burst in on the other refugees sitting hopelessly in the corner of the hotel earlier in the day. Now, they clogged the corridors, milling about, and calling out to each other. They stared at me as I passed, standing back to make room, then turned to talk excitedly to each other. I suppose they had been listening to the gunfire and rockets exploding on the structure of the hotel throughout the day. They understood very well the imminence of the danger they had been in, had the rebels broken into the hotel, but down in the basement they had been set apart from the reality. My sudden appearance presented them with the quite surprising manifestation of all their fears. I wondered if this was why soldiers are fêted when they are needed and, precisely because they set off those deep-seated fears in the civilian population – which many people may also resent to find in themselves – they are so often equally vilified when the fighting is over; a phenomenon perfectly expressed in Kipling's poem 'Tommy'.*

Exhausted, I hardly cared. I was filthy dirty, sweat-stained, my clothes in shreds from crawling round the roof, and I carried the GPMG on a sling over my shoulder with the last of the linked ammunition round my neck. I had taken everything I could find off all the Nigerian soldiers. I was down to maybe the last sixty rounds and the Red Cross had arrived at the last possible minute.

People pointed the way as I made my way through the crowds in the bare concrete corridors, as if they had read the script and knew where I was expected to go, and I found myself directed to an office in the bowels of the hotel. I opened the door and stepped from the sweltering closeness of the basement passages into an ice-cold air conditioned IT room. The room contained the electrical management systems for the hotel and the telephone exchange equipment for the switchboard in the little room above on the ground floor where I had called Murdo. There was no sign of the Red Cross people, but Roger Crooks, Steve Lawson and Martin Greenwood were there and waved me over to join them. Roger and Steve were sitting down talking on telephones, which surprised me. I suppose I had been so isolated in my own personal fight on the roof, running up and down the stairs to keep the rebels back from the hotel in the previous eight hours, that I had imagined everyone else to have been as cut off from the world outside as I felt.

In fact, Roger had been on the phone for hours trying to find someone to help us out. He had started with his partner, Oscar Wyatt. The founder and chief executive of Coastal Incorporated was a wealthy oil businessman whose wardrobe consisted of little else except grey flannels, white shirts and black shoes, but Roger said he had seven private jets, a couple of oil refineries and some rather useful connections in the US Administration.

---

* 'Tommy', the essential message being, 'For it's Tommy this, an' Tommy that, an' "Chuck him out, the brute!", but it's Saviour of 'is Country when the guns begin to shoot; An' it's Tommy this, an' Tommy that, an' anything you please; an' Tommy ain't a bloomin' fool – you bet that Tommy sees!'

Roger had left Wyatt in no doubt about the seriousness of the situation confronting over 1,000 people in the Mammy Yoko and Wyatt had started to pull strings. While I had been crawling round on the roof in the boiling sun to avoid being killed by RPGs and heavy machine gun fire, Roger, who was a former member of the famous oilfield Red Adair team, had divided his time between helping Martin and Steve put out fires started by rockets exploding in the middle floors and endless conversations on the phones down in this cold little IT room in the basement among hundreds of refugees. Roger had been talking to the great and good all over the world, including US Secretary of State Madeleine Albright in Washington, the British High Commissioner, Peter Penfold, who was in the centre of Freetown trying to broker a cease-fire face-to-face with the coup leaders at considerable risk to himself, and the International Committee of the Red Cross.

'Hi, Will,' Roger drawled, coming off the phone with his hand over the mouthpiece. 'You've turned up at just the right time. I've got the USS *Kearsarge* on this line and the British High Commissioner on that one.' He gestured at the phone Steve Lawson was holding. 'You know what's going on with those goddam maniacs outside the hotel; you've done all the work so far. You talk to 'em.' Very briefly, he explained that once Madeleine Albright had accepted just how dangerous the situation had become, she had ordered the US aircraft carrier USS *Kearsarge* to turn around from its course away from the Gold Coast and sail back to Freetown. This was the ship which had carried out the previous two American evacuations with such efficiency and the idea that there was a force of 2,000 US Marines a few miles off the coast ready to come to our help, just like the 7th Cavalry in the Wild West films, was suddenly and incredibly reassuring.

Roger handed me the phone. 'This is Anne Wright on the other end. She was the person who coordinated the other two evacuations on Friday and Saturday.'

'Hallo, Will?' said Anne. 'Was that you on the roof?'

'Yes, that's me.' I had heard nothing in the sky since the Hind Mi-24 helicopter had had a go at me earlier in the day, but I suppose that the captain of the USS *Kearsarge* had sent up his

Sea Harriers,* or a Super Cobra helicopter, high up above the hotel to see what was happening and confirm the stories about the rebels' attack which were emanating from the basement of the hotel. The resolution of US air photography was so good that high altitude 'overheads', as the intelligence community calls them, could show enough focus on a man's shoulder epaulettes to tell his rank. I had no doubt the Americans on the *Kearsarge* had been watching much of the last hour or so of fighting in real time from the comfort of their carrier operations room.

'Bit of a tight situation you got there,' she said, confirming my thoughts.

'I've been in worse,' I said matter-of-factly.

'I'd hate to hang out with you,' she replied, laughing. 'But we're glad to hear you've still got a sense of humour!'

There was a pause in which she was obviously talking to someone else at her end, then she added, 'I'm just going to patch you through to our briefing room. Will you talk to the officers there?'

Having been on warships before, in briefing rooms preparing for action, I assumed I was being put onto a loudspeaker in the marines operations room, so when I heard the connection go through, I said, 'Good afternoon, gentlemen.' I know that was a bit formal, especially after the day's work – even typically British – but it seemed to strike the right note and there was a responding chorus of deep masculine voices, 'Hi, there!'

'You keeping your head down over there?' one authoritative person wanted to know.

'I certainly am, sir.'

'Well, my name's Colonel Sam Helland,' the man continued, helpfully introducing himself fully in a manner typical of the American forces and in complete contrast to the often diffident style of the British. 'I am the Joint Task Force Commander of the

---

* AV-8B Harrier, V/STOL (Vertical/Short Take-off and Landing) multi-role 'jump jet' with weapons options (maximum load 3,856kg in short take-off) for ground-attack, support and interdiction roles, including free fall, cluster and retarded bombs, rockets and missiles, like Sidewinder; speed 550 knots and night-vision capability.

160

22nd Marine Expeditionary Unit here on the USS *Kearsarge* and I wonder if you could give us a situation report?'

'Yes, sir!' I smiled – this was exactly what I wanted to do. 'The rebels have been attacking this hotel since six o'clock this morning. I estimate they are now about 250-strong. They appear to have an endless supply of ammunition. They have fired at least 250 RPGs at us during the day, and God knows how many thousands of rounds of 12.7mm or 14.5mm. They're not very well trained. They are now about 100 metres away on the outer perimeter wall of the hotel.' I paused and then asked, 'Have you got an air photograph of the place?'

'Sure do.'

I wanted to describe to him exactly where the rebels were congregating outside the hotel and said, 'Okay, then imagine I am standing in the Mammy Yoko and looking across the road at the Bintumani Conference Centre.'

'Yes. I have it.'

I imagined them all in their marines combat uniforms poring over a large, usually 40-inch square black and white air photo. I went on, 'On my right, about half right, I can see a small mosque, approximately 400 metres away?'

'Yes.'

'Next to the mosque beyond the car park and on the other side of the road is a small building. It's white with a red roof.'

'Yes. Got it. We know where you mean.'

'That's where they are forming up. That's where the trucks bring their supply of ammunition and rockets, and that's where they have been assembling the weapons and preparing for their attacks. It seems to be their command post. From there, they move down through the banana plantation to a line of shanty huts from where they have been firing RPGs, and moving closer to the hotel all the time along a piece of hollow ground which you can probably see on your photo dotted with a few trees, opposite the hotel entrance.'

'Yep, I got it.'

'They've also been using mortars,' I continued. 'Probably 82s, but they obviously have no idea how to use them as the rounds have been going right over the hotel and landing in the sea behind us.' This was just as well, since in competent hands those mortars, probably Soviet 82mms* judging by the sound, would have landed rounds directly on the roof and ended the battle in short order.

'These fired from the forming-up point?'

'I think so.' I was less certain about the mortars than I was about the heavy machine guns which had been on target for hours. I told them, 'They've also got 12.7mm or even heavier 14.5mm machine guns set up in the anti-aircraft role, on tripods. They know how to use these and they've been firing at us all day, ripping the roof to pieces. That's why I've had to keep coming off the roof to find somewhere else to fire from.'

'Right thing to do,' drawled the marine commander. 'What are they dressed like?' This was another typical military question, so the marines could be told what their enemy looked like on the ground.

'They're a rag-tag mix of combats and civvy clothes they've stolen from shops in Freetown,' I replied thinking of the mad appearance of the rebels I had seen. 'Some are wearing several shirts at once, brightly coloured T-shirts, and they stick things in their hair.'

'In their hair?'

'Like sticks, bits of tin or pieces of broken mirror.' I did not think Colonel Helland needed to know right then about Jom-bobla rituals and woven strands of pubic hair.

'What about their tactics?'

'They had no idea at the beginning of the day,' I told him laconically. 'They all bunched together, chanting and singing in the open, but since mid-morning someone with a bit of knowledge must have turned up because they began to use cover and got their act together. They've had some sort of game plan as they've been trying to get round the back of the hotel, to outflank us.'

'I see,' Helland mused. 'And what's your position?'

'I've got a GPMG but only maybe fifty or sixty rounds left. And a couple of grenades.'

---

* Soviet M1937 82mm medium mortar, barrel length 122cm, weight in firing position set-up 56kg, range 3,040m and rate of fire 15–25rpm.

There was a long silence.

'Well,' said Helland, trying to sound optimistic. 'We'll do everything we can.'

I was used to this sort of remark. It often meant there was lots of talking and good intentions but nothing happening. I had no idea what the Red Cross visitors could do for us, but I knew that there were still over 250 rebels outside the hotel itching to get inside for murder and mayhem. I wanted action. I laid it on the line for him, 'One short dash across the car park and they'll be among us inside the hotel. Any chance you can bring in an air strike?'

There was another pause and then Helland admitted, 'As much as we'd like to, we can't.'

I grunted, 'Right.' Maybe the 2,000 marines were close, but not close enough.

'I'm real sorry,' he said apologetically. 'But we don't have the clearance or jurisdiction for offensive action right now.'

Red Tape: never much use for stopping lunatics with AKs. I glanced at Roger and, to hide my disappointment, I asked practically, 'So what are your options then?'

'We'll have to come back to you,' replied Helland obscurely from way out at sea.

I felt let down. What were the Americans going to do for us? Whatever it was, if they did not do it quite soon, they would be too late.

Steve passed me the other phone and I had a similar conversation with the British High Commissioner, Peter Penfold, explaining what had been happening. He said he would do his best to encourage the *Kearsarge* to come to our help. He also said he had been working to broker the assistance of the ICRC. When I put down the phone to Penfold, I asked Roger, 'Where are the Red Cross people?'

As if on cue, the door opened and a tall, slim man in his early thirties, with long, thin flaxen hair, in slacks and a white shirt came into the room. 'Hi, I'm Lauren,' he said with a distinct Swiss accent. 'I'm from the International Committee of the Red Cross.'

Roger introduced us, looking from Lauren, clean as Swiss mountain air in neat shirt and slacks, to me in my sweat-stained,

163

bloody and torn clothes. He said, 'What's the deal, Lauren?'

'I have been negotiating with the Revolutionary United Front and they have agreed you can all leave the hotel under the flag of the Red Cross. We shall all go out through the front.'

I said nothing but Roger drawled, 'I need more detail, Lauren. If we leave this hotel, where exactly do we go to?' He was acutely and properly aware that this was his hotel and as manager he still had responsibility for the people as long as they were under his roof.

'You'll be taken to the centre of the town under our protection and there you will be segregated.'

I had no idea what he meant by that but the idea was not appealing. I joined in with, 'That doesn't sound like negotiation to me. Sounds more like capitulation.'

'I don't understand.' Lauren's pale blue eyes switched to me and he stared unwaveringly, politely enough but with obvious distaste. We were poles apart. I represented everything he disliked, a reality he abhorred and the very antithesis of the ideals of the Red Cross. Like a crusading evangelist in dark heathen lands, he had come to save us and we should blindly follow. The ICRC was always right.

'Speaking for myself, I certainly don't want to go into town,' I told him bluntly.

Lauren insisted that this was the only route out.

'What d'you reckon, Will, for all these people?' Roger interrupted.

'I know we can't hold out here much longer,' I told them. 'But I don't relish the thought of being taken into the middle of the town by the rebels and paraded around. And I can't imagine anyone else in this hotel wants to either. We don't want to be doing that, Lauren. All these people have come here precisely because they wanted to get away from those lunatics in town.' I thought about the young man whose heart had been ripped out of his chest on the road by the mosque. 'I don't think we'd last very long.'

'But you will be under the Red Cross flag!' Lauren repeated, exasperated.

Suddenly, I heard the sound of firing again, faint as we were in the basement but none the less distinct. The cease-fire which Lauren had negotiated for one hour was over.

'I've got work to do,' I snapped grabbing the GPMG, and I ran out. While they talked, I had to keep the rebels at bay. I ran as fast as I could back up all the flights of stairs to the top floor, crawled breathlessly onto the hot roof again on my hands and knees and peered through a drain hole. As I feared, a group of rebels had begun to sneak forward from the hollow ground towards the hotel entrance. I fired a short burst at them, hitting a few behind the white perimeter wall. The others ran back for cover and I let them go. I had to conserve every bullet. I worked my way around to the topside of the hotel to check the rebels' attempt to cut around the back, and reflected grimly that for ten long hot hours we had had no idea what would happen to us and then in one short hour no less than two potentially excellent solutions, the Red Cross and the Americans, had been presented to us and just as quickly snatched away.

I was exhausted, drained, desperately short of ammunition yet I was back to struggling about on the roof and time was running out fast. If the Red Cross or the Marines did not come up with something good very quickly indeed, the rebels would be wreaking havoc among the hundreds of refugees long before nightfall.

Once again, the rebels tuned in their heavy machine guns and pinned me down under a tremendous weight of fire smashing into the parapet above my head, as if they wanted to tear the hotel down brick by brick, floor by floor. Pieces of broken concrete showered around me, bullets snapped through the metal air conditioning ducts by the water tower, ricocheting off the walls and pipes, and I could feel the thud of RPGs exploding into the hotel in the floors below me. It was as though they were furious that they had been bamboozled by the Red Cross and regretted agreeing to a cease-fire at all. They seemed more determined than ever to kill me and everyone else in the hotel. After about ten minutes of this there was a slight lull in the firing and I wriggled back towards the front parapet dragging the gun with me. Suddenly there was a colossal explosion out on the hill which rocked the hotel. The rebels' fire stopped abruptly and I peered through a drain hole to see a towering column of black smoke rising from the other side of the big baobab tree at the T-junction. Smoke billowed out, hiding the house with the red roof and the mosque, and pieces of debris rained down on the banana leaves and the tin roofs of the shanty huts.

When the smoke drifted away I saw the rebels' command post and forming-up position had vanished, trucks were wrecked and bodies lay about all over the road out beyond the bananas. I had not heard any planes but this had to be an American Sea Harrier from the USS *Kearsarge* using the accuracy of a laser-guided bomb. The explosion was right on the spot I had described to Colonel Helland in my target indication during our conversation earlier. I guessed they had aircraft watching us all the time from on station in the sky far above the hotel so the noise could not be heard. When the cease-fire had ended and the rebels recommenced blazing away at the hotel, they had probably thought it was time to even the balance in our favour with an explosion which they could deny if necessary and claim was the rebels blowing themselves up.

'That was handy,' I said to myself, absolutely delighted. This was a tremendous boost to my morale, but it did not eliminate the menace. Within a few minutes, the rebels started firing again, first AK rounds but then the steady thud of a 12.7mm joined in, and soon it seemed we were back to normal.

After about an hour the firing stopped again. Once more, I waited several minutes to see if this was real. An eerie quiet descended on the hotel broken only by a discreet rustling of wings as the vultures jostled each other for space on the branches of the big tree behind the hotel. Cautiously, I crawled back to the shadows of the stair well and trotted all the way down the stairs to the basement.

As I walked along the corridor towards the exchange IT room, I passed an open door marked 'Wine Cellar' and glanced in to see Ken sitting on the floor inside. He had Sonya on one side of him and Didi on the other and he was leaning against racks of wine bottles stacked to the ceiling. Normally, this set-up would be his perfect solution to life, but he looked despondent. I had completely forgotten about him and asked, 'You okay?'

He nodded glumly without moving.

There was nothing more to say and no time to waste so I nodded and carried on.

I found Lauren with Roger in the icy cool telephone exchange room. Lauren had spent the last hour negotiating on his radio with the rebels and this time he simply assumed that he, as the ICRC representative, was in charge. He adopted a snappy Teutonic tone and said, 'You must all come with me through the front door of the hotel.'

Once more, Roger turned to me and asked for my opinion.

There was no doubt in my mind and I told them, 'The rebels have been attacking us since six o'clock this morning. They have shown not the slightest regard for our safety in the last twelve hours. They've been shooting at us, firing rockets and mortars at us and trying to kill us all day long. What on earth makes you think they're going to abide by any agreement and not try to kill us when we leave the hotel?'

Lauren was about to answer but after being on the receiving end of the fighting, I was dog tired, I had no patience left and I shut him up with, 'Secondly, once we go into the centre of town, and we're surrounded by the rebels we will become hostages!' Throughout the guerrilla fighting in previous years, the RUF rebels had seized and held numerous hostages for months in appalling conditions against ridiculous demands. They had all been terribly mistreated and many had been killed. 'What happens then? The Americans might be able to do something for us now, because we're still in command of our own destiny, but they'll find it impossible to help us if we're captured by the rebels in the middle of Freetown. I'm not going to put myself in that position, or give the rebels the chance to chop my arms off like they did to a boy in town a few days ago. Or worse.'

'Yeah, you're right,' said Roger. Steve Lawson and Martin Greenwood nodded too.

'You must!' Lauren insisted, his voice rising. 'You have to come with me! I've negotiated it.'

'We don't have to do anything you say,' I told him. I was polite but blunt.

'We ain't coming,' Roger added.

'You must!' Lauren repeated, determined to make us agree.

'You will be under the protection of the banner of the Red Cross!'

His messianic conviction of the perfection and power of the Red Cross was impressive, but like so many missionaries he blithely ignored the realities of the situation. I told him sincerely, 'Lauren, I very much admire your bravery in coming here today, and the risks you've taken personally to negotiate with these madmen outside, but there's no way I'm going out of that front door under anyone's banner! That's the end of that. I'll go my own way, and you can go your way.'

'But you must come my way!' he said obstinately. 'The Red Cross have negotiated your safety and if the Red Cross say they are going to do something, they do it.'

'Fine, let the Red Cross do it,' I told him conversationally, without getting irritated as there was really no issue in this for me. 'But I'm not doing it. No way.' I had no intention of handing myself over to the rebels. I turned to Roger and the others and said, 'I suggest that the people who want to go with Lauren can go out the front door to the rebels, and the others can stay and take their chances with whatever the Americans can do for us.'

'So where will you go?' Lauren interjected, unable to believe that there were actually people who did not want to commit themselves to the Red Cross irrespective of the circumstances.

I shrugged, 'We'd probably have to escape out the back of the hotel, out of sight of the rebels in low ground towards the beach.'

This infuriated him and he burst out, 'I have put the reputation of the Red Cross on the line! I must tell the rebels that everyone is going to come out of that front door!'

'You don't have to tell them anything.'

'I do!' He was adamant and threatened, 'If you go out through the back door, the reputation of the Red Cross will be at stake and I shall have to tell the rebels.'

Suddenly, this put a different complexion on the discussion. I had not spent ten desperate hours fighting on the roof to have this lunatic put me and all the others at serious risk for the sake of someone's reputation. Very coldly, I stared at him and said, 'If you do that, Lauren, it will be the last thing you do.'

'What d'you mean by that?' he said, taken aback.

'I'm just warning you,' I told him quietly, looking him right in the eyes.

He said nothing and there was a silence. One of the phones rang. Steve answered and said after a moment, 'It's Peter Penfold. He wants to speak to you, Will.'

In extremis, everyone had assumed I was in charge. I took the phone and the High Commissioner said in a friendly tone, 'This is Peter speaking, Will. You all right?' He had been watching the battle all day through binos from the roof of his High Commission in Spur Road.

'Yes, okay, thanks,' I replied and asked, 'What's happening with the Americans?' They had had an hour to sort their options. I was sure they had carried out that one air strike on the rebels' command position, but that was not enough on its own to stop them storming into the hotel and we were now desperate. The Red Cross option had absolutely no appeal and quite simply there was no other option.

'I've spoken to them and they've told me you must leave the hotel where you are now and then they will pick you up from the beach.'

'Why can't they come and get us now, from this hotel?' We were safer inside the hotel than wandering about in the open when we would be sitting ducks for the rebels.

I suspect Peter Penfold agreed but he explained the US position, 'They're saying that if you go down to the beach, they can help you.' It was an absurd legal point, but it seemed that if we stayed in the hotel there was nothing to say we were in danger, so we had to show that we were trying to escape from our attackers before the US could intervene to protect us in open ground. 'They will protect you if you are fired upon.'

'So they've got gunships in the air?'

'I can't say if they have or not, but I suppose so,' said Penfold. He probably did not know any more than me, but after the air strike on the rebels' command post, it seemed likely.

'What d'you think of this plan?' I asked him. He was the man who had spent all day talking to the Americans and negotiating with the rebels.

'I don't know,' he countered. 'You're the man on the ground.'

Once again I was being left with the decisions, and it irritated me that all these people who would in quieter moments be so forceful with their opinions stepped smartly to the rear when the shooting started. 'I know that, but I'd like to hear your view.'

He repeated, 'I've been told that if you make your way to the beach, the Marines will come to pick you all up.'

'And if we're attacked on the way?' I glanced at Lauren and wondered what he would say to the rebels if he went out the front.

'The Americans will react if you are fired on.'

I shook my head. It was the wrong way around. 'That doesn't give me much confidence. What guarantee do we have that the Marines will come to the beach if we do go there?'

There was a slight pause and Penfold said, 'They won't say exactly, for reasons of international law or perhaps because of their own rules of engagement, but that's what I believe they will do.'

His tone was supposed to sound bullish, but there was a hollow ring to it I did not like. I would have liked it even less had I known then that in fact Peter Penfold had been given no guarantee whatsoever by the USS *Kearsarge* that the Marines would come to pick up any refugees from the beach or anywhere else. He was an experienced diplomat who had seen similar situations before but he was none the less gambling on forcing the United States into action on moral grounds and the only way to make them react was precisely if we were attacked on the beach in open ground. He was trying to help us, but this was like tying a goat to the post and telling it that the only way the hunter could shoot the lion and save it was if the lion came along and started to eat it first. We would not have been impressed had we known.

I sat staring at Roger and the others and ran through the options in my mind. Should we leave the safety of the hotel, or put ourselves at risk on the beach, where the Marines might not turn up? They all stared at me in silence, expecting me to decide. I asked Penfold a last time, 'What d'you suggest?'

He would not budge and said, 'You're the guy on the ground, Will. You must decide.'

'Right!' I said, making up my mind. This was no time for faffing about. 'This is what we're going to do. Those who want to go with the Red Cross will leave by the front door with Lauren. Those who want to take their chances with the Americans will follow us out of the back door down to the beach. We'll leave the hotel simultaneously.'

'You can't do that!' Lauren burst out. 'You can't use the Red Cross like that!'

'I'm not using you,' I said. Lauren was boring me.

'Yes, you're using us as a decoy!'

'No. We're just leaving at the same time.'

'I'm not going to do this,' he snapped.

He may have negotiated a truce but it was only temporary and he was fast proving more of an obstacle than a help. I said, 'What are you going to do, then?'

He shook his head obstinately and repeated his threat, 'I must tell the rebels what you're doing, going out of the back door.'

Bureaucracy, blind adherence to rules, or just plain cussed, this was stupid and dangerous and I told him again bluntly, 'Listen, Lauren, if you do that you put all of us at risk, so I'm warning you for the last time!'

He did not reply, but stared at me resentfully.

'Let's solve this the way Will suggests by asking the people themselves,' interposed Martin Greenwood in a diplomatic and practical tone of voice, and he led the way out into the basement corridors which were by then crowded with people waiting to hear what was going to happen. Martin found a chair and Lauren stood on it to offer the Red Cross option of going out with him through the front door with the rebels into town. Then Martin stepped onto it in turn and repeated the alternative, 'All those who want to go to the beach, where we think the Americans will come to help us, should go with us out of the back of the hotel at the same time.'

It was hard to tell what the response would be as there was a short delay in which the marshals went round the hotel to pass the word to all the emergency locations where people had been hidden all day. Then the hotel came alive with movement. Hundreds and hundreds of people started appearing from all directions, in corridors, on the stairs, men carrying suitcases or bags with their last remaining and most precious possessions, women

171

carrying babies or shepherding small children and others just hurrying along with nothing more than the clothes they wore. It quickly became clear what people thought of the two options.

Out of over 1,000 people, only about 250 gathered in the front lobby with Lauren and his assistant, a tall thin woman clutching a radio. They included the Lebanese with white sheets over their heads whose leader had tried to do a deal with the rebels to kill me on the roof in exchange for being allowed to go free. They were stupid enough to think that the rebels might still respect the arrangement, but their attitude irritated Martin so much he shouted at them in a very direct Yorkshire style indeed and made them take the sheets off.

Lauren was deliberately rushing his group to leave as soon as possible to stop us escaping out the back when he was going out of the front, so Roger and I wasted no time either and went off at once to find a suitable route out of the hotel. He showed me a way from the service entrance at the basement out past the rubbish bins under the canopy, round the tennis courts and across an open area by the dance bandstand to the perimeter wall nearest the beach.* I checked all the way that we could keep out of sight of places I knew the rebels had been in all day. The route took advantage of the hill which sloped towards the sea and seemed to be in 'dead' ground but I seriously doubted that such large numbers could slip away unnoticed. Roger and I were both very conscious of how vulnerable we would all be once we left the Mammy Yoko, but we had no option, nor the luxury of time on our side any longer. We had to go.

We ran back to the hotel and found everyone gathering ready to go in the corridors and stairways. Lincoln Jopp was in the basement corridor, leaning unsteadily against the wall, the same dirty shell dressing round his head in his torn and bloodied uniform. He had spent the whole day lying on the floor in a stuffy little room in the basement with more than a dozen wounded Nigerian soldiers. He was looking pretty grim. His face was caked with dried blood and he was badly dehydrated. No one had paid

---

* See sketch map on page 55.

any of them much attention in the last hours and two of the Nigerians had bled to death.

'How're you feeling?' I asked.

'Terrible. I feel really sick.'

'You look terrible,' I said cheerfully. 'How about some rehydrate?' Earlier during the first cease-fire, I had raided the hotel's first aid cabinet with Roger's help and found some sachets of Dioralyte, containing special replacement fluids and glucose in powder form which made me feel a lot better. I made up some more drink for Lincoln, telling him to sip slowly, and he began to perk up immediately.

As he drank, I realised that if the rebels saw him in his uniform, he might be in trouble. I told him I would try and find him something else to wear. I had another purpose in mind too. I ran upstairs to the first floor, kicked in the door of the first room I came to, went straight to the bathroom, switched on the shower and stood under it in all my clothes. The feeling of water running over my face and body was delightful, like a gentle cooling massage. My face was black but there was no time to waste, so I washed and stripped at the same time, rubbing soap as much over my wrecked shirt and trousers as over me. I dried off and nipped out into the corridor where there were several abandoned bits of luggage which had been too heavy for people to carry. The foyer was full of them. I ripped off the zip of one likely looking bag, rifled through by feel as the corridor was rather dark and grabbed a white shirt and jeans for myself, as mine were in rags after being scraped about the roof for hours, a natty blue baseball cap and what looked like a fine pair of Levis for Lincoln.

Back in the basement, I made him change. He looked ridiculous. The Levis were far too short, leaving a long stretch of skinny leg between the trouser bottoms and his British Army-issue jungle boots on his feet. However, there was no time to find anything else. Lauren was already through the front door with his group and we had to leave at once. I pulled on my cap and squeezed past the crowds to the service entrance at the back to lead them out of the hotel to the beach.

Just as I left, I handed the GPMG back to a young Nigerian soldier standing near the door. He had his combat helmet on, with all his webbing, and his large white eyes looked pathetically at the files of refugees leaving the hotel. I felt quite sorry for him. All the Nigerian detachment had to give themselves up to the rebels. The rest of the company was lined up outside the front entrance of the hotel in front of their colonel who stood very alone, utterly disconsolate, as I waved him goodbye. The fighting was over for them, they were waiting to surrender to the rebels and looked understandably miserable. I did not fancy their chances of good treatment under the rules of the Geneva Convention, certainly not in the light of Johnny Koroma's view about prisoners as a cadet at Sandhurst.

The GPMG was useless without ammunition but I kept the two grenades in my pocket and a Makarov pistol I had taken from a Nigerian earlier which I hid in my belt under the shirt. I had no intention of being caught out in the open without something to defend myself with.

The light was fading as I led the way from the hotel, which helped. If the rebels did attack us, we would have some protection in darkness and might get away. I walked round the tennis courts and past the bandstand, out through the white perimeter wall and across the road which ran along the seafront. To avoid people missing the route, I went straight to the beach, keeping left of a beach bar, and stepped onto the sand. Roger had suggested we went to the Hotel Cape Sierra, which was about three hundred yards along the beach on the point at the top of the estuary. While I had been busy with Lincoln he had told the High Commissioner and the Americans on the *Kearsarge* that that was where we would be.

As I walked along the soft sand in the last light of the day, the sun slid into the sea on the horizon, casting a broad path of golden reflections and painting sharp orange lights over the faint wisps of white cloud in the pale blue sky. Behind me, a long snake of hundreds and hundreds of refugees trudged wearily over the sand. It was a bizarre sight. Those carrying bags stopped from time to time to rest, dumping their load to give their aching muscles a moment's rest before hoisting them up once more to walk a bit further. Others carried suitcases on their heads. Women clutched small children to their chests and marched stoically on, one foot in front of the other on the soft sand. There was not much talking but the occasional crying of younger children carried faintly on the warm breeze. They were numb with the events of the day, still terrified of what might happen if the rebels got to them and silently determined to buckle down and do whatever was necessary to save themselves and their children. The coming darkness would help, but it would be a miracle if we were able to move more than a thousand frightened people without the rebels knowing and then hide in the Hotel Cape Sierra without them trying to get at us as they had in the Mammy Yoko. If the rebels were engaged with Lauren's group for the moment, it was only a matter of time before they turned their attention back to us. I just prayed the Americans really were in their planes high overhead watching our last desperate attempt to avoid being assaulted, and I prayed they would forget their 'jurisdiction' issues and act. As soon as possible. An emergency evacuation might work well under the cover of darkness while the rebels were celebrating their victory and doing God-knows-what to the 250 people who had gone off with Lauren.

As the strip of beach between the bar and the Hotel Cape Sierra filled up with refugees, a large bus appeared round the corner of the road which ran down past the Hotel Mammy Yoko further up the hill. The driver, a local Sierra Leone, pulled up on the side of the road by the bars and a dapper man with smooth dark hair in a white shirt and clean slacks stepped out. He turned out to be a Lebanese diplomat. In typical Lebanese style, some of the Lebanese refugees in the Mammy Yoko had been secretly busy on their radio telephone negotiating their own private solution which was as different and contrary to Red Cross diktats as our own. The Lebanese had used personal contacts with their embassy in Freetown, which had in turn negotiated with the rebels to drive a bus through their front line surrounding the hotel and remove certain Lebanese families to safety. They drove the bus through at exactly the time Lauren's Red Cross group was surrendering to the rebels, using them as a decoy. In amazement, we watched about forty well-dressed and obviously wealthy Lebanese men, women and children crowd onto the bus, with the diplomat fussing around them, and then drive off up the coast as if they were off for a day at the seaside. I wondered how much they had paid the rebels for this convenient *laissez-passer*.

'Interesting shirt,' observed Steve coming up behind me as we walked along the sand.

'What d'you mean?'

'Nice embroidery on the back. Choose it yourself?' He laughed as I took it off and saw that in the darkness of the corridor where I had found the bag, I had not seen that these were women's clothes. What I had thought was a white shirt turned out to be pale pink with charming *broderie anglaise* on the back, and my jeans were hers too.

'I'm sure Sylvester Stallone wouldn't be seen dead in gear like that,' said Steve delightedly.

'You look lovely,' agreed Martin.

I grinned and we carried on up the beach, enjoying the joke at Lincoln's expense as well. He looked absurd in his short Levis, as if he had rolled up the trouser bottoms to go bathing. We looked a right pair!

As we approached the drooping palms surrounding the Hotel Cape Sierra, a small knot of people came through the trees holding up a bed sheet attached to poles. They had watched the attack on the Hotel Mammy Yoko all day and felt that this was the best way to greet us. I suspect they were worried that some of us still had weapons and might take them for rebels.

There was a tangible lightening in the atmosphere among the refugees when they reached the Cape Sierra. The endless line struggling along the beach ended at the top of a few steps up to the entrance of the hotel. A continual stream of dozens and dozens of people spilled over these steps into an entrance courtyard. They filled this area in front of the hotel, dropped their cases and began to relax, confident the Americans were on their way and rescue was imminent. Suddenly, there was a sharp explosion like a grenade going off. Everyone ducked or dropped to the ground in panic, looking round to see where the attack was coming from now. What they saw was a man standing awkwardly by the fountain in the centre of the courtyard with an enormous suitcase which he had just smacked down on the concrete in the middle of them. The tension disappeared and they stood up again, laughing and talking.

People recognised me from earlier in the day, or before, and kept coming up to shake my hand. I found this embarrassing, and I did not share the sense of relief sweeping through the mass of refugees who had reached the Cape Sierra. I wanted to get away. Lincoln led me round the back of the hotel to another building where he had been living in an apartment during his stay in Freetown. I remembered the place from my first night in Sierra Leone, when Murdo and I had been to find Fred Marafono talking to his diamond dealer contacts in another apartment there. It was a large place, with several rooms overlooking the sea. While the people massing around the hotel congratulated themselves on getting away, we wanted to find out whether the Americans really were coming to help us, as the British High Commissioner had said.

One of the journalists with Corinne Dufka, a dark-haired Reuters staffer who had been all the time in the Mammy Yoko, had a portable satellite phone set up outside the hotel. Satphones do not work inside so we had put it on the ground outside and fiddled about turning the large dish on its extended legs so it faced the satellite for the best reception. Lincoln's first call was to the USS *Kearsarge* to hear what they had planned.

After a longish time, he came back and announced, 'They aren't coming till tomorrow morning!'

Corinne and I stared at Lincoln. This was bad news.

'Are they coming at all?' I wanted to know.

He shrugged and said, 'They say they are. But they're not coming for us tonight. I couldn't tell whether they're still having problems with their rules of engagement and jurisdiction or whether they simply prefer to pick us up in daylight.'

I could see some sense in that. Putting more than 1,000 tired and shocked people on to helicopters in the dark for a flight over the sea to land on an aircraft carrier deck at night might lead to all sorts of problems. However, my fear of another attack by the rebels was suddenly very real. It was seven o'clock and we had twelve hours or more to wait in the hope that the rebels were too busy with the Red Cross group and looting the

Hotel Mammy Yoko to bother with us yet.

When we went back to the main part of the hotel to tell Roger, Steve, Martin and all the rest, the atmosphere changed at once as the implications of the US Marines' decision sank in. They all realised they were not out of trouble yet. The laughter died away and they began to spread out around the Cape Sierra in a very sombre mood indeed to sit out the night. The situation was still very serious. They lay about among their cases and bags talking in muted tones, like passengers delayed at an airport, all nervously straining their ears to hear the slightest noise outside the hotel which might warn them the rebels were on their way.

Lincoln gave me one of the spare rooms in his apartment. I showered, properly this time, and began to feel more human. All the time, the events of the day and the risks we still ran buzzed round ceaselessly in my head.

'You like me to look at those cuts?' I asked Lincoln. He was really a mess. Gratefully, he took off his shirt, wincing as it pulled at the dried blood, and sat down on a chair. I inspected the damage. He had been badly peppered with dozens of bits of shrapnel on his front and back. None had caused deep wounds as far as I could see with such a superficial examination, but the bigger cuts on his head were different: black, swollen and unpleasant. I used lots of cotton wool and disinfectant to dab off the blood and dirt round each cut and then stuck a plaster over it, gradually working my way all around him. He needed some proper attention from a doctor but this would do for the time being.

'We need a beer,' he said when he had showered and changed too and we walked round to the hotel bar for a couple of beers with Roger, Steve, Corinne and Martin. Soon a crowd had gathered round talking about the day. They were effusively grateful to me, pumping my hand and thanking me. Some I recognised but most were just faces in the crowds. One English woman pulled me to one side to say how indebted she was to me for saving her two young children. 'They'll appreciate what you did for them for the rest of their lives,' she said.

I would be a liar to say I did not enjoy all this attention, and I thanked her but I warned, 'It's not over yet.'

'Never mind,' she replied stoically. 'Thanks to you we'll make it.' I have no idea of her name, and she disappeared back into the crowds as abruptly as she had approached me.

As the last faint light of the day faded into night and darkness enveloped the Cape Sierra, a feeling of barely suppressed panic gripped all the people squashed into the hotel. We hardly needed to advise the hotel manager to keep all the lights switched off and everyone lay in total darkness trying to make as little noise as possible, nervous and tense, all hope suspended for the night. They had escaped the horror of the rebels that day, but they had a long frightening night ahead of them before the next step to freedom – if the Marines did come. Once again, there was nothing they could do except wait. There was nowhere to go from the spit of land we were on, and nothing any of us could do to protect ourselves if the rebels came. I imagine a lot of those people came to terms with themselves that night, because our fears are always worse in the small hours of darkness. Perhaps a good many others just lay miserable, sweating through the warm night in blind panic. I really do not think anyone slept much at all.

Before leaving the hotel bar, one of the journalists working for the BBC, Liz Blunt, said she had left her satphone in the Hotel Mammy Yoko. I volunteered to go and fetch it for her.

'Really?' she asked. I guess she found it impossible to believe that anyone would go back to the hotel after so much violence there. 'What about the rebels? They'll be all over the place.'

'I'll keep my eyes peeled,' I promised her. Judging by the rebels' military skills I had seen so far, I doubted very much that they would have proper sentries on the lookout. Once inside, they would be so busy robbing everything they could lay their hands on, I thought they would hardly notice someone else there, unless I actually ran into them in a corridor. For that, I had the Makarov and the grenades.

We found a couple of local men to volunteer to come with me as Liz said the satphone was very heavy and, just as I was leaving, she asked, 'You sure you want to do this?'

I nodded. The fact was, I had seen what the rebels were like all day, and I knew I was better than them. I was still working on a high plane of efficiency and excitement.

I was right. The two local lads were good value and we crept carefully back towards the Mammy Yoko keeping our eyes wide for enemy movement. There was nothing. Some of the rebels had gone off to town with Lauren's group and the rest were rifling through the hotel rooms stealing as much as they could carry from the bags left all over the place. They were not the slightest bit interested in fighting any more.

All the same, we made no noise and stayed very alert as we slipped into the hotel again through the service doors in the basement. We used the service stairs to reach the third floor, and all around us on upper floors we could hear the rebels banging about, shouting and laughing. Fortunately, they were looting from rooms at the front, topside of the hotel, and Liz had left her satphone at the back where she had spent the day in her emergency station allocated by me. We had to avoid a couple of groups whose racket made them easy to hear along the corridors, and found Liz's satphone where she said it would be.

It was heavy, as she had said. We shared out the bits between us, nipped back downstairs and out into the sheltering darkness. The walk back was tiring along the beach sand, but uneventful. Liz was soon assembling the satellite telephone for a transmission to London all about the events of the day which was broadcast on the BBC *News*.

I went back to Lincoln's apartment and relaxed with him and the others on chairs overlooking the sea, listening to the sounds of surf breaking on the beach, with a glass of whisky in my hand.

There was not much else we could do which had not been done. We spoke again to Peter Penfold, the High Commissioner: he was optimistic about the Marines coming for us next morning, but it was beyond his power to confirm the operation. Nor would the Marines on the USS *Kearsarge* commit themselves when we called them late on for a final promise of rescue, presumably because they were worried about giving away operational details.

Lincoln and I felt this was over-cautious. Although the rebels had kept up their attack continuously all day, neither of us considered they would be a match for the US Marines with their fighter ground-attack airpower floating on call in the sky above, whether the rebels knew when and where they were coming or not. However, our chief concern was what might happen before they came.

'I'm afraid we're in the shit if these loons catch us,' mused Lincoln.

I had no doubt I would be, if they caught me. There were enough people among Lauren's group to identify me as the person who had stopped them all day and killed dozens of them. If they came, they would be looking for me.

As I sipped my whisky looking over the beach and white flashes of surf into the darkness over the ocean, it was hard to believe it had all happened. The elations and terrors of this long hot day washed over me, like the relentless waves breaking on the sand, and I felt a stunning disbelief that I really had survived. The delicious sense of composure I had experienced after I recovered from that really bad moment with myself on the roof under intense heavy machine gun fire was still with me. Exposure to extreme danger for so long – and time is always the essential ingredient in this priceless annealing of the mind and character – had produced an exquisite sense of detachment which allowed me to savour every aspect and tiny detail of what I had been doing. Even – and especially – the bad parts. Post-combat trauma, so favourite a topic among journalists and a ready excuse among so-called veterans claiming mental damage, has no place in this calm and rarefied state in which the mind has been improved and strengthened by the experience, expanded and empowered by the extreme tensions. This was strength of spirit, amounting to faith, like steel hardened in fire. I had never felt better. My delight in succeeding, so far at any rate, at helping the people stuck in the bowels of the hotel and bringing them to the beach where, if our luck held, we might be rescued, was beyond words. Best of all, I was still alive to enjoy it.

We turned in. I put the Makarov under my pillow and slept the deep sleep of the damned.

Tuesday 3 June

At six o'clock the following morning, I snapped awake at the first faint thump of rotors far away on the still morning air. Thoughts of the Hind Mi-24 which had attacked us the day before flitted through my mind. I concentrated, my head down to hear better, listening for other more discreet sounds of men sneaking up at us on foot. All I could hear were rotors. They were out at sea, and there was more than one.

I called Lincoln, grabbed his binos and ran to the terrace. I looked out towards the noise, shading my eyes against the reflection of the bright early sunlight off the sea, then I saw them. Five CH-46 Sea Knights with their distinctive twin rotors front and back, like the army Chinooks, were beating their way towards us low over the water, closing with the shore very fast. This was the confirmation we wanted. The US Marines tooled up for war and riding over the horizon in their 'birds' to scoop us to safety at the last moment.

The helicopters shot over the beach in a deafening roar about 500 metres from the Cape Sierra, lifted slightly as they slowed and dropped among the palm trees blowing dust and sand everywhere. Marines hanging in the open doors as they landed hardly waited for the wheels to touch down before they jumped out with their M-16 assault rifles, wearing helmets and in full battle order. Platoon sergeants shouted orders, their lieutenants ran forward with radio operators struggling along behind, the antennae waving about over their heads, and marines followed, doubling across the rough grass between the palms and seafront bars to secure higher ground and dominate their beachhead. In moments, they had established M-60 machine gun positions facing down the

183

road and across at the buildings opposite where rebels might form up to attack. Behind them, the choppers lifted off the ground, washing the grass flat, blowing grass and bending the drooping palms with the powerful downdraft from their rotors, leaving piles of equipment on the ground. As soon as they were off, marines ran forward to pull away and sort the boxes of ammunition, radios, barbed wire and other stores before the next wave of choppers landed.

As the Ch-46s swung away to the flank, turning over the beach and setting course back to their mother ship out to sea, another three single-rotor helicopters, the bigger CH-53 Sea Stallions, called Jolly Green Giants in their army role, flew in behind them and landed side by side in the beachhead to land more marines and equipment.

A different, harsher noise grew out to sea where marine hovercrafts* were speeding from the carrier over the glistening water leaving white tracks of foam in their wake. The racket rose to a crescendo as they smashed through the surf and lifted up the beach to the grass by the road. Then they settled, like beasts lying down, as their sacks deflated and ramps dropped to the ground at the back. Marines waved their arms shouting instructions, and eight-wheeled armoured personnel carriers† and Hum-Vs eased from the belly of each hovercraft out on to the ground. Engines whining, the eight-wheelers trundled off to pre-designated positions on the perimeter of the beachhead to boost firepower at the control points on the flanks and the Hum-Vs burbled off among the palms.

Overhead, two Super Cobra attack helicopters circled at 4,000

---

* Landing Craft, Air Cushion (LCAC), these transport hovercraft move ship-to-shore at up to 50 knots with loads of 75 tonnes which allows the mother ship to remain over the horizon.
† Light Armoured Vehicle (LAV-25), based on the Canadian 'Piranha' design, this eight-wheeler is a very versatile all-terrain armoured personnel carrier, armed with an impressive 25mm chain gun which destroys just about everything except a tank. LAVs can be equipped with TOW anti-tank missiles (Tube-launched, Optically-tracked, Wire-guided), an 81mm mortar with a range up to 5,700m showering out fifteen rounds per minute, or anti-aircraft missiles like Stinger.

feet, black dots in the sky watching like protective eagles, instantly ready to swoop down in the ground-attack role and batter the rebels with their cannon and rockets. With them, but much higher still, the USS *Kearsarge* had positioned two Sea Harrier VTOL ground-attack fighters for serious backup with bombs and missiles.

I must admit I could have done with some of this the day before. In less than half an hour, the USS *Kearsarge* had landed 300 heavily armed US marines, Hum-Vs, armoured vehicles, radios, ammunition, battle stores and gear to secure their beach-head against anything Sierra Leone could possibly throw at them, and the biggest emergency evacuation the US had carried out since the Vietnam War was on the road.

In the Hotel Cape Sierra, everyone was up, talking excitedly of the Marines' beach landings, now at last daring to believe they would be saved. They gathered with their belongings – the few bags they had been able to carry over from the Mammy Yoko – and waited in clusters all over the ground floor and outside round the hotel. Many of the local Sierra Leones were convinced that if the Americans rescued them, they would automatically find themselves carried all the way to the United States where some were already dreaming of new lives in America.

After a cup of coffee by way of breakfast, we all went round to the hotel to find that Steve Lawson, Roger Crooks and Martin Greenwood had already set up tables in the courtyard at the top of the steps to the beach as a control point. We recruited the marshals from the Mammy Yoko to help again and with instructions from the Americans told them to organise all the evacuees into sticks of seventeen people each. As before, the plan was to ferry everyone out to the USS *Kearsarge* in helicopters.

The Americans explained they would lift out all the non-African expatriates first – the Americans, British, French, Germans, Indians, Lebanese and others with foreign non-Sierra Leone passports – and then take as many expatriate Africans and Sierra Leones as they could. People who had been in the Cape Sierra joined us and others had sneaked in under cover of darkness during the night so the crowd assembled in the hotel was now back to 1,200 or more. We made all the arrangements, put the evacuees in sticks and in order. The marshals went off to

185

make lists of everyone in the Hotel Cape Sierra which they gave to us at the control point in the courtyard so we could prioritise the sticks by nationalities.

All this time the continuous sound of helicopters down the beach fuelled the excitement. Finally, the word came from the American central control point to begin sending sticks along the beach to the take-off point in the beachhead among the palm trees.

We called up the first stick and a mixed group of Americans shuffled forward to our desk by the steps. One by one, we ticked off the seventeen names on our list as they moved slowly past the desk, carefully checking the nationality of each person. Once they were registered on our lists, and had shown us their passports, they went down the steps on to the beach and they could not come back.

We gave a copy of the list of names in the stick to a marshal who led the first group along the beach following the same path we had taken the evening before when we had escaped from the Hotel Mammy Yoko. After the beach bar, passing the Mammy Yoko on the left uphill through trees, they walked on another couple of hundred metres to the marines' checkpoint. Tough-looking marines in full combats had set up a barbed wire barricade round the perimeter of their beachhead on angle irons driven into the ground and they stood around prepared for riot or worse, their armoured cars ready behind them, but this was hardly necessary with evacuees who just wanted to put the chaos of Freetown and the terror of gunfire and rockets behind them. The marshal gave the list of the stick to the marines and left them at the checkpoint to go back for another stick at the Hotel Cape Sierra. Soon, little knots of people, seventeen in each, sat dotted about on the grass under the palm trees in the sun, heads down against the blowing dust and sand, waiting their turn to move forward to the helicopters.

The marines led them towards the big CH-53 which stood ready on the grass, its rotors turning lazily. Other marines stepped forward and gave each person a white helmet against the noise inside the chopper and an orange lifejacket, carefully helping to fit these on a couple of children and an old man. After the two previous evacuations, the procedure was slick and the marines for

186

all their combat readiness behaved with enormous consideration, conscious they were rescuing civilians who were tired, hungry, and at the end of their tether. Once they were equipped, the marine in charge on the ground led them to the rear of the helicopter landing area and got them to sit down again, the sticks in rows side by side.

A CH-53 swept in over the beach, hovered briefly and landed, blasting everyone with dust. The big ramp at the back dropped to the ground and the air loadmaster waved.

The marine controlling the stick of evacuees waited, his hand raised, till the chopper crew was ready. The air loadmaster appeared again on the ramp of the CH-53, one hand on his helmet, listening in the earpiece for the pilot's orders. He whipped up his other hand, thumb up. Ready to go!

The marine dropped his hand, turned, and waved two sticks on board, leading the way up the ramp and into the dark belly of the aircraft. He ducked away with a shout of encouragement to the loadie, and the ramp closed upwards, shutting out the bright sunlight. Inside, everyone was helped to find a place on the canvas bucket seats and safety belts were fitted. The powerful engines wound up the rotor to an ear-splitting din and the big helicopter lifted into the air, tilted forward and accelerated out across the beach to sea in bright sun.

Already, the next sticks were kneeling ready to embark the next chopper, and behind them more. The constant din of helicopters landing and taking off filled the air, the palms bent and waved in the downblast of their rotors, and the marshals shuttled back and forth along the beach with their lists, taking stick after stick to feed the helicopters. After about an hour and a half of this, over 500 people had been airlifted across twenty miles of blue sea to safety on the *Kearsarge*, including twenty-one Americans, 208 British passport holders and European citizens, Lebanese and others.

There had been no sign of the rebels, but tension was still high among the hundreds and hundreds of refugees crowding forward to our control table in the courtyard. Apprehensive, sweating in the heat, they watched the groups of expatriates snaking along the beach one after the other and they were beginning to wonder if the Americans would take them at all. Finally, after more than two hours, they cracked. Suddenly, the Sierra Leones and others surged forward, smashed through the tables we had set up as barriers and crushed me against the hotel's perimeter fence at the bottom of the steps. I tried to push them back, shouting and fighting to regain some order and stop myself being trampled underfoot as they struggled to clamber up the fence.

'Will! Let them go!' Lincoln shouted at me from a low roof top overlooking the courtyard. 'The marines have secured their beachhead. Don't worry!'

He was right and I was anyway powerless. I ducked sideways out of the way, shoving and pushing to safety at one side. I joined Lincoln on the roof and we watched hundreds of locals scrambling over the fence and running up the beach shouting and screaming towards the helicopters. The marines had set up their barbed wire barrier for just this eventuality and stopped them dead, rifles at the ready. Hum-Vs and armoured cars growled into position, the marines shouted and jostled them firmly back, and within a short time they had reassured the mob that they were going out to the carrier as well. This was all the crowd wanted to hear. Their panic subsided as quickly as it had boiled over and they allowed themselves to be divided into long lines and sat down under the palms in groups of seventeen to wait their turn.

In the Hotel Cape Sierra, we were suddenly left with nothing to do. The US Marines had everyone under their control, their firepower meant the rebels would not attack us now, and for the first time in days I felt the pressure lifting. Steve, Lincoln and I hung around for a while at the hotel and then strolled down the beach, chatting. We found the British High Commissioner and his staff, Colin Glass and Dai Harris, and the Defence Attaché Lt Colonel Andrew Gale.

The High Commissioner and most of his staff were whisked away on the next lift. I found myself in a group with Dai Harris and sat down to wait my turn with the few hundred Sierra Leones left. All of a sudden, after leading and coordinating the effort to protect and rescue all these people around me, I found myself just one of the crowd. Now we were all in the capable and efficient hands of the US Marines and I slipped into the background again, my services no longer required.

Late in the morning, our stick was finally called forward. Dai and I were the last expatriates to leave. The marines fussed us along to receive our helmets and orange lifebelts and we walked up the ramp into the darkness of the CH-53. I have parachuted from these helicopters, and this was familiar and always exciting territory. The racket of the rotors built to a crescendo, the chopper lurched into the air, tilted forward and roared out over the beach to sea. I peered through a square perspex window at the retreating coastline, picking out the hill rising from the centre of Freetown to Spur Road and the pink walls of the Hotel Mammy Yoko pock-marked with black fire damage where the rockets had exploded. Then, Sierra Leone disappeared.

In minutes, we were over the broad grey expanse of the USS *Kearsarge*'s flight deck, pulling round in a slow turn to glide in and land down one of the yellow marker lines. Immediately, the ramp went down, and crewmen appeared in navy fatigue trousers and white fireproof jackets to show us where to go.

In the sunshine, Dai and I walked away from the turbulence of the rotors to a reception desk. From there, we were passed on to another crewman by the carrier's superstructure who waved us over and signalled us through a metal door down a gangway. We walked down a gentle slope, for vehicles, through a wide door after the others on our stick to a lower deck, through another big metal door and into a vast hangar. Around the sides, I noticed armed marines standing silently out of the way just in case any of the rebels had got onto the choppers and caused trouble inside the aircraft carrier. In front of us, under a high ceiling of wiring and pipes running end to end of the hangar, all the other evacuees sat on hundreds of chairs set out in rows across the deck.

This was the reception for the emergency evacuation, where every evacuee was processed and recorded. As the people at the front moved slowly through the control desks answering all the questions, everyone behind them got up and moved to the next chair along, endlessly standing up and sitting down, drawing closer and closer to the head of the queue, like an enormous game of musical chairs.

Dai disappeared off somewhere and I sat down at the back.

The process was most efficient and every detail had been considered to calm the evacuees through this long and boring wait. At the end of each row stood a table loaded with soft drinks, peanuts, snacks and junk food and a TV screen playing videos. As I shifted from chair to chair, I watched *Babe*, a film about a pig that talks to sheep, and a greater dislocation from the realities of the last week would be hard to imagine. The commercial success of the film might be explained because in spite of the utter banality of the plot, we were all completely absorbed in it for hours.

Caught in this typically American piece of robotics, I was just another cog in the machine they had cunningly prepared to receive evacuees still suffering from the traumas of so much violence. I was quite happy. I really began to download from the tensions of the previous days and let all the problems slough away. For once, I did not have to think about anything at all; there were no decisions to make; I could relax and I enjoyed being part of the crowd again.

Finally, I reached the line of desks at the front and a woman in a crisp navy white shirt reached for a fresh form and began asking questions, 'Have you got a passport?'

'Sort of,' I told her and handed over the sad, ripped and sweat-stained relic which was all that was left of the new passport Dai Harris had given me less than a week before. It had been in my trouser pocket while I was crawling and wriggling round the roof of the Mammy Yoko.

She looked at it with extreme distaste and said, 'Jeez! How'd it get like that?'

'I was . . . erm, busy and fell over,' I told her.

She gave me an old-fashioned look, only faintly amused, and said, 'Keep it. You'll need another. Meantime, please fill in this form.'

There were lots of forms.

Registered once more as an evacuee, all questions correctly answered down the line of desks, I nipped straight over to a canteen serving hot food which I had been watching for ages, trying to keep my self control. I was ravenous, and the smell of what was undoubtedly the finest meat curry of my life was driving me mad. I picked up a plate, advanced to the servers and reached out my hand for the plate to be filled to the gunwales with good wholesome curry.

'Will?' A woman called from behind me.

I looked round. Martin Greenwood was advancing through the crowd with a woman he introduced as Anne Wright. She was the American coordinator of the previous two US evacuations and I had spoken to her on the radio telephone from the IT room in the basement of the Hotel Mammy Yoko. We shook hands and without preamble she said, 'Follow me!'

I hesitated, looking longingly at the serving dishes full of hot curry, and said half to myself, 'What about all this food?'

'Nah, don't worry about that,' she replied dismissively and set off determinedly among the crowds of evacuees across the hangar.

Martin shrugged, grinning, and gave me a slap on the back. It had taken me two hours to get to the grub and now I had to leave it.

'Shit! I'm starving!' I told him fiercely and stamped off after Anne before she disappeared from view among the crowds.

'I'm taking you up to Heaven,' she said as if to compensate for pulling me away from the food.

I had been on a carrier before and knew that this was what the Americans called the top decks in the superstructure and the captain's bridge. The US Navy are probably fiercely proud of this, but just then heaven for me would have been a plate of curry.

I was back to work again. In a small office on one of these upper decks, Anne introduced me to a US Navy intelligence officer. He had been involved in the rescue operation; he had been watching the latter stages of the rebel attack and Martin had already told him what I had been doing. He asked me for more detail. All I wanted was something to eat, and I rushed through the day's fighting in about forty minutes while he made careful notes.

'Any chance of something to eat?' I asked rather desperately when I had finished.

'Sure thing, Mr Scully!' he boomed and took me along to their officers' dining room where some of the chopper pilots were eating. 'I'll take you to the officers' mess.' This sounded promising, but when we got there, he glanced along the servery display and said, "Fraid there's nothing left but salad.'

I felt cheated. The Americans were being so helpful but all I wanted was that hot curry down in the hangar and some peace and quiet with the other evacuees. I fiddled about with some salad, eating what I could and the intelligence officer called up a Marine NCO to look after me.

'This marine will assign you a cabin and look after you,' he said, excused himself and disappeared. I had served his purpose and he had other things to do. My minder, a smartly dressed US Marines NCO with a No. 1 haircut down to the wood, looked me up and down and asked, 'What d'you want to do first, sir?'

'I'd like a wash, please.'

This time, he stared at my pink shirt and woman's jeans, and re-phrased his question politely, 'Perhaps you'd like to change your clothes?'

He took me down metal stairs and we walked noisily along metal corridors to the PX, the US services' store. 'Pick out what you want,' he told me.

'I've got no money,' I admitted. I had lost everything I had brought to Sierra Leone, even the clothes I had been wearing in the Mammy Yoko – all except the little green daysack which I had over my shoulder. I was quite sure my bags in the compound in Yara had long vanished into various mud huts in the village where the locals would now be better dressed than ever before. Everything else had gone from Cape House in the coup.

'Don't worry. It's on the Navy.'

I went shopping. The choice was somewhat limited: a pair of US Navy tan slacks, a USS *Kearsarge* T-shirt and a cheap watch to replace the one stolen by the rebels. I found a jumbo pair of designer underpants by 'Boss', presumably for those triple-extra-large US sailors with a fashionable eye for the catwalk. I tried them on. The marine burst out laughing but it was all they had so I pulled the trousers over the top and put on the T-shirt.

He took me to a pilot's cabin. I was looking forward to some privacy and ready for sleep. It seemed I had no sooner lain down on the bunk and begun to drift off to sleep when there was a bang on the door. Another marine stuck his crew-cut head inside the cabin and said, 'You Mr Scully? You gotta come with me! And bring your bag.'

Wearily, I swung my legs to the floor, heaved myself up, grabbed my daysack and followed him. We clattered up and down more ladders, stepping through fire control doors along narrow corridors, to a helicopter loading bay on the level of the main flight deck.

'What's the plan, mate?' I asked him.

'You're going by chopper to Guinea,' he explained. 'You're one of the VIPs, so we're flying you to Conakry straight away.'

'Oh, right,' I said, flattered. 'Thanks very much.' With 1,400 extra people on the ship, their facilities were stretched to the limit and this was the best option.

The loading bay was a low-ceilinged steel room with cargo doors on one side which gave onto the flight deck. Boxes and equipment stood fixed at the back where a group stood, including some familiar faces from the Mammy Yoko: Martin Greenwood, Graham McKinley, a former British Defence Attaché who had spent all day in the Bintumani Conference Centre during the rebels' attack informing the British High Commission of the progress of the battle, the Nigerian Deputy High Commissioner, Mr Keshi, who had been with the Nigerian colonel in the Mammy Yoko when the three rebels stormed into the lobby – and who had spent the whole day sitting in the basement in his underpants – and a half dozen other people. Among these was the Nigerian High Commissioner, Chidi Abubakar. Mr Keshi brought him over and introduced me. 'This is Mr Will,' he said to his High Commissioner. 'The man who helped our troops in the hotel yesterday.' We shook hands. A nice way of putting it, I thought.

Chidi Abubakar was very well-spoken. He had worked hard all week helping Peter Penfold negotiate with Johnny Paul Koroma and the coup leaders and he thanked me effusively for helping his Nigerian soldiers. 'We are indebted to you,' he told me smoothly. I wondered what on earth the Nigerian colonel had told him.

I went to sit down on a metal box to wait for our helicopter to Conakry.

Abruptly, loudspeakers on the wall blared metallically: 'Listen up! Here is a broadcast to the entire ship from the US Ambassador in Sierra Leone, Mr John Leigh Hirsch.' There was a slight pause, then I recognised the voice I had heard in Yara when Duke and I had been glued to the HF set for any news in the first hours of the coup. I met him later in Conakry. He was a small wiry man, good company, with glasses so thick he would need good eyesight to see through them. He had done a great deal for Sierra Leone, especially supporting the UN aid programmes, and he had condemned the coup as a major setback for the country's democratic development.

He made a good speech thanking the officers and crew of the USS *Kearsarge* for coming back up the coast for the third time to rescue so many people. 'The evacuation from the beachfront is now complete and we owe this entire ship's complement a big debt of gratitude. This was the third emergency evacuation mission the USS *Kearsarge* has conducted from Sierra Leone inside one week, and Captain Michael Wittkamp tells me this ship has taken off no fewer than 2,516 people, including 430 American citizens and people from forty other nations. I believe everyone would agree that the evacuation missions have been fast, safe and efficient and the US Marines and the US Navy have done an outstanding job for us all.

'He also says that over 1,261 people were taken off the beach today in less than four hours, and that makes this operation a record. This was the biggest single evacuation the US has carried out since the Vietnam War.' He paused and said, 'I was in Freetown and I saw the orgy of looting and violence there. Many of you on this ship who were rescued have some terrible stories to tell. I hope time will heal your memories. I am sure all of you would want me to thank the marines, the pilots and the sailors who pulled us out of there. In due course, I hope too that those of you who have left your homes and businesses will be able to return to Freetown in safety and take up the threads of your lives once more.'

He thanked a variety of others, including the UN Special Envoy, Desmond Luke the Chairman of the Peace Commission who had stayed behind, and the British and Nigerian High

Commissioners who had attempted to negotiate with the rebels. Then, he finished with, 'There's special thanks as well to some of you among the evacuees who did so much to help this record-breaking operation go so smoothly, like Roger Crooks, the manager of the Hotel Mammy Yoko where you all spent a terrible day yesterday, Steve Lawson his deputy, Graham McKinley and Martin Greenwood from England.'

He paused a long moment, and then his voice echoed round the metal walls of the loading bay as he added, 'There is someone else we need to thank, and I apologise because I don't know this man's second name, but all of you know him as just "Will". From what I hear, without this man's special commitment these last frightening days and particularly yesterday, very many of you would have suffered far worse and might have lost your lives. So, Will, if you can hear this, here's a real big thank you from us all.'

A crackling noise in the background resolved itself clearly into clapping and cheering among the people in the room where he was speaking somewhere high above us in the ship's upper decks. Martin and the others round me in the loading bay nodded vigorously, smiling at me. I had not expected this public thanks, and I was quite moved.

The PA system snapped off. As if on cue, the hangar doors swung open. We walked into the sunlight across the deck to the chopper, for the short flight across brilliant blue sea along the Gold Coast to Conakry . . .

We are the Pilgrims, master; we shall go
Always a little further: it may be
Beyond that last blue mountain barred with snow
Across that angry or that glimmering sea.

. . . Always a Pilgrim.

Afterword

Will Scully found Murdo McCloud waiting for him at the helipad in the port of Conakry, just as he had said he would on the phone, and much as he had been only two weeks before on the helipad at the Hotel Mammy Yoko. This time, however, Will had no luggage except his battered green daysack. Murdo took him to the Novotel which in the days and weeks following became a hotbed of diplomatic, commercial and entrepreneurial activity. Conakry filled with a hotchpotch of politicians, businessmen, mercenaries, rogues, and villains who had fled the violence in Freetown, along with thousands of ordinary local people whose lives had been turned upside down by the coup d'état, their homes wrecked and their belongings looted.

From among them, word came out about the fate of the 250 people who had opted to go with Lauren under the flag of the International Committee of the Red Cross. At first, they had been escorted into Freetown unharmed but then Lauren had lost control of the group, many had been separated from his protecting influence, dragged off by the sobels who were furious at their losses that day, and they suffered badly.

Peter Penfold moved his High Commission into temporary quarters in Room 503 and, with the American Ambassador John Hirsch, tried to bring international influence to bear on Johnny Paul Koroma to end the violence and return Sierra Leone to its civilian government. Kabbah and those of his cabinet who had succeeded in escaping also based themselves in Conakry, agitating for the coup leaders to step down, while Sam Norman, ex-Defence Minister, busied himself with action plans to over-throw the coup leaders. The Nigerians, for once basking in the

197

bright sunlight of reflected democracy, sanctimoniously echoed these sentiments but added in typically bombastic tones that they intended to take military action to reinstate the deposed government and sent another two warships to stand off Freetown. Koroma's AFRC and Foday Sankoh's RUF took no notice and the violence spread from Freetown inland. Freetown's businessmen did their best to keep their businesses alive, without knowing how long they would be out of Sierra Leone, or if they would ever get back. The Lebanese disappeared into the narrow streets of Conakry, like water into sand, wheeling and dealing again, at home anywhere a telephone and percentage could be found.

Roger Crooks and Steve Lawson set about finding alternative interests to their hotel business. Sanctuary of the refugees and embattled all that Monday, the Hotel Mammy Yoko was wrecked, the top floors shot to pieces, the lower floors battered with rockets, burned inside and out. The rebels had stripped it bare, even taking the kitchen sinks which the Lebanese chefs had used for that last meal cooked with the food Will brought from town. Taking his cue from the tide of refugees trying to make the sea passage from Freetown to Conakry, Roger decided to invest in ferry boats and disappeared to Spain to buy a second-hand hydrofoil and then on to Ireland where he put money down on a more traditional steamer.

Steve stayed in Conakry, saw an opportunity with the sudden influx of displaced but well-off people from Sierra Leone and started a string of night clubs with his attractive Sierra Leone girlfriend Jennaba. She had been with him and helped throughout those few dramatic days in the Hotel Mammy Yoko, they came out together on a helicopter with the Marines to the aircraft carrier and they married later that summer.

Martin Greenwood returned to his beloved Yorkshire where he tried to keep in touch with events in the mining areas where his investments lay vulnerable to the RUF rebels who were wrecking and robbing everything. The lure of diamonds was strong and he planned to return sometime. James Marshall, who had helped Steve and Martin fight fires set off by the RPG attacks in the Hotel Mammy Yoko, stayed on in Conakry as well, trading in rice and clothing imports, both of which were desperately needed by the refugees, and keeping an eye on his interests in a bauxite mine. Others like Graham McKinley, the British ex-Defence Attaché, went home.

Meanwhile, conditions deteriorated in Sierra Leone. All political debate was suspended in a wash of looting and violence which spread to all parts of the country. The civilian population unanimously boycotted the AFRC and its marauding sobels. People stayed at home in a campaign of civil disobedience organised by the labour congress and refused to recommence normal commercial activity in spite of Koroma's absurd entreaties to carry on as normal. Inland, the Kamajors counter-attacked the sobels at towns across the border from Liberia, first Zimmi, about 250km from Freetown in the south-east, then north around Kenema which is only about 80km from Kono. More than fifty people were killed in the fighting. Not surprisingly, Koroma blamed Sam Norman.

In Conakry, Murdo kept in touch with Norman, more than ever hoping to cement a contract to support him in his hour of need, making plans and lists of equipment they would need. In fact, everywhere in bars and restaurants in the town, little knots of expats in safari suits and bush gear met to plot and scheme how to cash in and make their fortunes from diamonds or gun running – including Zief, a Jewish arms dealer whom no one liked but who always seemed to know where to obtain anything to satisfy any customer; numerous fit, crewcut South Africans who came and went in handy squad-sized groups; and a group of Israeli mercenaries led by a tough, hard-as-nails, bronzed ex-colonel of the Israeli Defence Forces who got on with Will and tried to persuade him to join his plan to swoop on the diamond mines in Zimmi like some real-life action-man from Francis Ford Coppola's *Apocalypse Now*!

Murdo wanted Fred Marafono out of Kono, which was imminently threatened by the rebels who wanted the diamonds themselves. Fred, his Canadian industrialist, the Executive Outcomes mercenaries working for Branch Energy protecting the diamond mines, and Martin Greenwood's miners were all in danger. Murdo found the Russian pilots of the two Mi-17s which were busy operating out of Conakry, finally brokered a deal to fill all the seats, and they flew right across the jungles and mountains of Sierra Leone to lift everyone out to safety in Guinea. Needless to say, the arguments about who had paid what and for whom dragged on and Martin found himself with invoices for rescuing his miners from both Murdo and Tim Spicer of Executive Outcomes, each believing they were still owed money.

Duke MacKenzie emerged from the jungles of Guinea after his own epic escape from Sierra Leone. After his last call to Will on the HF radio, he had decided to make his own way out by road. He took the old Landrover and drove to the border in the Kuru Hills, skirting Makeni and Pendembu towns en route. Then it all went wrong. The Guinean border guards robbed him of everything, including his shoes. Wracked by malaria, he walked barefoot for days along jungle tracks to Conakry where he was found and taken in by a group of American missionaries whom Will had helped in the Hotel Mammy Yoko. He left Conakry before Will had a chance to see him again and went back home to New Zealand.

Ken went home too. He had had enough. Murdo generously paid for his flight but he did not take Sonya with him: she stayed in Conakry and Will saw her from time to time plying her usual trade, 'night fighting' in the clubs of the capital.

In all this anarchy, the Nigerians' ulterior motives for removing the AFRC by force were decidedly in question. Anger that 300 of their troops had been taken prisoner by the sobels was not excuse enough since they were soon released and, gradually, they increased their forces at Lungi airport to 4,000 troops, their warships blockaded the coast and they were suspected by everyone of increasing Nigerian hegemony along the Gold Coast as the most powerful African country in the region. At the end of June, ECOMOG announced that the Nigerian forces were no longer part of the peace-keeping forces.

Koroma's AFRC was totally isolated by the international community and there seemed no end to the chaos in Sierra Leone. Refugees flooded into Conakry having dared the fourteen hour long sea journey from Freetown and the adventurers saw a chance for new enterprise. Murdo, ex-RAF Harrier pilot and squadron leader, made the rounds of the British High Commission and the

US Embassy almost daily, while Will's courageous defence of the hotel was the talk of Conakry. Together they made a good team and soon found plenty of lucrative work bringing people and assets out of Freetown.

Will made several journeys by sea for various people and became an expert on the coastal waters between Conakry and Freetown. One time, the Americans asked him to bring out Desmond Luke, who was Chairman of the Peace Commission and who had helped Peter Penfold during the first negotiations with Koroma and the AFRC. Will found his was not the only boat on this stretch of coast. By this time, the sea was littered with the possessions of refugees trying to escape Sierra Leone who had come to grief in stormy weather: or ambush. Local pirates boated out from the coast and the Nigerian sailors on their warships were not slow to see the opportunity either, often stopping refugees to rob them or demand a toll for 'protection'.

Another time, Will took Roger back in a motor boat to fly out a light aircraft he had left in a hangar at Hastings, the old wartime airfield for Freetown. Called a 'push-pull',* the plane was ex-US Army and had been used in the Vietnam War for reconnaissance. Will's hired motor boat broke down after fourteen hours at sea, so when they reached the Aqua Club Roger went off to see about his plane and Will went to look at Dai Harris's boat. Dai was still with the High Commission in Conakry and he had asked Will, if he had the chance, to bring out his smart, sea-going motor boat which was moored at the jetty in Man of War Bay, between the Hotel Cape Sierra and the Hotel Mammy Yoko. This was Dai's pride and joy, arguably the best ocean-going fishing motor boat in the Aqua Club, and he wanted it back. However, the manager of the Hotel Cape Sierra, Paolo, had co-opted the boat for his own personal use in case he had to make a run for it. He was very unfriendly, flatly refused to let Will take it and

---

* These aircraft had a turbo-prop at both ends of the pilot's cabin, one at the front which pulled and the other at the back which pushed, hence the name. The tail assembly was at the end of twin fuselages running back from the wings.

ordered several muscled locals he had employed as guards to shoot Will if he tried.

Fortunately, Will had been able to see over the motor boat and discovered the engines were misfiring and unreliable. The guards posed no serious threat but Will decided Dai's boat might very well not reach Conakry anyway. The idea of being stranded adrift off the mangrove swamps along the coast did not appeal, as he would find out later, so he chose to fly back with Roger in the push-pull.

While Roger prepared the plane, Will went to find Mike North and Mike Phillips, as planned. They were still holed up in the same house but this time Phillips was waiting with a small bag packed. His local girlfriend had disappeared and he had finally decided to go on his own, whatever North said. Mike North preferred to stay on in Freetown to sit it out and wait for better times. Often, long-term expats like North settle roots so deep in odd places that they leave themselves nowhere else to go.

Will and Phillips drove back to Hastings to meet Roger. The streets were still cluttered with refuse and patrolled by rebels, but their euphoric madness in the days immediately following the coup was gone, replaced by a gloomy sense of desperation. By this time, there was virtually no food in Freetown, no services worked, supplies were blockaded and the place was in stagnation. The sobels had power but nothing else.

The airfield was heavily patrolled by sobels so Will kept his baseball cap firmly down over his face just in case any of them recognised him. In fact, they were quite cheerful, perhaps because Roger had bribed them liberally with whisky and cigarettes to let him onto the airfield and fly out his plane. Five of them squashed into the little cabin on canvas seats: Will, Mike Phillips, Roger and a Sierra Leone partner of his who also just happened to be an ex-Minister and Klaus, the pilot.

Klaus was an East German in his sixties, lean, brown and very Teutonic. He had served Erich Honecker's communist regime for years on secret missions in various countries before finally ending up in Freetown and settling down with a local girl. Roger paid him, but Klaus was an adventurer at heart and perfectly happy to fly them back to Conakry in the push-pull. The flight back was uneventful till they approached Conakry, where the whole coast was obscured by thick sea mist caused by warm air rolling off the humid tropical hills inland over the cooler sea and turning into fog.

Very fortunately, Murdo was waiting patiently for Will again in the simple building which passed for the Conakry air traffic control tower and, an ex-pilot himself, he knew the push-pull was in serious trouble. There was nowhere else to land except at Conakry. He took command in the tower and began to talk Klaus down through the fog. He did not know that although they could hear him in the plane, on a loud-speaker, they had no headsets because these had been stolen by rebels and there was no means of replying to him.

Peering up into the fog, Murdo heard them pass over the tower. He warned them to avoid a huge pylon near the runway and, speaking into the silence, told Klaus to bring the plane round on a bearing to land. Inside the cockpit, the tension built as they lost altitude in a wide turn. Will strained to see through the all-enveloping white mist which seemed to press against the windscreen. Klaus's eyes flickered between the white outside and the instruments. Murdo's calm voice told Klaus to lose more altitude, to break through the cloud so he could see the runway. In grand German style, Klaus could not be told and flew on. In the mist, he lost his sense of direction, missed the runway and came down too low. Suddenly, mud flats appeared and they almost smacked down on them. Desperately, Klaus pulled the plane up to avoid disaster.

No one said a word. Grimly, Klaus levelled the plane above the white sea of cloud, swung around and tried again. There was no alternative. This time, he listened very carefully to Murdo. At the last moment, they broke through the mist, the runway appeared beneath the wheels and he dumped the plane on the tarmac.

Will did another trip back with Roger, this time to fly out an Mi-17 from Lungi airport where it was parked on the tarmac between the Nigerian troops defending the airport and the rebels surrounding them. They made the long sea journey in a motor boat with a South African pilot called Jube, who had worked for Executive Outcomes in the fighting in Sierra Leone in '95 and '96, and an Egyptian mechanic to check over the helicopter before they tried to fly it. They landed on ground near Tagrin which was controlled by the Nigerians who were distinctly unhelpful, until the usual bribes changed hands. When the soldiers realised this party of foreigners wanted the Mi-17, the price went up exponentially and Will parted with several hundred dollar bills before they were allowed to approach the helicopter. The Nigerians did not come too. It was parked on open tarmac in no man's land between the opposing forces and rather uncomfortably near the rebels who were back to being unfriendly this time.

In baking sun, Will and Roger hid all day in the shade of the chopper, watching Jube and the Egyptian mechanic checking the Mi-17's systems while the sobels and Nigerians observed them lazily from a distance on either side. Late in the afternoon, Jube declared the chopper fit to fly. They tried to disguise their final preparations – test-running the engines several times so the sobels grew bored with the noise – but as soon as the rotors began to turn in earnest and bite the air for take-off, the sobels perked up and shots began cracking overhead. Jube took no risks attempting a vertical take-off. The rifle fire intensified dramatically. He got the wheels off the ground as fast as possible, tilted the machine and ran headlong down the runway away from the rebel positions to gain airspeed. They shot off the end of the tarmac, over scrub and the beach and out to sea before he pulled up for some altitude and set course for Conakry.

Undeterred by this narrow escape, Will agreed to help the Americans. They wanted him to take Stuart Wilcox, a US aid worker, an ex-marine with Nicaraguan experience, back to their Embassy in Freetown and destroy documents which they had not had time to dispose of before. They supplied a twin-engined motor boat and gave Will a nicely worded *laissez-passer* signed and stamped with the United States eagle in case the Nigerians stopped them. The trip gave Will the chance to take Klaus back to Freetown. He loved it. His German pilot's peaked cap at a jaunty angle, ramrod straight, he snapped orders at Will all the way back, about currents, wind and bearing, as if he had been a sailor all his life, and became convinced a new career as a ship's captain lay ahead of him. After Will and Stuart dropped him back in Freetown, he was so impressed with the excitement that he bought a boat and started his own business ferrying people back and forth between Conakry and Freetown.

The mission continued well. After Stuart had destroyed the documents at the American Embassy, he and Will picked up another passenger and began the trip back to Conakry. Brian Mohawk claimed to be an aid worker and was involved in diamond mining. He had an interesting little bag which he never let out of his sight. In the boat, he sat down, clutched the bag on his lap and waited for the trip to be over. It took longer than they imagined. Within a couple of hours of Conakry, they ran into a storm of blinding tropical rain which reduced sea visibility to nothing and pushed them inland. Somewhere out to sea near Kabak Island, the boat ran solidly aground on mud flats.

Will and Stuart argued back and forth about the best plan, whether to swim to the coast or stay put. Stuart estimated they were three kilometres out and said the mud flats would give them a chance to rest on the way or even more or less walk in. It was already late afternoon and the idea of spending a night at sea did not appeal to him, whereas Will wanted to stay with the boat which was undamaged and float off with the tide. Brian took no part in this discussion. He declared he could not swim, but he probably meant he would not swim carrying his precious bag, and he had no intention of leaving that behind even if his life depended on it.

Stuart was determined to swim, so reluctantly Will decided to go with him in case he got into trouble. From habit, he had a plastic bag inside his old green daysack which he tied off to make a flotation aid and he wore his North Face waterproof against the cold, wrapping it round him to catch air in the back. Then he slipped over the gunwale into the water. For a time, he and Stuart called out to each other as they swam towards the distant shoreline. Then Will lost contact with him as darkness fell. The water was cold and several times in rougher swells he had to concentrate to stay afloat. Later, Stuart reckoned they were in the water more than two hours and the distance was nearer six kilometres. Miraculously, they beached together but Stuart was freezing cold and at the end of his tether.

Will led the way inland, picked up a track off the beach and followed it to a village. At first, the villagers were helpful, and an old man agreed to go back at once in his pirogue to find Brian. Stuart was too exhausted and cold, so he stayed in the village while Will guided the local back out to sea in the dark. Eventually, they found Brian huddled up in the motor boat under a light Will had had the foresight to switch on before jumping overboard. The boat was still aground, so they left it and returned to the village where the chief had decided to take them all hostage and demand no less than $100,000 for their release! Brian clutched his little bag all the tighter. However, after lengthy discussions, Will reduced these fantastic and criminal expectations to a more commercially realistic $200.

The following day, they returned to Conakry in the pirogue. Brian Mohawk sat rigid in the narrow, wobbly boat, terrified he would fall in and lose his diamonds in the sea. When they slipped into the *Petits Bateaux* harbour and tied up, Brian vanished into the side streets. Will heard later that as soon as Mohawk landed in Conakry everyone was out looking for him: a strange reception for an aid worker.

Will made several more journeys but as summer passed it was plain that Koroma's AFRC could not be unhinged in the short term. The Nigerians continued to make aggressive noises from their enclave around Lungi airport, there were more clashes in the interior with the Kamajors and the international community were solid behind Kabbah's civil government. The opportunities for good business in Sierra Leone depended on Sam Norman and he was Minister without power for the time being. Will thanked Murdo and returned home to England in September, pilgrim no more along the Gold Coast . . . at least for the time being.

Murdo stayed on, then took to travelling back and forth, and during one visit to London he married Beth Dunne.

In the autumn, the British Government announced various honours for those who had distinguished themselves during the hectic and dangerous days after the coup. Colin Glass was made Commander of the British Empire, Dai Harris an Officer of Order of the British Empire, Lt Colonel Andrew Gale was awarded a Queen's Gallantry Medal, and Lincoln Jopp a Military

Cross. Surprisingly, Peter Penfold, the High Commissioner, received nothing, though his activities and influence during the negotiations with the AFRC were critical. Arguably his role in persuading the Americans to come for that final beach evacuation was vital, and made in circumstances quite as testing and dangerous as any of the rest of his staff. Much later, in May '98, there were demonstrations by civil groups in Freetown outraged that the Foreign Office had not recognised Penfold's significant personal contribution. And there was no mention of Will Scully.

Sierra Leone suffered through the end of the year, blockaded and pariah of the international community, its shops empty, its prisons full, its people starving and commerce at a standstill. All this time, the Nigerians built up their military capability at Lungi and the stand-off between them and Koroma's sobels continued into '98.

In Conakry, there were long, hot, sticky months of intrigue. Kabbah and Sam Norman in exile turned once again to the mercenaries for help. Kabbah was worried that the Nigerians were too powerful, and since his own army had been wrecked as a force for good by Koroma and the RUF, he needed another to balance the Nigerian Army in Sierra Leone. Once again, he turned to the Kamajors. As the Nigerians built up their forces under the ECOMOG flag, Kabbah and Norman drew up plans to arm and train the Kamajors . . . and they probably deeply regretted not having done so long before through Murdo and Fred Marafono.

However, this time Kabbah seems to have turned back to the Executive Outcomes stable, perhaps because they had been so effective in '95. He found a wealthy Indian financier to bankroll the plan, and Tim Spicer used Sandline International to buy a 35-ton consignment of arms in Bulgaria and fly it to Sierra Leone to arm the Kamajors.

Spicer claims to have discussed this plan with British and American government diplomats and agents, including Penfold, but he seems to have underestimated the Nigerians. Surprisingly, considering the purpose of the arms was to counter Nigerian hegemony in Sierra Leone, he flew them via Nigeria. When the plane carried on to Lungi, the Nigerians promptly seized everything, locked it up in their armoury and thereby eliminated the

Kamajors from the picture at a stroke.

Then, on 10 February 1998, the Nigerians attacked Freetown. Within two days, Major General Shelpidi commanding the Nigerian forces said Freetown was under his control. Koroma, by this time self-promoted to colonel, claimed junta troops had repelled the invasion but he was nowhere to be found. As before, thousands of refugees fled the fighting by sea and many drowned when their overloaded boats capsized. Aid workers said Connaught Hospital in Freetown was 'bursting at the seams' with wounded.

With overwhelmingly superior forces, the Nigerians consolidated their grip on the town but the fighting continues inland as this book is finished in May, and the Nigerians claim they need another 6,000 troops to retake the diamond mining areas. Peter Penfold went back to his High Commission in Freetown and President Kabbah returned in late February to quell rumours that General Abacha of Nigeria was in fact using his forces to annex Sierra Leone. Kabbah's efforts to train the Kamajors failed (again) and he can only stay in power with Nigeria's help. At what cost? It is still unclear who will ultimately control the rich diamond deposits but there seems no doubt that new deals will be struck; and equally little doubt that much of Sierra Leone's wealth will be smuggled out as before. The misery of the ordinary people in this country is not over.

In Britain, satisfaction that the properly elected government of Ahmed Kabbah had been returned to power was abruptly overshadowed by controversy. Lord Avebury, a liberal peer, revealed that the arms had been flown to Sierra Leone in breach of United Nations resolution 1132, which Britain itself helped to draft, and claimed that the Foreign Office had known all about it.

Suggestions that government departments did know that Sandline was involved surfaced rapidly in the glaring light of media enthusiasm for political drama. The Ministry of Defence said several reports naming Sandline were sent to the defence Ministerial team; the *Sunday Times* of 10 May published photographs of mercenaries standing round Sandline's Mi-17 helicopter (the same one Will liberated from the rebels at Lungi) while it was being serviced by Royal Navy mechanics off MHS *Cornwall*; Graham

McKinley, the former British Defence Attaché, said he had been asked by intelligence officers for his views on the matter, adding Penfold would not have agreed anything with Spicer without informing London; British officials admitted they had known Sandline was 'running air operations' to assist Kabbah's return but denied they had known Sandline was in breach of a UN resolution; and Tim Spicer repeatedly affirmed that he had discussed his plans in detail with British diplomats and intelligence officials. The Foreign Secretary, Robin Cook, robustly denied there was any knowledge of this at Ministerial level.

Kabbah said that he thought the UN embargo was directed against Koroma's illegal regime, not against his own 'legitimate government'. The British Customs and Excise dropped its investigation into allegations that Sandline had broken UN resolutions, and, as this book is finished, the Government appointed a two-man committee to report on the affair.

Whatever, this 'scandal' highlights the eternal gulf between actor and critic, between those with balls enough to work in places like Sierra Leone and those who stay safely back at home and pass judgement, so the last word must be about Will Scully. There was much talk in Conakry and later in England about his singular part in protecting so many refugees in the Hotel Mammy Yoko. Steve Lawson, Lincoln Jopp, Peter Penfold and others wrote uncompromisingly in his support. Will went to Sierra Leone without pretensions, as a civilian, he did what he did at the hotel expecting nothing, he employed his skills with deadly professionalism, as the spirit of his regiment will always expect of him, and he sought no recognition nor reward. He was hugely impressive. However, he is a hard man, an adventurer and no plaster saint (who really wants its SAS Pilgrims any other way?), and for a long time there was doubt that the British Government could bring itself to recognise the intensely committed, vital and brave role he played.

Finally on Thursday 2 April 1998, the *London Gazette* published a new list of honours and awards in which William James Scully was awarded the Queen's Gallantry Medal. The citation was headed with the simple but wholly accurate reason, 'For saving lives during a coup'.